SAMUEL JOHNSON'S
ETERNAL RETURN

TWENTY-THREE

SAMUEL JOHNSON'S ETERNAL RETURN

— A NOVEL —

MARTIN RIKER

COFFEE HOUSE PRESS

Minneapolis

2018

2392510029

Coffee House Press books are available to the trade through our primary distributor, Consortium Book Sales & Distribution, cbsd.com or (800) 283-3572. For personal orders, catalogs, or other information, write to info@coffeehousepress.org.

Coffee House Press is a nonprofit literary publishing house. Support from private foundations, corporate giving programs, government programs, and generous individuals helps make the publication of our books possible. We gratefully acknowledge their support in detail in the back of this book.

LIBRARY OF CONGRESS CATALOGING-IN-PUBLICATION DATA

Names: Riker, Martin, 1973– author.
Title: Samuel Johnson's eternal return : a novel / Martin Riker.
Description: Minneapolis : Coffee House Press, 2018.
Identifiers: LCCN 2018004534 | ISBN 9781566895286 (softcover)
Subjects: LCSH: Future life—Fiction. | GSAFD: Allegories.
Classification: LCC PS3618.I532 S26 2018 | DDC 813/.6—dc23
LC record available at https://lccn.loc.gov/2018004534

PRINTED IN THE UNITED STATES OF AMERICA
25 24 23 22 21 20 19 18   1 2 3 4 5 6 7 8

for my wife and son

SAMUEL JOHNSON'S
ETERNAL RETURN

1.

The Susquehanna is a pleasant avuncular river that winds down through Pennsylvania toward the Chesapeake, past airy forest and farmland, and these days, of course, past those endless suburban expanses. But if you drive north along the edge of it, under Harrisburg's small-city skyline, then purple mountains sliced away at the ends by the highway administration, past the last Amish fruit stand and tiny beleaguered college town, you will eventually arrive at what is left of William Penn's once-illustrious woods: a sylvan paradise, empty of humans, thus of human concerns. Continue on, along a narrowing road beneath a sky of leaves and branches, and soon you begin to imagine, or half imagine, that this place, these woods, are everything that exists in this world. Whatever you'd meant to accomplish, whoever you'd hoped to become, all you'd previously called reality seems suddenly a distant memory . . . And as the last thought of human society extinguishes itself, as your last worldly expectation slips away, if at that point you turn right and continue on for about twenty more miles, you will come to the town where I was born, called Unityville.

It is an idealistic name, Unityville, and well earned, in my opinion. There is great, near-total unity in Unityville. There are also only about thirty people, all of them religious zealots, or rather there were thirty at the time when my parents first moved there, that time being very long ago now. Today the number is probably closer to forty-five.

My parents, who were also religious zealots, arrived in the town eight months pregnant, having lived full lives in the world of society and come to see that world as nonsensical if not pernicious, and certainly no place to raise a son. I've often tried to imagine how they felt that first day, having ridden for miles through thick forest to arrive, at last, at our single dirt road, our shabby houses and garden patches, finally to park before our white slant-roofed church with its barn full of livestock out back. Were they pleased or disappointed by its smallness? Disheartened or emboldened by its shabbiness? Its isolation, at least, they'd signed on for, and I imagine them awed by it, and by their own resolve, convinced they'd accomplished something deeply profound by finding such a crummy place to live.

They were not long in town, however, before my father discovered that a stockpile of righteous indignation is no substitute for a job. And so it came to pass that every weekday morning of my childhood, my father climbed into a blue Studebaker station wagon to depart for the impossibly distant-seeming city of Williamsport, where he worked for the phone company, doing what I don't know. Each night he returned, visibly crumpled. Far from escaping society, it seemed, he'd only increased his commute. My mother, faced with shouldering both halves of our family's churchly burden, immersed herself in religious activities to which I was invariably dragged along. My childhood, then, was spent largely alone, waiting out activities that did not personally involve me, leafing through my lessons in the church foyer or loitering among the pews, where I proved to have as little aptitude for religious belief as for any other sort. Days were blank and formless. Weekends filled with church and chores.

Year followed year, and if I was never particularly oppressed by feelings of discontent or dissatisfaction, it also never occurred to me that there existed a reality either better or worse than the one I'd been born into, or a person more vibrantly alive than the dullard I seemed destined to become.

I should clarify that when I say I was alone, I don't mean that there were no other children in Unityville. There were several, but they held no interest for me, or no more interest than anything else. There was one girl in particular, Emily, who was close to my age and fond of me. She was an imaginative, enthusiastic young woman, always trying to engage me in one activity or another, and the perfect indifference I showed her is as good an illustration as any of my personality at that time. A loner. A mope. Whether I'd brought it into the world with me or picked it up along the way, mine was a magnificent vapidity, an unprecedented nullity of spirit. I was a compulsive nonengager, a natural-born audience member, a couch potato who'd only to discover his couch.

The event that brought an end to this mortal stupor and determined forever my fate was the arrival, one autumn morning in my twelfth year, of a television set. By what star-crossed circumstance a television came to be in Unityville is a story I will tell in a moment, but suffice it to say that at a time when television was still new, when programming was scarce and sets not yet ahead of sofas in the hierarchy of family furniture, the arrival of a television in Unityville was less likely than a stigmata, and considerably less welcome. What interest had these people, who sought nothing so much as escape from society, in watching an idealized version of it? No interest at all. In fact, the argument that arose among the townspeople—the first argument I'd ever witnessed in that town—was never about whether the television should be *used*, since all agreed it should not be. It was simply whether the set should be disposed of outright or secreted away and forgotten.

Why the latter course was deemed more prudent is what I'll now attempt to explain.

Although citizens of Unityville were sometimes forced to venture outside our small community, the only people who ever visited *us* were from a large Amish colony some miles south. These people, having lived apart from society far longer than we had, were considerably better at it. They lived without electricity, for example, something the people of Unityville would never even attempt. They were also quite handy, so conveniently so that Unityville had become grossly reliant upon them, even for basics of survival. They built our houses, helped plant and cultivate our crops. We paid them, of course, and thus a relationship had grown up between our two communities. It was strictly a business relationship, but courteous and respectful, and beneficial for everyone involved.

But there was one among these Amish called Brother Abram, a huge muscular boy-man of perhaps twenty at the time I'm recounting, whom the people of Unityville secretly referred to as "the bad one." He was not bad in the sense of being angry or devious, but he fit poorly into our understanding of what an Amish person should be. He was not a bad *man*, in other words, but simply a man who was not good, we thought, at being Amish. He was very outgoing, for one thing, even gregarious, and took a somewhat aggressive personal interest in our community and way of life. Generous with his time, always offering to help in one way or another, often for no payment, always teaching and advising, and more than once he had been the solution to some great crisis or other. In short, "the bad one" was quite good to us. And while there were certainly those suspicious of the interest he took in our lives—and particularly his interest in the period lived *prior to* Unityville, the lives our citizens had left behind them—and while these suspicions occasionally led one or another townsperson to suggest that Brother Abram had questionable intentions and distinctly un-Amish ambitions and would for these reasons be best kept at arm's length, still, at the end of the day, even the most cautious among us had to acknowledge how greatly we benefited from his particular combination of enthusiasm and expertise. Dubious, no doubt, but we were beholden to him.

Thus when "the bad one" arrived one brisk autumn morning, after the leaves had already turned their fiery colors but before they'd all fallen to the ground, with a television weighing down the back of his buggy, the citizens of Unityville were not sure what to do. It was a light, crisp morning, in my memory it still is, a morning both chilly and bright, with both breath-clouds and birdsong, and we watched him ride up toward the church steps as all of us were wandering out. He rode up and stopped and stood on the driver's bench, arms spread wide. He gestured with pride toward the back of his buggy and seemed almost childishly disappointed when the townspeople scowled at what they saw there. He spoke then, and while he did not say where he'd found the television, he said a great deal else. And if I remember his speech distinctly, with perhaps here and there those embellishments that memory inevitably tacks on, this is because it was the largest number of words I'd ever heard spoken by an Amish person, and because it was the first truly memorable thing that had ever happened to me.

"Brethren," he began, in his Amish way of speaking, "I have ridden me all over creation, o'er hill and dale, through holepots and downwet to gift to you this heathen lichtbox. Yay, well nough I know vhat you'd say! But, Brother, you say, ve left us long-go the crotch of vorldlitude, what need us this demon's fernhoodle? Whereforhowever I say unto you, in none but goodvill and friend-veeling, that the lowchance of use in yourn Christian hands out-wroughts the nochance of use in mine own! For though ve Amish use no lectrical vices, yet you good Christians do keep a steady lectric supply, vhich maketh this costly piece of modern lectrical furniture somewhat fruitfillier in yourn than in mine own keeping! And since I have been a good friend to you, and good and hand-lending neighbor, I trust you vill receivedeth that vhich I have ridden me o'er hill and dale, through holepots and downwet at no small cost and convenience, and keep it vell and grossie safe, that even twould you maketh no use upon it yourn ownselfs, no less so twould you save it up for company, and"—actually, I will summarize what he said.

In summary, then, what Abram said to the people of Unityville was that he wished his "gift" to be housed there, in our electrically wired town, where he himself might make use of it, regardless of what the rest of us did. He never explained or justified his interest in the television but pummeled away instead on the question of why we should house it, or rather how we should, in what manner. *This* was the question he had ostensibly brought to us, and he proceeded to offer, as solution, that he would build a special dwelling, at his own expense and by his own hand, a "good neighbor haus." Set far off in the woods, this "haus" would be near enough to receive electrical current but far enough to remain out of the town's way. Opened to all, visited by none—what say we? He stopped short of enumerating the consequences were his proposal to be poorly received.

His speech over, Abram at last lifted the television—an enormous wooden console; truly he was a mountain—placed it upon the ground, and rode off into the morning chill, leaving at our feet both the television's fate and, in some unspoken yet clearly understood sense, our own.

There followed a hush, then a kind of group fidget, and even, for a moment, the semblance of a split. Those who'd warned of Brother Abram's dubious intentions allowed themselves to bask in the satisfaction of having their suspicions confirmed; yet their glory was short-lived, and soon they, like the rest, became morose with the moral perplexity before us. How did the necessary good of Abram's labor weigh against the relatively ignorable bad of his television set? What constituted a compromise of our values, versus a Christian respect for values not our own? Does the Bible address directly the question of *proximity*? Of where lines get drawn? Or does the need to draw a line at all mean the battle is already over, that goodness and righteousness have already lost, and that all of us were doomed to some horrific fate simply for entertaining this topic? The next day Brother Abram returned and, finding the television still among us, smiled warmly, but not too warmly—he did not overperform "warmth"—attempted to lay hands upon shying-away shoulders, then cheerfully took to the woods, scouting locations for his "haus."

This is the point at which I at last enter this story, for among the very few pieces of useful information to be found in my head at that time was an extensive explorative knowledge of the town's surrounding geography, and Abram, who knew the area poorly, or at any rate claimed to, very pleasantly asked me along. Thus began what quickly became a sort of apprenticeship, for after the site was chosen, Abram continued to involve me, throughout the planning, the building—he showed me things, taught me things. And in a very short time we had erected together, about a hundred yards from town but surrounded entirely by forest, a two-room "haus" with a large antenna.

Oh fateful little house! I picture you now as clearly as if I were back there in the past, when you were still in my future. Your cleared-away plot, your stray boards and tiles. Whitewashed walls, the whole strange sight of you. What did I think of you then? If only I'd known! Future site of all my life's happiness, as well as my failures, my regrets, and ultimately my undoing.

The outside, being windowless, was a bit grim, but inside included a main room with a small kitchen area and a comfortable sofa and chair, as well as a back room whose purpose was initially unclear to me. At the center of the main room stood the television, always off while I worked there, and which Abram never once suggested I might watch. It simply stood there as we worked around it, this wood and glass object, the first true "object" of my imagination—it seemed I had an imagination after all—curious to me both for its exoticism, having come from the world outside, and for what I understood it to do. Part magic, part invention, a box that opened with light and exhaled infinity, through which a fantastic pageant of voices and images beamed into the room, lives "out there" beyond our small town, not real, exactly, but created in reality's image, a vision of life through a window to another world.

As construction neared an end, Abram's visits to Unityville became more frequent. Daily, in fact, and never with his Amish brethren, but always alone. He would appear in the morning and work through the day—for food, on various projects—then in the evening retire to his "haus," where I now know, but at the time did not know, or perhaps simply did not bother to acknowledge for myself that I knew, he almost certainly spent his nights. I, at any rate, would see him only during the day, as I continued to work alongside him and in fact took on an increasingly useful role. For whereas previously I had done mostly lifting and hauling, by now I'd acquired such abilities as to handle more skilled work, which Abram happily relinquished to me, even while failing to take upon himself any of my own menial labor, so that increasingly I found myself doing *all* the work while Abram sat by, talking about television.

Not that I minded! On the contrary, I was always encouraging and prompting him for descriptions of the various programs he watched. There was a grown man named Miltie and a puppet named Howdy. There was a dog named Lassie and a singer named Perry. There were things called "game shows" where people answered questions for money, and there were dance programs, and news programs. I tried to imagine them, those living pictures, those fantastical scenarios, but my field of reference lacked acreage, and there was not enough varied material in my head to create for myself a vision even half as stimulating as Abram's descriptions themselves.

By now the reader will have assumed that I eventually made my way to Abram's "haus" to insinuate myself on the sofa there—and of course, yes, I did. But what you may be surprised to learn, as indeed I was very surprised to find when I arrived late one summer night of my thirteenth year, having at last summoned the courage to squeeze out a back window an hour past my parents' bedtime—the figure I was surprised to find perched upon the couch, beyond Abram's doorway silhouette, her face washed gray in the television's flicker, was Emily, the girl who always tried to get my attention, the one I'd largely ignored. I'd never seen her with Abram, nor even imagined her with him—yet now the sight made such an impression upon me that it would remain in my head forevermore. Before I first laid eyes upon a living screen, I saw the glow of that screen on a human face. There was Emily, whom I barely knew. There was Emily, watching television.

"Emily?" I said.

She looked back, broke away from that television to smile at me. She said: "It's you!"

Meanwhile Abram was turning from one to the other of us, caught in a rather ugly scowl, as if his face had momentarily forgotten it was visible to those around him. Finally he shrugged. "In you come."

It seems they had been expecting me for months—Emily explained, much later, that this was what Abram had told her—and had been often disappointed that I continually failed to arrive. Now I was there, however, and the next stage of my life began.

Tuesday was Uncle Miltie with Martha Raye; Thursday *The Lone Ranger*; Friday *Rin Tin Tin*. Lawrence Welk, whom I never cottoned to, was Saturday at nine, while Lucy, whom everyone loved and whom I loved more than I loved any actual person, was nine on Monday, later moving to Wednesday at seven thirty. By that time there was *Wagon Train* and *Father Knows Best*. There was *Perry Mason*, *Dick and the Duchess*, and *Gunsmoke*. Next there was the Beaver—how I loved the Beaver! There was Zorro and Pat Boone. When I think about them chronologically, one thing I've noticed about those early years of my television viewing is that the programs seemed to mature in subject matter at more or less the same time I did, from childish pie-in-the-face variety programs to the antics of bowl-cut young men to the adolescent romance of Western adventures. The culmination of this trajectory was a season sometime in the late fifties that saw an unbelievable concentration of *Bonanza*, *The Rebel*, *The Lawman*, *The Alaskans*, *Maverick*, and *Wyatt Earp*, with the Beaver—whose brother, Wally, was so close to my age that I was able to imagine him aging right alongside me—having moved by then to eight thirty Saturday from his previous Thursday spot. One tends to think of watching television as a solitary activity, if not downright isolating, the opposite of wholesome social interaction. In its heyday, though, television was often the very site of such interaction, connecting direly inhibited individuals across impossible social voids. And when you consider the sort of person *I* was, or rather the nonperson I just barely personified, you can see why my residence on Abram's sofa represented a great upward turn in my development as a social being.

It was not that Abram and Emily and I discussed what we watched or held other conversations of any length or depth. In fact, if either Emily or I presumed to talk during a program, Abram quickly shushed it away. No, what we shared was a time and a place and participation in an unsanctioned activity. Passive activity, it's true, but we shared it. And not for a night or a week or a month or even a year, but for the several years that we met this way, on our regularly scheduled evenings. And this was how I came to have what might properly be called a life. A life with people and a life with television. A life with people and television.

This brings us up to 1960. It was the year CBS's Sunday lineup ran *Lassie*, *Dennis the Menace*, *Ed Sullivan*, *GE Theater*, *Jack Benny*, *Candid Camera*, and *What's My Line?*, and the year my fate took its next definitive turn.

I was eighteen, was now well into my life with television, and had little sense of, much less ambition for, a life beyond—when one night Emily and I arrived to find Abram gone. It was a vibrant, fresh-scented evening, the sort that fortifies the blood in the exhilaration of springtime thaw. I'd met Emily along the path to the "haus," and we'd been talking a bit about the programs for that evening—in fact, we'd been speaking more and more lately, not just about television but other topics as well, and not just along the nighttime path but on chance meetings throughout the day, or when Emily, not at all by chance, would stop by my workplace to chat, until Abram would grumblingly remind us of the work that needed to be done. But there was a pleasantness there, is all I mean to say, and it was a lovely spirited evening, and so we were quite unprepared, emotionally, to arrive and find Abram gone. Of course each of us had been sick or otherwise absent on countless occasions over the years, but this was something else. He was gone. The television was on, as was usual when we arrived, yet set atop the console were several pieces of yellowish paper that turned out to be a rather long note.

I apologize in advance for its wordiness, but as it has always been an important document for me, one I've given a great deal of thought to over the years, I include the entirety of this letter below.

Yungins,

Many a nite-an-day haf I pourt myself a hedful of thinkings bout this telefussin, and vhy gut Christian mums and dads get acheybelly and knickertwist ofer a thing so entrataining and gut-joyable and plessur-making and fine. I doubtnot you have vundered such yourselfs. Tis true that vatching you much telefussin can bit-tarnish normalife and make normadays appear saemwhat dullish—I disputeth no part nor paece of this claim. Yet to unterstant in full telefussin's awe-filt Got-like power to sow into souls many insatsfaxons, we need us first consiter how a mudern peeples mostdays are liffed. And this is vhy I haf prepared me this note of my own thinkings for your considering.

In truth, the vorld we lif in is mostpart filler, like a Viener schnitzel, scrappl, or uttervise low-graed vurst. This VURST VORLD is made most of scraps and feddyparts, with oft whole years past tween meat-filt goings-on. Nay, yout not belief yourselfs to see it, but even hi-adventuring peeples out in this mudern vorld knoweth only the teenymost chunk of tru lifeiness, hopped in there amongst the scrappl fat of the everydays. The mudern vorld is just this and thers no uttervise posbil.

Now, if telefussin shown not but the fanciest mudern lifes but *shown the full bits* of them, there then twould be naet for Christian mums and dads to spaek boo over. Yet the awe-filt Got-like power of telefussin lieth not in the parts it showeth, but ruther in the parts it leaveth out.

Spaken plaen, telefussin takes away lifes dullish parts, the scraps and feddyparts, and makes any life atall seem intrusting. Yay, vere it posbil to liff a telefussin life, you could be any soul atall and twould not matter, insomuchas how intrusting yout be. Vere it posbil to liff a telefussin life, all your moments twould be momentious, all your thinking twould be profownd, all your choosing twould be of grossie and everlasting import. Nay, put none can liff a telefussin life, and the raeson is a thing I stall myself from telling. Long haf I stallt from discusing vith you this matter, but now I do feel in my hart and hed that you haf grown old nuff vhere you is better off hearing than not hearing it.

Tis Got. Yay, I spake it plaen. For Got wrote the Book of Life, and He writeth it still, and He doth not removeth from out His Vorks noneparts vhatsoever, not the feddy nor the meat-filt parts naether, nay, nor doth He stand for othersome to removeth such parts, as do question the purfection of His Vorks. Yet the programs you vatch on the telefussin, by *not* showing the full bits, do *not* gift full Grandur to His Vorks, His VURST VORLD in all its allness, but rather moldeth and shapeth mostdays life to fit peeple's self-magining. It createth from true life meer idols of self-delisation. It melteth down the mettle of Got's VURST VORLD and make instet a goltin calf to vurship! Vhich is HERESY, plaen and simpl. Nor doth it matter if the telefussin program be true or falsht. It matters only that we *selecteth* from His Vorks. We stareth in the mouth Got's Gift-Hass. Beggars tho we be, we Choos!

Such is the sin for vich we are punisht vith perpetul insatsfaxons. Yet as to the *faerness* of it, I do atimes vunder. If Got Himself did removeth from out His Vorks some bits of the feddy, mudern life vould be a faer bit more entrataining, not to say gut-joyable and plessur-making and fine.

Yungins, the raeson I haf writ me this note of my own thinkings for your considering is that you are now grown and changt much, and our cowch has alast becum overcrowtert. It is time I adventur into this VURST VORLD, the vorld beyond the telefussin, to discover vhat destiny holds in stor. Much as any mudern man, I feel insatsfaxons of all sorts, yet I knoweth too a truth: that there is not so much choosing in this vorld as He vould haf you belief. Therefor, if you can liff in Gots VURST VORLD and be gut-happy here, vhy, you most surely should. They call that "grace," and peeple can only haf it long as they know not vhat it is. Once you know, then try as you vould, normaday life forevermoreafter dissatsfies, and you forevermoreafter prefer you the telefussin sort. May be I just ruint it for you by telling.

Gut luck!

Abram

In the coming years I would reread this letter many times, on many a self-questioning evening. On this particular evening, however, in the understandable intensity of having a great surprise suddenly thrust upon me, I failed to take in much of Abram's letter at all. I was preoccupied instead with the sheer fact of it, the shock of the sudden absence that had occasioned it, and also with something else, quite unrelated—an even more pressing development, which I'll now do my best to explain.

We were sitting on the sofa, holding the letter, sitting in our normal spots but without Abram's body between us. Emily had turned off the television, our attentions more occupied, for once, with the reality at hand. Yet as the smoke of the situation began to clear, and as we ourselves settled, she now got up and switched the set back on. I did not make much of this gesture, assuming she meant simply not to miss any more of our program, or at most to divert us from the various worries we'd been discussing. Only later did I realize there was more to the gesture; a diversion, yes, but not from worries. Rather, it was her effort at dissipating the uncomfortable emotional situation that was already developing in the room. A shift in the air, in the social dynamic. For it was not simply Abram's absence that hung heavily in the air that day; it was also the newfound presence of our aloneness together, a before-then-unheeded tension between Emily and myself, which I tried to attribute, as we settled into the program, to Abram's absence, the shock of it. Impossible to discuss or outwardly acknowledge—yet this tension continued to grow stronger, even as the television's characters paraded past. It swelled in the space where Abram would have been sitting and was soon so oppressive that I began to feel nauseated by it, as if by the onset of a sudden, inexplicable illness. No longer able to follow the program, utterly oblivious to the television's images and sounds even as my brain passively received them, I watched my body shiver as if cold, felt my pulse elevate; I sensed the onset of a vomit deep down and would have hastily excused myself to the woods had Emily's body not appeared to me, in that moment, to be suffering the same condition. Eyes met, and rather than vomit we gave ourselves over to a wave of passion that carried us far out to sea, to a place we had never gone, had barely imagined, and from which there was—one instantly knows—no returning. It was a churning, disorienting wave that twisted our bodies into brilliant reckless contortions, a calamitous journey outside of time and bereft of perspective, and when at last it subsided, I felt as if ages had passed. We found ourselves floating, still clinging to one another, surrounded in all directions by a new placidity, a transcendental calm, with a great dark emptiness beneath us, a thrilling and terrifying depth, and with the muffled voices of our favorite television characters just barely reaching out to us from some distant, long-forgotten shore. It was my first experience of being inside of life, of attending life's essential performance not as spectator but as fully engaged participant. I knew then that my childhood was over, though I hadn't the slightest idea what came next.

Nine months later, when Samuel Jr. was born, and when my dear Emily died giving birth to him, I experienced again this extraordinary feeling, not a "bad" or "good" feeling but a powerful participatory one. After that, I felt it quite regularly in the daily up- and down-surges of life with my son, until the day came when I lost it forever, which we are getting to soon enough.

It will seem all too befitting Unityville's Edenic pretensions that the first major event of my adulthood was banishment. In fact, it was a rather mild banishment, as banishments go. Nor was it Emily's pregnancy that earned us this sentence—that was reconciled with a quick wedding that we both agreed to happily enough. But it was the inevitable revelation of our longtime clandestine affair with *the television* that led several in the town to suggest that Unityville might not be the ideal location to start our new life together. There is a generous interpretation to this suggestion and a less generous one, but I will not bother with either, since other circumstances made the question largely moot. There was a child on the way, after all, a child who was heartily welcomed by Emily's parents, perhaps slightly less by my own, a tiny human still innocent of the world and deserving every sort of stability and care. And so, to balance these various considerations, it was decided that Emily and I would move together into the now abandoned "haus," whose location would once more prove providential, being near enough for grandparents but far enough for lives of our own.

Thus began the most pleasant, carefree months of my life, spending mornings and evenings with Emily and during the day providing semiskilled handiwork for the town, where Abram's sudden departure had left more than enough opportunities for his "apprentice" to regain the approval of the citizenry. And outside of town, Emily and I were left to grow our relationship in whatever manner made sense to us, whether that meant watching television or discussing television or, as was increasingly the case, spending hardly any time at all with television, and instead taking walks, and making love, and holding long conversations about our future, the seemingly wide-open possibilities of our new life together. The world I had once imagined, a world "out there" on the far side of television, was now of little interest to me, unless it was to travel there with Emily, for "with Emily" was the only place I wished to be.

And when my son was born, and was placed naked and tiny onto my trembling chest; and when, holding my son, I watched my wife watch us both, even as she herself bled out onto the table; and when I saw her face fill with horror at what I assumed was the same thought I was having, that she would die, that she would not be around for him, that she would not be around for me, that we would be abandoned and this beautiful child would be deprived of the one thing no child should ever be deprived of, his lovely mother, his mother who loved him more already in that instant than most people are loved in a lifetime; and when she spoke no words but only watched us until the pain was too great and she succumbed—in that moment I was filled with the pure light of life. I personally contained more life, in that moment, than any person should ever be asked to.

Emily, my wife, I wish we had had more time. Who knows what would have happened, the people we might have become. I wish everything had had more time. I am writing this for Samuel, our son, but also for you, of course, in a way. I mean to say that there is the bond of husband and wife, and the bond of parent and child, but there is also a bond between parents, the unspoken bond that says that everything you do for your child you also do for each other, that all the love you give to your child you also give to each other. And I think it also says that anything you *would have* done, any love you *would have* given, that, too, is for each other.

And then we were alone, my son and I. Emily was gone, had been taken from us, and I was instantly filled with the most powerful need to protect him. I whose life had never known anything like "ambition" or "direction" was suddenly more charged with purpose than I would ever have thought possible. Where before I had let whole years slip unheeded through my fingers, now I would seize the day so firmly I'd need to take care not to choke it. This was life, this child in my arms. I would never leave his side, never fail in my attention to him. For the first few days, I did not even let his grandparents near. I carried him with me at all moments, slept with him on my chest, though in truth I did not sleep for fear I might roll over and harm him. But I was determined we would live this way, two hermits in isolation even from that isolated town, my love lording over us to the end of our days.

Understand that if I take pains to emphasize the *severity* of my love, its unhealthy possessive nature, my purpose in doing so is not to glorify it nor to extract pity for the real duress I was clearly suffering. Rather, I underscore my emotion and conviction during this time so that you might comprehend how deeply perplexed I felt, not many days later, when anxiousness and boredom reentered me.

Of course a human being is a vessel with many compartments. Of course one's heart never holds just a single feeling, no matter how strongly that feeling is felt. I had learned this lesson at the moment of my son's birth and my wife's death, yet in the days and weeks that followed, I discovered that in fact my body could maintain over very long periods the most profound contradictions, watching and loving this beautiful child, unable to imagine a more perfect being or a place I would rather be, and at the same time exasperated by his cries, overwhelmed by his constant care, and wondering, with increasing frequency, how I might manage to take a break from him. At such times I began bringing Samuel to his grandparents (Emily's parents), who were extremely understanding if not outright joyful to see what they assumed was the natural fading of my (perfectly understandable, they said) irrational possessiveness and the burgeoning of a healthier, more responsible, more sharing sort of fatherly love. For my part, I allowed them to hold on to this hopeful interpretation of my mental state, though I knew it to be false. I knew that my love had not been tempered either in type or degree; it still raged in my heart with all its surety and power; simply that it contended, now, with this other force—I thought of it as fatigue rather than laziness—a force that did not lessen my love or calm my heart but simply interfered with and frustrated it. Every time I left Samuel's side, no matter for what duration, I would swoon with guilt at the inconsistency of my actions, the inconstancy of my resolve. But while relinquishing neither my passion nor my guilt, I would explain to myself—I thought of it as being reasonable rather than making excuses—that it was a matter of exhaustion. My brain could provide only so much attention at one time, I told myself. I could sustain that level of engagement for only so long, and the speed with which I found myself going from profound immersive joy to direly needing a recess was in reality a testament to the profundity of the joy, since the more profound the joy, the faster it would consume my mental resources, as a more intense flame burns more quickly through its wick. Mine was not a peculiar combination of laziness and obsession, I told myself; rather I was too loving, my emotions too raw and burdening. And I would need to learn, for the sake of my son, to temper this affection, to parcel it out, so that I would not be so often forced to take a break from it.

Yet I was not able to temper my affection (the fatal flaw of a too-loving father, I told myself, though I'm afraid this was as much a self-compliment as a criticism), and as my need for distraction and "downtime" increased, along with the explosiveness of my caring, I found myself edging back toward the television.

The television, from which Emily and I had been slowly disengaging. The television, which in fact had been pushed back into a corner months earlier to clear a play space for Samuel, and at one point had even had a tablecloth draped over it. The television, which now made its way back to the middle of the room, where it shared Samuel's space in such a way that I could watch both simultaneously. It demanded my attention just as my son did, but unlike my son, it demanded precisely nothing else. No emotion, no real consideration, no responsibility whatsoever. It was an escape from life, from my son, from everything that mattered. And the more I watched, the more I felt compelled to watch, swooning all the while with self-loathing.

How had I become this way? Had television done this to me? Had it sewn into my soul a restlessness so pervasive that even the most profound wonders of real life were to be ruined by it? When I looked at myself now, I saw a man who expected every instant of his life to be compelling, who, when faced with a moment that was not immediately compelling, felt desperate to replace his own life with someone else's, with the life of some character on television. Nor did I improve as Samuel grew—no, quite the opposite. I would spend an entire afternoon playing with my son and would to the outside observer appear to be a generous and loving father, attentive to my son's wants and needs. Yet at the end of the day, I would realize, with something like shock, that I had not *enjoyed* a moment of it (well, moments, of course), but had spent the entire time counting down the minutes until it was over, until I could escape again to the thoughtless engagement of my television. As if my son were some horrible torture I was being subjected to rather than the joy of my life and the only living thing I loved! To be fair, the games he came up with were extremely boring (the game "neighbor" in particular was torturously dull, with "school" and "family" tied for a very close second); yet when you consider that the very sight of this child was enough to fill me with a sense of euphoria—and yes, I would often flash with euphoria throughout these incredibly boring days of playing, when I looked into that handsome little face and saw there the embodiment of beauty and wonder, and it would be extremely strange, this mixture of boredom and euphoria, this simultaneous living-in-the-moment and wanting only to escape it—all of this was, I've said it already but I have no other word for it, exhausting. My love was exhausting; my boredom, presumably caused by my exhaustion, was exhausting; my exhaustion was boring and guilt-inspiring, yet never did this accumulation of frustrated feeling lessen any part of the enormity of my love.

Oh, to have known, back then, even for a moment, the tragedy that would soon befall me! To have seen, not just my shortcomings, but how perversely I would be made to suffer on their account! But would I have improved myself, even with that knowledge? Or is it my *self* that I have always been condemned to, the inescapable limits of my nature, of which the rest have been merely results? These are the sorts of questions I have asked and re-asked over the years, and continue to ask all the time. For befall me that tragedy did, with no time for thought or reflection, on a winter night in 1965.

It was just a few days before Samuel's fourth birthday, and I was watching television. I could probably list for you the complete programming from each night of the week for that season, but the schedule that will air forever on the Guilt-and-Despair channel of my conscience is Monday's mixed-bag lineup of local news, *To Tell the Truth*, *I've Got a Secret*, *The Lucy Show*, *The Andy Griffith Show*, *Hazel*, and *The Steve Lawrence Show*, though I never got past Mayberry that night, for three-quarters of the way through the nine o'clock slot was when catastrophe struck.

My son was, as usual, not watching with me. He hated television, always had—I'd never been able to convince him to watch even the kiddie programs. That night, I'd put him to bed, or at least I'd taken him to the bedroom an hour earlier and assumed he was either sleeping, now, or else playing, but quiet in either case. I was always amused by *Andy Griffith*, its lighthearted characters in their small-town adventures reminding me a little of Unityville, a better, less dreary Unityville, where life was always interesting even though not much ever happened—and so I was quite disturbed when that evening's episode turned out to be largely about guns. It was a bank-robbery episode, and included a lot of talk about guns, the virtues of having or not having them. *Guns in Mayberry?* And I wondered for a moment whether anyone in Unityville kept guns, a thought I'd never had before and that later seemed impossibly timely, in light of what was about to occur. For no sooner had I formed this thought than a voice out in the woods suddenly called my name—"Samuel Johnson! Samuel Johnson!"—and, startled out of my daze, I rushed to see what it was.

No parent could be prepared for the sight that met me. If any parent could have been prepared, it would have been me, who over the years had created in my mind every sort of terrifying paranoid scenario that could possibly befall my child. But those were mere nightmares, tricks of the parental imagination, and when reality struck, they'd not prepared me in the least.

Here was my son, out in the night wearing only his pajamas (how had he gotten out without my noticing? Was I truly that distracted?), being physically restrained by a lunatic, a crazed long-haired man with my boy in one hand and an actual gun held over his head with the other. There was no time for thinking, there was not even a "me" to think, for nothing existed, suddenly, except this man and the two things he was holding: all of life in one hand, and in the other, nothing but death. The one I lunged for was the gun, and there was a struggle, and the sound of it firing. Then there was more struggle, and noises in the dark, then even greater darkness, and suddenly my son was standing next to me screaming as I looked down upon—myself? There I lay, shot through the chest, my eyes wide, my body quite obviously dead. What was happening? Was my death happening? Was my son, whom I tried but failed to reach out to, for I no longer had control of my movements—was it possible that my beautiful motherless son was now without a father as well? How had this happened? How had I failed him? What could I do? Until at last my soul turned and flew away from there—away from my life, away from my son, *away*—and I was not even able to look back.

2.

What happened next happened quickly, and in my shock and emotional confusion, I took for granted that everything passing before my eyes was part of the standard procedure for a soul departing this world. I failed to wonder, as I sailed over the forest floor, why my flight was horizontal rather than vertical, or why I seemed to be headed into town rather than in a more heavenly direction. Not until later did I recall a noise like hyperventilating, or notice that the voice in my mind shouting "Samuel Johnson!" did not particularly sound like my own. Even when I tripped and fell on the path, even then I was in no state to wonder why a soul would trip and fall, and only when that same soul fumbled with its keys to start a rusty truck parked by the trailhead was I at last struck by the odd turns my path to the afterlife was taking. In fact the thought that finally broke through to me was simply that I did not know how to drive. "Samuel Johnson!" cried the voice meanwhile—and the hands, the grungy hands scrambling, the heavy wheezy breathing, the truck's unmuffled revving that brought lights on in the houses, and *Thank goodness*, I thought, *they will see that something's happened, they will check on Samuel, he will not be alone* . . . And when the truck then plunged into darkness, it was not the darkness of death, but a darkness with headlights, unless death also had headlights, perhaps it did, how would I know, who'd never before died, who'd barely even lived, and *Oh God*, I thought, *I'm dead* . . . "Samuel Johnson!" cried the voice while the night's black vacuum sucked me ever deeper in the only direction that road traveled—*away*—my soul ferried ever farther from my son, mile after mile, until the terrible Charonic truck pulled out onto a much larger road, a highway bright with moonlight, then south—*away*—the moonlight flittering, on my left, off the great wide river, already farther than I'd ever been from home, now farther and farther still . . . Until at some point my soul's grubby hand grabbed and twisted the rearview mirror and I found myself facing not my own ghostly visage but rather the very-much-living visage of my lunatic killer, the man who'd just orphaned my boy! "Samuel Johnson!" cried the voice, and in that moment the truck veered, flew through the left-side guardrail off a low cliff and down into the moon-shimmering waters below. Then blackness, and blackness, and finally silence and stop.

When I next "came to," I was looking down upon the dark Earth from far above, at the tiny dots of light that mark the larger roads and scattered houses of rural Pennsylvania at night, and at the blacker black of the Susquehanna cutting south over the land. My movement was gentle, like oozing. There were no sounds but a comforting hum, no feeling but stillness and peace. I had just died again, it occurred to me, two deaths in quick succession, which was bewildering, yes, but this time it seemed to have stuck. And as I floated over the sleeping planet, trying to pinpoint which patch of forested darkness might contain my son, I told myself that things would be o.k. for him, after all, that his grandparents would care for him, and that the lunatic, whoever he'd been and whatever he'd wanted, was now gone. Samuel would be safe, I thought, with a good life, a warm and loving home. He would not be "better off"—how could my boy be better off without his father?—but there was nothing to be done about that now. His future was out of my hands . . . Yet no sooner had I begun to make peace with my fate than my entire field of vision was once more interrupted. My soul suddenly turned, tilted, and I saw that I was not floating heavenward at all, but rather was sitting in a long dark compartment surrounded by seats and sleeping bodies. I'd not departed this mortal coil, but had simply been looking down out the window of what I now recognized—having seen them on television and as specks of metal overhead—as a commercial airplane in flight, speeding me away from my son with near-sonic velocity. I'd not made peace with my fate; I was, if anything, more lost than ever!

Alone there in the darkness, with no sound but the plane's low rumble and the soft snores and rustling about the cabin, I eventually forced myself to calm down. So abruptly had I been yanked from life to death, then from one death to another, then from what I believed was a heavenly trajectory back to this mundane sphere, that I felt wholly overwhelmed. *Why am I here? What happens next?* A man's balding head rested inches from my shoulder, yet I had never felt so alone. I told myself this was clearly a dream, and I should simply wait to wake from it. But as my eyelids closed, and remained closed, and were quickly joined by a slower, heavier breathing that seemed also to belong to me; and since, despite my body having fallen asleep, my mind remained perfectly awake, there in the darkness, with nothing to see or do; and since I stayed in this wakeful state for what felt like days and was in reality perhaps two or three hours, I did eventually begin to take stock of my situation.

Upon death—I surmised for myself—my soul had flown into the lunatic killer's body, and upon *its* death, I'd flown again, presumably into the body closest by. That body, this one, belonged to someone seated in an airplane flying overhead—and here I was.

Was I a ghost? If so, I seemed unlikely to haunt anyone, having apparently neither a voice of my own nor any other means of expression. Unseen, unheeded: that appeared to be the state of things. Trapped, in fact, in the darkness of another person's head, a person being carried in a metal cylinder through the emptiness of night, night itself being nothing but the default state of a planet floating meaningless through space; and I began to suffer something like vertigo, my thoughts in danger of spiraling into pure chaos, when fortunately the eyes I saw through opened, and my body rose from its seat, squeezed past its sleeping neighbor, and made its way by the tiny floor lights—everything about this environment entirely new to me, bear in mind—to a cramped metal closet that was apparently the bathroom.

My first look—there, in the bathroom mirror—at the human form in which I'd been stranded was a little surprising, and caused my mind's eye a hard blink, because the young man looked so much like me, my living self. He was a few years younger and better groomed, but in height and weight, skin tone and hair color, he might easily have been my twin. He was more fidgety (I was never fidgety), and as he proceeded to use the toilet, I saw that his stomach was flabbier, his whole body hairier—in fact in time I became aware of so many differences that I no longer saw any resemblance at all—but for a moment, at least, I could not escape the déjà-vu-like feeling that I had somehow become trapped inside a saggier version of myself. I later decided this was purely coincidence, but at the time this feeling fueled my imagination (although clearly reality had already out-imagined me by a considerable margin, and I was merely catching up), and I began to consider that there might be a purposeful Design at work. Perhaps the events transpiring were not random, but rather shaped by Reason, or by particular reasons, by an intention of some sort.

A punishment from God—it must be, what else?—a punishment for failing to believe or having sex out of wedlock, for my shortcomings as a father or watching too much television, one or all four, since these were the only sins I'd committed that seemed at all worthy of God's attention. And they *were* serious sins, I supposed, and deserving of punishment, perhaps even a punishment like this—were it not for my son. For although sometime earlier, while floating over the Earth, I had told myself Samuel would be safe without me, that was only because I'd assumed I would be gone. Whereas now that my fate had proven otherwise, I was again convinced my son desperately needed me, if only because I was still here for him to need. To remain in this world, to continue to exist on the same mortal coil as my boy and yet have no means of protecting him—the situation struck me as indefensibly sadistic. Surely no power in the universe was so pointlessly malicious? Surely events would soon conspire to return me to my son?

Well, and why *wouldn't* I return to him? I went on, my body by now back in its seat and sleeping, so that I was once again speaking to myself in the dark. Was the world so large (at that time I did not actually know how large the world was) that fortune would not soon land me back with him? True this airplane was taking me away, but airplanes, I knew, also returned, and the same people who took them in one direction tended to take them back in the other. Surely I would soon return to my son with as much haste as I now sped away!

For hours I went on this way, and by the time the pilot came on the loudspeaker to announce the plane's descent, I had fully deluded myself with hope for a swift and sympathetic conclusion to these profoundly unsettling events. The cabin lights came up, and now my body awoke, as did the other bodies around it. The plane then landed, followed by a long period of taxiing around the runway, during which my neighbor, the one who had been sleeping by my head, spoke to my body as if they were already acquainted, as if perhaps they had spoken at the start of the flight as well. Thus I learned that his name was Burt ("by the way") and my name—the name of the young man I was stranded in—was Christopher. I learned that Burt had come to California (this was how I learned we were in California) to join up with his wife and daughters, who'd moved here some months earlier while he looked for a job. I learned many other things about Burt, who spoke continuously throughout what ended up being an incredibly long tour of the tarmac, until at last Christopher was asked what brought *him* to California, and a voice that was not mine said:

"Oh, I—That's a very long story. I was involved in—How to explain? I was doing well in college, very well, in fact, not that I'm bragging, hardly! Of course that doesn't—only that I tend to be rather introverted, or bookish, happily, I should say, and yet! Somehow trouble manages to—Well it's really been my whole life, hasn't it? Happily reading, or writing, 'steering clear' and—But then, *then*, for reasons I will no doubt never understand, a moment comes, it always does, when I question the very—I panic, that is, that I'm making a terrible mistake, cheating myself of a 'normal life,' not that I'd particularly want one of *those*. But before I can come to my senses—alas!—I've launched myself into the social sphere, where something goes wrong, it always does, upon which I erupt, that's what my parents call it, an 'eruption,' it's the same every time. Only in this present case—that is, my parents, for various reasons—It seemed prudent that—You see, they arranged, out of the 'kindness of their hearts,' so to speak—or perhaps, to be fair, out of the actual kindness of their actual hearts—This morning, that is, I'm to set off for a year aboard a *ship*—not a passenger ship, an actual shipping-type ship, so no pool chairs or shuffleboard, I'm guessing—still, I'm off to 'see the world,' as my parents put it—I told them I've no intention of seeing any such thing ha ha—At any rate, there you have it!"

Soon I would learn firsthand quite a lot more about Christopher Plume—more than I wished to know, more than anyone should ever be forced to know about another person's daily existence. In this moment on the airplane with Burt, however, with Christopher still new to me, as I listened full of hope for how his plans might bring about my swift return to Samuel, I stopped short on the words "set off for a year" and "see the world," and my mind's heart collapsed. I spent what remained of the morning's journey in a kind of hate-filled daze. The situation was too ripe for mere coincidence, and it occurred to me that Fate, or God, or whatever force could be behind this (for I have always believed some force must be responsible for the heinous conditions of my afterlife; I believe it even now, all these years later, with still no evidence either way), whatever force was orchestrating these atrocious events was in fact more viciously ironic than I could ever have guessed. Clearly its intentions were set against me, and rather than return me to my son, it was steering me as far away as possible.

Reader, then and there I decided the course of my future, along with my purpose in this world. As we arrived at the docks and stood in the shadow of the enormous vessel, watching Christopher's luggage lugged up a wobbly wheeled staircase to an opening in the ship's flank, while dinghies and sailboats sailed out around us toward the largest body of water I had ever seen, I swelled with the most absurd optimism, and for a moment almost forgot I was dead. I imagined myself embarked upon a great tragic-heroic adventure. *Whatever the way back to Samuel,* I declared, *I will find it myself.*

That achieving this goal would prove infuriatingly improbable, but not technically impossible, and would set me on a quest spanning many years and many lives, through vast deserts of boredom, perilous droughts of despair, and occasional saving oases of friendship and love, is the story I intend to tell in these pages.

3.

Christopher Plume was the only child of a wealthy Boston couple, busy but not unloving, who regretted how little time they had to spend with him. He'd done well in college but had developed an oddly humble sort of arrogance about himself, in that he felt he knew more than everyone around him, yet also felt he knew almost nothing at all. He believed himself to be extremely ignorant by any reasonable standard, but saw the current standards for education—whatever those were in 1965—as so ludicrously underwhelming that despite his own ignorance, he still knew more than everyone else. He was sheltered and snooty, more awkward than mean-spirited, and loved nothing so much as being alone. He would happily have resigned himself to a life of the mind but for one ill-fated quirk of his character, that every once in a while, for one reason or another, he would suddenly panic that his natural inclinations were all wrong. That in withdrawing from society he was cheating himself of a fully human life. He would then plunge headfirst into society, where something terrible would happen, each time more terrible than before. So when this latest incident at college (the nature of which I never learned, as after his conversation on the airplane with Burt, he never again mentioned it) led to expulsion, and his parents suggested he spend a year working for his uncle's shipping company, Christopher had jumped at the chance. It was not the prospect of high-seas adventures that enticed him so much as the hope of escaping "adventures" once and for all. Of losing himself in stoicism and bookish isolation. Which unfortunately for me was more or less what happened.

In fact, now that I think about it, my time with Christopher Plume is probably the worst place to start the tale of my own adventures, aside from the fact that this is where they actually started, since it was easily the dullest episode of my entire afterlife. Not only was Christopher's work on the ship the most menial possible (countless hours of mopping and scrubbing, the only jobs he was qualified for), but he was a social outcast from the start. It probably did not help that when the crew first invited him to join them off-shift, he replied, "Oh no, that's—You see I'm here more to *read* than anything—It's nothing personal, of course. I'm sure you're all very interesting!" Or that he was inept at everything, or that his uncle had ordered he be given a cabin all to himself when everyone else had to share. To his credit, Christopher did not seem bothered by the crew's contempt, nor did he even mind all the tedious labor, since every moment *not* spent working—or sleeping, eating, talking to himself, or staring out his porthole at whatever new exotic location the ship had traveled to, though never once bothering to go ashore—he could spend reading books.

So many books! More than I had previously known existed. Rhymeless poetry, impenetrable philosophy, bulky incomprehensible novels, and others I would not even know how to classify because I could not understand them at all. He read and read. He slept and read. He mopped, scrubbed, brooded, masturbated, and read. Stranded on a floating island surrounded by semihostile natives, he tried to live as if he were alone in the world. And he would have been very disappointed, I think, to learn that he was not even alone in his room, that I, Samuel Johnson, was there with him, seeing only what he saw, hearing only what he heard, and being left, when he slept, with just the sound of his breathing in a darkness with no dimension; just the beating of his heart in an emptiness without space; just the nighttime noises of a mortal plane I no longer belonged to but somehow still occupied, to what end I could not imagine. Surely there was no situation so awful in all the world, and I the most pitiable creature living or dead!

You see, despite my confidence on the airplane that I would find a way back to my son, on the ship I quickly discovered I had no actual means of doing so. Though I could see and hear, I could not taste, smell, touch, speak, or affect anything whatsoever. I tried every possible escape . . . but what was there to try? No actions to take, no choices to make. Just awareness of myself as a being in nonspace, witness to a life that was not mine and had nothing to do with me. It was an afterlife unlike any the Bible had mentioned; in fact, more than anything it resembled (I could not help but notice) watching television. And in my fury I told myself this must be the point: as punishment for my failures in life, I was being made to suffer a television-like purgatory . . . but eventually I decided that didn't make sense. Christopher's life was so much more boring than television, after all. If the point of my "punishment" was to make me regret watching television, it was having the opposite effect. How badly I wanted to watch television! Though even that would have been torture, only incrementally less excruciating than the unremitting awfulness of those endless nights and days. Television didn't *matter*, after all. Christopher certainly didn't matter. Only my Samuel mattered, returning to my son, which, however, there was no way to do!

In fact there *was* a way, or would be in the near future, but since back then I did not know that, my defeatist impulses rather quickly kicked in. I passed the first few months in a rage of furious impotence, but eventually, without even quite realizing it, I gave up. My conviction wore away. I forgot what I was supposed to be doing. Or not forgot, but one day I failed to bring it to mind. And then I was out to sea, so to speak. I was no longer the tragic hero I'd imagined myself on the dock that day, but only a bored hopeless soul doomed by Fate to an eternity of dullness, circling the globe without ever seeing any of it, reading book after book without understanding a word, having lost first my hopes, then my goals, and finally even my problems. Until for all intents and purposes I *was* Christopher Plume. We were both Christopher, in our different ways, even if he was the only one happy about it.

But life, I have noticed, only goes around in circles for as long as you don't want it to. Once you've forgotten your aspirations and grown comfortable in your existential inconsequence, life jolts you forward, usually for the worse. And sure enough, after nine months at sea, Christopher's cocoon life was suddenly interrupted.

First, his social standing improved. As awkward and inept as he somehow had managed to remain, still he could not stay a newbie forever. He did his work without complaining, which was at least something, and one day, without anything being said, the rest of the crew started treating him better, simply because he'd been around so long. For Christopher it was a confusing moment. For the longest time he'd been pleased to be ignored and excluded, wanting nothing more than to be left alone, yet now he found himself feeling— this was the second thing that happened—as if perhaps he ought to be a little more social after all. Was it the crew's small encouragement? Or had solitude finally taken its toll? Perhaps he was simply exhausted by the constant effort of living mentally apart from people he had no physical way of escaping? Whatever the case, little by little he entered their ranks, allowing himself to become the person they preferred him to be. Amenable. Self-deprecating. Slightly dumb. Happy to take an interest in subjects he found utterly uninteresting. Willing to listen to the same stories over and over, to accept mockery without taking offense—and advice! There was, in our ninth month, a great deal of advice.

"You know, your problem is"—it always started with "your problem is"—"you're too" fancy or stuck-up or snooty or intellectual. Or "You're too nice," though where they got the idea that Christopher was nice, I can't imagine. "You got to get *dark*, kid."

"Dark?"

"Like, *serious*. Also, loosen up."

"You're so right," Christopher would reply, downhearted. "What is it about me? It's how I've always been! Why can't I just" go ashore or smoke or invite everyone to hang out in his cabin and get drunk?

Of course they were already drunk in his cabin for these sorts of conversations.

"You know what ain't in your books?" says one of the advice-givers. "The whole damn world. Adventures, dangers. Out there! You meet it staring or it swallows you up. Believe me. *Believe* me. Things I've seen . . ." Brows harden recalling everything that's been seen. "And out here's worse than anywhere. You go it alone out here—well, nobody should go it alone anywhere, but least of all *out here*."

"That's right," someone else says. "Man's right about that."

"Course *we* love it out here. But it's the worst. Out here, you learn to love the worst. *That's* dark."

"For me," says Christopher, who has been only half listening, "it's more that—Well, I get these ideas in my head, ideals against which I pretend to evaluate lived experience, when really it's more like I don't wish to be bothered with—with anything, I suppose—with everything! But is that any way to live?"

"Not out here it ain't."

"Not anywhere, but *especially* not out here."

"Because *life*, I've come to realize—and by the way it's spending time with you fellows that has allowed me finally to come to this realization—but *life*, I think, is largely *about* being bothered. What a strange revelation! And yet so true!" His voice very animated by this point. "Life is about being bothered!"

"Not sure that's how we'd—"

"Not comfort and happiness, oh no no! It's about forcing yourself beyond those familiarities to talk to people and do things and try things even when you don't wish to, even when, not only do you not wish to, but also you know perfectly well you won't enjoy it when you do! But we *do* these things, or you fellows do at any rate, these are the sorts of things normal people do. But me? I'm flimsy. Weak. I've always been—"

"*Weak*, that's a better word for it. That's what we were trying to get at earlier. Not so much physically, though that too, but more it's your attitude to things, the way you walk around like a . . . You know chinchillas? I had a girlfriend once kept chinchillas. Soft, kind of stupid. They don't know a thing about anything."

"Which is true of me as well!"

"On top of your being snooty and snobby and so forth."

"I have all sorts of shortcomings!"

"But, *but*, listen. This is the important part. You need to hear this part."

"Tell me!"

"You're o.k., kid. You may not know a single thing other than books, mops, toilets, and carrying shit, but you try. You *try*. Unlike jackass Stuart over there. He knows everything you could know about sailing, he's one hell of a sailor, Stuart, but he's also a lazy fishshit. At least you ain't a fishshit, kid. That's something."

"That's—Thank you for saying that!"

And it went on this way, in the manner of this conversation, for about a month.

Oh ludicrous month! Christopher increasingly convinced of the wisdom of his crewmates and the deficiencies of himself . . . losing his own sense of purpose, just as I had long since lost mine . . . the days and weeks running together; time an immeasurable lump. And it might very well have gone on this way forever—or at least for the remainder of Christopher's one-year contract—but for an accident of circumstance, when one day his new "friends" invited him on an off-ship outing, where Christopher came to a rude awakening, and was faced with a fateful choice, and where this story of my time with him finally gets off the ground.

We'd anchored that morning off the island of Antigua in the West Indies. A clear day, and bright, the water impossibly blue, and we landed in a cove of such unusual beauty that for the first time in a very long time I, Samuel Johnson, was shocked out of passive stupefaction, and remembered myself. Not that I thought *about* myself, or my goals, my problems—only that I woke, at long last, to thoughts and feelings that were perceivably my own. For as soon as we'd cleared the docks it was down, first, to a long yellow beach, soft and powdery. Then a forest path—a wide swath of packed dirt— the sun cutting shadows through the treetops. Here were plants I'd never seen and flowers I'd never imagined, birdsong I'd never heard. Of the few places I'd traveled in life and death combined, this was by far the most vibrant, and I felt something like excitement, a rustle of anticipation . . .

Up a gradual incline and as we walked, a man named Dawson, who had been working on the ship longer than anyone and never failed to impart whatever knowledge he'd picked up along the way, informed us that the island's native name was Wadadli; that the locals spoke a mixture of British English and Caribbean Creole, the latter a sort of choppy English mixed with African words and inflec- tions; that the average rainfall was only forty-five inches, which appar- ently wasn't very much; that over the years he personally had come here more times than the rest of us had gone anywhere (which in my case at least was almost certainly true); and that the most important thing to know about the town we were just now entering was that it boasted the world's best cabana bar, where a few moments later we arrived.

What followed was disappointing (a sign of my growing self-awareness was how disappointed I felt), because in the midst of this natural paradise, when we might have gone off exploring or lain out in the sun, visited cultural sights or met and talked with local people, instead they did what they always did: they got drunk. Christopher was no different, except that he drank faster, spoke less, was poked fun at more, and needed to use the bathroom at least twice as often. In fact it was in returning from his fourth or fifth trip to the bathroom, after perhaps two hours in the bar, that Christopher discovered the others were gone.

"Isn't that spectacular," he said out loud to no one. "They've all left while I was in the bathroom! Left me here with nothing!" Which was not entirely true, however, because they'd left the bill as well. "And this!" He held it up.

Indignant, drunk, still he kept calmer than I would have expected. He gathered his wits, folded the insufficient cash he found in his pocket into the thickest wad possible, set it casually on the table-top as if it were unquestionably more than enough, and meandered his way out of the bar into the bright Antiguan afternoon. Then a quick right, a left, another right, before taking off at a sprint up the sloping road.

"Cretins!—Hooligans!—Jerks!" he spouted some moments later as he finally slowed down, out of breath from uphill running. "Gone from the table, what, three minutes at most? And the drunk fools forget you even—Or worse, they don't forget, they—probably left on purpose!" The scene of their departure unfolding for him as he pushed on up through the town, past shops, attractions; it was basically a tourist town, or at least we were in the tourist part of it. "Well of course if they left *the bill*, they must have left *on purpose*," he went on, "laughing, most likely, slapping each other's stupid shoulders, and—" And having established for himself that the others had definitely left on purpose, had mocked and poked fun at him and were no doubt still mocking and poking fun, his anger turned, now, on himself, for *he* was the one who'd allowed this to happen—how? "By being a fool, is how—a dupe! A rube! Falling in with them in the first place, then—listening to their self-important blather! Adopting their overwrought affectations, squeezing myself into the narrow confines of their ludicrous worldview, as if their 'ship life' were anything more than—As if it added up to anything at all!" Angry at himself but also at them, still. Angry at his own anger, and at the situation overall. Of course this was far from the first time the crew had demeaned him, yet it seemed (still climbing . . . the whole town was one big hill) that being away from the ship, being out on his own in a place so lively and open was giving him new perspective, or else old perspective, was reminding him of the person he preferred to be. "And how little it takes to see clearly!" he laughed, shedding, now, layers of that life that had so recently encrusted him. "How little distance we need to once again see the world writ large and recognize the smallness of the life we've been living! To stand before one's decisions, decisions that moments earlier seemed perfectly logical, but that we no longer recognize, or rather—Well, what *is* it, in the end?" Having by this point reached a spot where the road split left or right but where Christopher kept straight, leaving the road to climb some stone steps up the grassy hilltop. "Is my subconscious need for companionship overwhelming my conscious desires and preferences? Or is my *self*-consciousness thwarting my natural state? Have I so internalized society's prejudice against solitude that I doubt my own autonomy and place confidence in others, not because they deserve confidence but simply because, being others, they are *not me*?" But by now he'd reached the hilltop, and stopped, both walking and talking to himself, in the crumbly graveyard of an old church.

Here everything was quiet. There was no one else around, and from that height, on that day, you could see for miles in all directions. Below lay the town and the beach and dock, out further our ship, the ocean. Turning, we saw the island's interior, an expanse of green hills, a rolling skyline against a hazy blue horizon.

He sat in the shade of a knotty tree, more somber than before, possibly more sober, looking out at the world's green-blue enormity and pushing pebbles around with his feet. The only sounds were the breeze riffling the tree's small leaves and the scratch of the kicked pebbles. He was alone with his thoughts. I was alone with mine.

How strange to be out in the world! I thought, by now fully awake and experiencing, all at once, an exuberant rush of self-awareness, the flush of the fine weather, and overpowering relief at being free of that damn ship. *After ten months circling the globe,* I said to myself, *to be here, suddenly, in this spot, this spot among all others. Having come here for no apparent reason; having all but stumbled here in leaving the ship. Yet with a sense, too, of having* arrived *here—at the top of the world!* (Aside from the airplane, it was the highest place I'd ever been.) *Christopher is right,* I went on, *it really does take so little to see the smallness of life on that ship. A few hours on land, barely a mile between us and the water, but it's enough for the whole rest of the world to come rushing back in!* Then I thought of my son . . . and a wave of sadness rolled over me. I was sad but also happy, both emotions at once. And Christopher—his eyes had turned hazy. He'd started to cry. Not for me, obviously, but I thought I understood him. I felt sorry for him. And for myself. For a moment, I felt sorry for everyone.

It wasn't very much later that we started back down the hill, and the day must have grown hot, because even leaving the shade he was sweating. He did not hurry but labored along, having somehow ended up on a different road going back than the one we'd traveled up. It was less touristy, this new road, lined with wooden houses and plain storefronts, local people going about their lives. They were nothing like me, these people—yet how lucky I felt to be among them! They had dark skin (not the first I'd seen, as there had occasionally been black people on television), and their town was unlike anywhere I had ever been; yet it also felt familiar to me, this place, this new road, in a way the touristy road had not. *That* road (and the beach, the bar, the crumbly old church) had seemed like a fantasy, but this was more believable, an actual place people lived. And I remember thinking then (the sort of whimsical, expansive thought there'd been no space for on that claustrophobic ship), it occurred to me that the outside world was not actually as "outside" as I'd once imagined, back when I'd known that world only through television. For even on this distant patch of the planet, a road was just a road, the weather was either nice or not, nothing was more or less than it ought to be, for better or for worse, and—and my thoughts continued this way, and I was feeling very wise and full of myself, when Christopher came to a stop.

We were standing outside a small white house that was apparently also a shop. "Fortunes," the sign said, and "Palms Read." It was smaller than the buildings around it, and somehow ill fitting, as if it were thinner, or wider, or perhaps older? Certainly the inside, where we stood a moment later, was nothing like I would have guessed. No candles or beaded curtains or crystal balls, none of the "fortuneteller" props I'd seen in old movies on television. Just a cling-clanging of bells following us in from the door. There was a polished wooden table with some velvety chairs, an ornate lamp with a colored glass shade in the corner. On the far wall hung a large portrait of a black woman in a colorful outfit, but she was not the same woman who appeared a moment later in a fluffy bathrobe, wiping her hands on a paper towel.

"You have no cash," she said, upon taking a full look at us.

"I—" Christopher patted his pockets. "That's true."

"So?"

"Right, of course. I would need money. And I don't have any!"

"So?"

"I should be on my way."

"Wait!" said the Fortune-Teller. (I'll call her that since I never learned her name.) She puzzled over us a moment. "Huh," she said. "O.K., sit."

What happened next I cannot describe in any way that will seem nearly as fascinating to you as it was for me then. She simply stared at us, not briefly but for a remarkably long time. Whole minutes passed, and perhaps it was my philosophical mood, but I began to feel it was truly "us" she was staring at, not just Christopher but me as well—so penetrating was her gaze, so intent upon his eyes. When he started to speak, to mention again his lack of money, merely raising her finger was enough to silence him. In fact he was utterly cooperative the whole time, and tried hard to keep his eyes open, to sit still and not blink, as if he were sitting for an eye exam. Finally she spoke:

"Yuh on the ship."

"I am!"

"Course yuh on the ship. How else yuh come here? But life on the ship is no good for you."

"No, it isn't."

"You think it be good, but then, no."

"That's," said Christopher, "that's unfortunately accurate."

"But life is also no good before the ship. And before what comes before. Always, life is no good for you. Always you think it be good, but then, no."

"You—yes, you've—I'm afraid you've got me pinned!"

The Fortune-Teller shrugged. If I were to guess, I would guess she thought Christopher did not take her very seriously. Skeptic that he was, I couldn't imagine that he did, though he was in an odd mood, and the truth is I had no idea what he was feeling. Yet because I brought a very different perspective to these proceedings—because for me the so-called paranormal was by then normal to the point of being mind-numbingly dull—I personally could not escape feeling that something extraordinary was taking place.

"So." She sat back. "What you want?"

"What do I want? What do people usually want?"

"Advice."

"That's what I want, I suppose."

"I am afraid you will not like it."

"Really?" Christopher sounded more interested. "Why on earth not?"

"Can't tell yuh that without giving yuh the advice."

"Right!" He laughed. "A conundrum!" And wagged a playful finger, though it came off more as awkwardness and nerves.

Then she stood. She walked the room, musing. She appeared— if I can offer more interpretation, since of course I was extremely interested and following all of this very closely—to be legitimately fretting. At the very least, she was weighing whatever it was she had to share. And she apparently decided, in the end, to go ahead with it, for when she sat back down, she very slowly and very deliberately said:

"You got no life. You think you have life before, and that you lost this life, but you got no life before either, so you lost nothing. You lost nothing and you got nothing to lose. Wait, wait. Although you got nothing, inside yuh's a mon who lost something. He had something and lost it, and it is a real thing, and he is suffering this loss. His suffering is great, and he is stuck inside yuh, this suffocating mon."

"Yes, that's how I feel . . ."

"You misunderstand. You are not this mon. He is a mon inside yuh. A jumbee. Nothing I can do for you, but him we maybe help. Will you help this mon?"

"Yes. I want to help him!"

"You still misunderstand. To help this mon get back the thing he is missing, you got to give up the one thing yuh have. You got nothing, but everybody got one thing. But the mon inside yuh, he wraut up. He does not have the one thing yuh got. Yuh cannot give it *to* him, but give it up *for* him, that yuh can. And maybe this way he gets back the thing he is missing."

"I don't understand at all!"

"Nah, but me words been very literal. If you choose to help this mon, that is your choice."

"But you haven't even told me what to do!"

The Fortune-Teller fell thoughtful again. She mumbled out a discussion with herself, mumbling first to the right, then to the left, until one or the other gave up.

"Buss off the ship," she said. "You cannot go back there. There is nothing for yuh."

"No, there isn't."

"Take a plane from the other side of the island and fly to a place I will send you. I will send you to this place and give you stuff to eat when you get there. If you eat this stuff, then the mon inside yuh, the suffocating mon, maybe can do what he must to get back what he is missing. This mon, he needs to be brave. He needs to do what he must. He will understand when the time comes. But you, you will not understand. No matter. Me words have been very literal, and I give them to yuh free, to do with as you wish. Chances slim, but there is nothing to lose, because you got nothing. So?"

When we left the Fortune-Teller's house, we had with us a small bag containing a mixture of herbs and a scrap of paper upon which was written the name of the special place she was sending Christopher. Reader, can you guess what that place was? She also gave directions to the Antigua airport and pointed the way, a twelve-minute taxi ride across the island. Christopher had no money to pay for a taxi, or for that matter an airplane ticket, but it occurred to me in a moment of dizzying hopefulness that perhaps he could collect-call his parents, make up some story, and get them to wire the amount. I felt desperately eager for this possibility and anxious to know what was going on in Christopher's mind. Was he planning to go back to the ship? Forget the ship and head to the airport? Even now, I cannot tell you how much he believed of the Fortune-Teller's speech or how well he even understood it. I can tell you only that the sun was well to the west, the late afternoon already turning to evening . . . that people passed by as we stood there, paying us no attention at all . . . and that we were still standing outside the Fortune-Teller's shop when the deep groan-like *wumph* of the ship's horn finally warned us we would need to start back. And I can tell you, too, that when at last Christopher turned and started walking—*away* from the docks, toward the island's interior, the road, the airport!—I was filled with the most extraordinary feeling, and knew in my mind's heart that Christopher was as well.

For while there may be only a few moments in each lifetime when a person chooses to affect his own fate, and fewer for some people than for others, nonetheless there are such moments, they do exist, and Christopher had finally found a way forward that was not a poorly conceived "eruption." He'd found a chance to participate in the actual occurrence of his own life: to exercise freedom, to engage in action, to embrace change, to demonstrate courage! Or at least that is what I told myself he'd found as he set off in the direction of the Antigua airport. Filled with joy, I naturally assumed Christopher felt likewise. I also perhaps understood on some level that things would turn out bad for him, one way or another, and I wanted to think that for this one magnificent moment, he'd found it all worthwhile.

In fact, what followed was probably the single most enjoyable hour of my afterlife. So little has been even bearable, these many years, far less enjoyable, but that hour I will always remember. After ten months trapped on that monstrous boat, we were out in the world, striding with open arms as a wave of life's special energy washed over us. The ship's horn *wumphed* again in the distance, sounding its final warning, but for us it sounded a far more profound departure (Christopher now stepping at a brisk clip), a headfirst plunge into the uncharted waters of existence. The sky orchestrated a gorgeous backdrop to this scene, a dusky swirl of red, orange, and yellow, like the skin of an enormous tropical fruit. Truly, I had never seen such a sky. Most importantly, we were—I did not understand all the details, but I was quite certain of the fact of it—we were en route to my son. My son. Across this island, I told myself, awaits an airport. Simply follow this road, a mere ten or so miles . . .

The road quickly left the town behind and wound up into the hills beyond, but staying in sight of the ocean, and as we climbed we passed among clusters of small houses and a great variety of trees. Some of the houses were shack-like, others much nicer and modern in design, like houses in American suburbs I'd seen on television, but transplanted to this foreign place. Soon we'd reached the top of a long slope and could see that the road on the far side turned away from the ocean, wound down through the hills into the denser vegetation of the island's interior. That Christopher chose this spot to stop for a moment seemed reasonable enough, and I assured myself he was not faltering in his resolve, only that he was in terrible cardiovascular shape and needed to rest for a moment against a wire post fence along the roadside. He stood gazing down a great wide hill of short grass, straight and green as a golf course, that emptied below into a vast yellow meadow, which ran long and flat as far as the sea.

As it happened, his timing was fortuitous. For after only a few minutes standing there, enjoying the spread of dusk's colors over the water, we were unexpectedly witness to a sight of a different sort. It was our own ship rounding the edge of the island and sailing out to the horizon, away. How strange its slow crawl through the water, its ugly lumbering through that shimmering sea. The contrast between nature's beauty and man's depravity has never seemed so startling, and we followed the ship's path until at last it was such a small blip in the distance that you could no longer call it a blip at all. There went my captivity, my purposelessness, that cyclical, ineffectual destiny I thought I'd be trapped in forever. There went, too, some version of Christopher that he was happy to be free of and wished never to see again. Bon voyage! Adiós! Arrivederci, terrible life!

Then suddenly, to my surprise, Christopher had hopped the fence. Before I even understood what was happening, he was up and over and already halfway down the long hill, sounding his loudest yawp as he stumblingly hurled himself over rushing green, aiming, it seemed, for the sprawling yellow meadow, perhaps even for the ocean beyond. Air swooshed past his ears and each time he fell (he fell several times), he seemed to get up again with greater vigor and even louder yawps, as if to yawp his way through the pain of his tumbles.

Well, he deserves this, I told myself. Whatever "this" was. This eruption. I felt happy for him. Just that we had also, of course, an airport to get to.

Then into the meadow, its grass waist-high and whistling past, its expanse somewhat longer than it had seemed from above, longer and more exhausting. And as we slowed down on the verge of hyperventilation, I saw there was suddenly a building in front of us, a structure I hadn't noticed until now. It was not a house or dwelling but just a small shed, such as we used in Unityville to store tools for the gardens. Surrounding this shed, however, was a low, shoddily erected barbed-wire fence, and barely contained by this fence were two of the hungriest, meanest dogs I had ever seen. They were not even full dogs, only fangs and rib cages, snarling and flinging themselves at the barbed wire. Instantly Christopher switched from fast-forward to slow-backwards, sputtering calming words aimed seemingly at himself. We'd backed up this way perhaps thirty feet and were turning to run the other direction—back across the meadow to the hill, up the hill to the road, down the road to the airport—but when we faced around we found, standing in our way, an enormous, and I mean simply enormous, an enormous and determined-looking *bull*. It was lean but more than large enough to disembowel us, and seemed eager to do so. So back toward the sea we turned, running again, past the shed, the dogs, and we had just come in reach of the water—why the water? Was the water safe? Do bulls and dogs not like water?—when my field of vision did a backwards somersault through the air. I saw, all at once, the sea, the sky, the bull, and the distant hill behind us. Then all was black, and stayed black for some time. Until at last I was standing above Christopher, from the outside looking down, and this time there was no confusion. I knew what had happened and what it meant. It meant no airport, no journey, no son.

I considered ending this chapter here, with Christopher's death. I thought, in particular, that I should probably devote a separate chapter to my time inside that bull, if only because it is the most unusual circumstance I have found myself in, and readers might theoretically learn something from it. (*Is that why you're writing this,* I asked myself, *for readers to learn things?*) But the truth is, I was inside that bull for less than forty-eight hours, and there was nothing about the experience that would be of use to anyone. In fact, it was just one uneventful night, which I personally spent in anguish, and by the next day, and from then on, that particular bull's life was not typical in the least. The man who owned the bull discovered the scene in the early hours and immediately hid the animal away, hoping to save it, or himself, from an ignoble fate. We spent an hour in a claustrophobic trailer truck, then were stowed away in a barn. But the nature of Christopher's injuries must have been utterly apparent, so that we were soon discovered by the authorities and moved to a holding pen in an incredibly filthy facility that I assumed to be a slaughterhouse, and there we awaited our fate.

It was late that evening, my second in Antigua, while the body I was trapped inside trod small circles round and round the pen, like Christopher's ship sailing round and round the globe, as if even this brute beast felt obliged to describe for me the pattern my existence would forever follow, when the Fortune-Teller came to visit.

"Is big news," she said, leaning over the fence, "what happened to that boy. I heard it on the radio. That is how I knew to seek yuh. That boy was rich, got a rich family. Too bad he had no cash for taxis, you think? Ah, feel no way, I made new arrangements. Another mon is coming. He will take yuh on this quest. This new mon is gahn een—sick. Anyway he says so. I tell him 'Drink still-beating bull blood.' Ha! He is a crazy old mon and I think he will do it. Then I tell him, 'After yuh drunk the bull blood, take a *special quest.*' I give him the same stuff, same instruction. I think he will do it. But now, listen. When you get back to this place, you got to do the thing. You check? This mon is a bad mon, dogheart, so don't feel no bad feelings. That rich boy was not so bad. Hard to do the thing to that boy. So this turned out good—safe. This bad mon got no love. He's sick, a crazy mon. So if you got to make him dead, no worries. Everybody gets dead. You dead. There is nothing special about this. Love is a special thing. Rare thing. Rare things worth more. Simple. You check?"

Of course I did not really know, that night, what to expect of the following morning. But as the Fortune-Teller sauntered off into the darkness, I felt toward her a deep pang of warmth and the most overwhelming swell of gratitude. That she had seen me, bothered to notice me, to let me know that she knew I was there. That she had even chosen to *help* me, and with so little cause, really no cause at all!

I wished I had more time with her, could have thanked her. I wished I could have asked the million questions stored up inside me, or at least gotten some clarification on her incredibly vague instructions. But mostly, of course, I was full of anticipation. And joy! How extraordinary to be back in the world! To feel myself again a participant in existence. To know I was no longer alone. That there was hope. That whatever else happened, there was now at least possibility.

4.

Orson Fitz's first order of business, upon settling into the plane, was to down as much booze as the stewardess would bring him. This was hardly surprising, considering how chaotic his morning had been.

He'd arrived just after dawn at the slaughtering trough (or whatever it's called), looking less like a crazy old man than simply a very drunk one, with little bloodshot eyes peeking out from his pink face, a nesty poof of white hair, a lanky frame stumbling forth in a bedraggled business suit. The Fortune-Teller was there, propping him up. He teetered this way and that. She helped him hand some money to a man in a bloody apron, and the next thing I knew, the bull's neck was in a wooden vise, and this pink man's watery red eyes were up beside me. There was a whoosh, a chop, and everything shifted: suddenly I was looking down upon *a head*—the very head I had so recently occupied!—now lying in a bloody pile, which we (the pink man and I) proceeded to bend down and drink from, but which thankfully only he could taste. After which it was into a taxi and back to a hotel, where I learned his name ("Good morning, Mr. Fitz!"), watched him vomit into a toilet, waited through a long shower, and finally left for the airport—all this in quick succession—where he was stopped by security over the bag of herbs the Fortune-Teller had given him and had to field some unflattering questions before he could finally board the plane. Once seated, he'd called for booze, then more booze, and now, sated, sat restlessly poking around the contents of the herb bag, and unfolding and refolding the slip of paper inside, upon which were written the Fortune-Teller's magical words of destiny, the ostensible destination of his "special quest": UNITYVILLE, PENNSYLVANIA.

Oh exhilarating words!

Though surely less so for Orson Fitz than for me, Samuel Johnson, who had spent the previous night puzzling over the Fortune-Teller's instructions and by now understood, or felt I understood, what she'd meant. She'd meant that in order to be with my son, I'd need to transport into a body close to his. His own body? A relative's? And by what means would I achieve this miraculous transformation? The answer was, clearly: I would need to kill the man who carried me there. The "bad mon," the "dogheart." *How* I would kill him I had no idea, and that I would be *willing* to kill him, that I could manage it *morally*, had filled me with anxiety all night. Now that I had met Orson, however, and spent time with him, I found myself in complete agreement with the Fortune-Teller on at least one point: if I *had* to kill someone in order to be with my son, much better this foul Orson Fitz. Much better him than poor Christopher! And I looked back with something like tenderness, then, to Christopher lying gouged in that field. Ineffectual, caddish Christopher, whom I hadn't actually liked, I supposed, but for whom I'd at least felt some sympathy. Whereas Orson Fitz, this horrible Orson Fitz, with his endless gruff mumbling, with his booze and his rudeness and his elbowy indifference to the poor woman seated beside him—*this* man left my morals unruffled and my thoughts unfettered, free to indulge, for the duration of that flight, in the unimaginable hope that I might indeed be returning to my son!

Yet when we landed in Philadelphia and Orson attempted to book a flight for Harrisburg, which was the closest to Unityville he could get, he found the flight was not for three more hours; and so great was his impatience, and so weak his resolve, and so fleeting, unfortunately, his drunkenness, that this meager delay utterly uprooted him; and in the ensuing fit, he rebooked himself for Pittsburgh, which is a little over four hours from Unityville by car, but which for my purposes might as well have been Timbuktu; thus, before I even quite knew what was happening, I found myself forced onto yet another plane, yet another flight away from my son, having in the course of the previous fifty or so hours gone from Christopher's seemingly endless stagnancy to a brief stint in an Antiguan bull to a sudden rush of forward momentum and the most unbelievable windfall of hope—of hope!—only to find myself now worse off than ever, heading toward Pittsburgh with horrible Orson Fitz.

That flight was short, and from the Pittsburgh airport we took a very dreary taxi ride into town.

I do not know if you've ever been to Pittsburgh (of course, I don't know anything about you at all, unless you are my son reading this—if so: your father loves you!—though probably you are not), but I can tell you that the late sixties through the midseventies was not a very good time for that city. All the lung-blackening industries were leaving or had left, and not much of anything was replacing them. Nor were my various personal experiences during my years there particularly wonderful, yet for some reason, to this day, I like Pittsburgh. I remember it more fondly than other places I have been. Is it the rivers and hills? They force the city into unpredictable patterns, hidden enclaves and streets that slope and curve. Each small neighborhood has its own tiny downtown, bakeries and pharmacies pop up in the oddest places, and when you wander around, it feels old, a place with a past, a lot of old houses and cemeteries. Not that I always like old houses and cemeteries—Orson's house, for example, which was both old and next to a cemetery, I hated from the moment the taxi dropped us off.

It was a narrow three-story with winding, steep stairs that ate up much of the available living space, a claustrophobic tower with mottled light, and if I say that the wreckage of junk and furniture stuffed into its rooms mirrored the inside of Orson's mind, you will understand this is a figurative expression, that I have no actual insights into the furnishings of the human mind, except to say that as far as I can tell it has no "insides" at all, and that I am only speculating about Orson's mind based on the life he lived, the ugly life I was forced to witness over the harrowing years I spent with him. The living room alone, where we spent the most time, held a sofa, four lamps, a coffee table, two end tables, three chairs, a television, a writing desk, two rugs, a filing cabinet, and four or five stacks of boxes filled with trinkets and doodads, papers and books, and every imaginable sort of storable scrap. On that first day I did not see any of this, however, for he stopped just inside the door, which opened onto the kitchen, dropped his bags, picked up and dialed the telephone, and:

"It's me."

"Oh hello, Mr. Fitz! You're back!" A young man, in perhaps his early twenties?

"Put David on."

"Of course! David, it's Mr. Fitz."

"Orson, thank goodness." Somewhat older: midthirties? "Are you back? Please tell me you're back. There's so much to go over."

"Stuck in Philadelphia. I'm calling but I can't really talk."

"There are just a few very pressing—"

"Tomorrow. I've got bigger worries at the moment."

"What about the meeting?" This was still David. "How did we—"

"I'm taking over the Mexico project. Who's been working that?"

"Elizabeth, but she—"

"Have her give what she's done to Elliot. I'll be traveling down there soon, so do it right away."

"You're going there? Orson, you should talk to her first. There've been problems with our Mexican partners."

"Thank you for that advice, David. There's no reason you would be aware of this, but I've been involved in this business for some years now. That name on the door is actually mine, unfortunately for everyone involved. And while I've no doubt that our resident genius Elizabeth has managed to screw up Mexico in ways I can't even imagine, I somehow doubt her evasive explanations will be a wonderful fucking help to me."

"Well, I don't think that's—"

"Put Elliot back on."

"Mr. Fitz?" The younger one again.

"Thirty minutes," said Orson, and hung up.

His car was much nicer than his house (I do not mean to over-gripe about his house, simply that it was awful and we spent so much time there), a powder-blue Lincoln Continental, long and wide with deep leather seats. We drove around aimlessly for a while, or to me it seemed aimless, aimless and hopeless and quite possibly endless, eventually arriving at a large downtown already closing for the day—the last shift hurrying home, the streetlights coming on. The sky between the high buildings was a heavy gray, nor had I ever seen a sky *between* buildings before. It was the most vertical place I had ever been, and no one seemed to live there. The shops and even the restaurants were closing, and while I assumed that Orson knew where he was headed among the maze of streets and avenues, still I could not help feeling we were traveling in circles, so identical did everything appear. Then suddenly we were parked. Suddenly we were entering a hotel and climbing into a red booth seat in a bar-restaurant with schmaltzy crooner music piped in—where Elliot, the young man from the phone, waited for Orson's bourbon and french fries to arrive before asking about his trip.

"My trip!" scoffed Orson. "What a goddamn waste. I go to this place, this so-called clinic, which is supposedly 'progressive,' whatever that means, and they say the same damn thing every other doctor says. They can't find anything wrong. Well, I can sure as hell *feel* something wrong, but apparently they're too 'progressive' for the idea that a person might actually be able to identify the feeling known as pain when it occurs in his own body."

"You went to a clinic?"

"I didn't tell you? Well, I don't tell you everything. Sometimes I save you the trouble of having to beg my forgiveness for not keeping your mouth shut."

"I . . . It's good they didn't find anything wrong, I suppose?"

Orson, fuming, flagged another bourbon.

"It's good if there *isn't* anything," he went on, "but if there *is* something, then it definitely is not good. Call me unreasonable, but I don't think it will be a great fucking consolation to me when I'm lying dead on a slab and the doctors decide that maybe there was something wrong after all. Oh, do you think so? What an interesting case! How fascinating! And you say he *saw it coming*? Too bad he only told us directly about it to our stupid fucking faces . . . Of course, then you and all my other employees could throw that party you've all been planning."

"Oh, nobody would—"

"I know what they say about me . . . So what've they been saying?"

"Well, yes, let me see . . ."

Now Elliot produced a notebook from under the table and began to report on everything that had been said or done in the office during Orson's absence: how projects were going, what partners were saying, problems encountered and mistakes made. It was only now that Orson looked at Elliot directly, and I was able to observe the young man up close.

A naturally nervous person, Elliot did indeed appear to be in his early twenties, though he might have been older and only made to seem young by his subservient demeanor. Short hair, rosy rounded features, and glasses unnaturally small to his face. His conversation was incredibly self-conscious, and careful if not conspicuous in avoiding any reference to Orson or Orson's work, or what the employees thought of Orson, or any fact that might be construed as critical of Orson, or might in any way incur Orson's wrath. He seemed more comfortable, on the other hand, when criticizing his fellow employees, often by referring to something Orson himself had said. A comment about a failed effort, for example, might be prefaced by "just as you suspected" or "you won't be surprised to learn," and would devolve from there into an elaborate finger-pointing, as if the object of the meeting was less to report on problems than to compliment Orson on predicting them. Nor did Orson seem to mind, and before long, and with all the drinking he did while Elliot was talking, Orson's relative stiffness yielded to something warmer, a conspiratorial friendliness. A calmer Orson calmed Elliot in turn, and by the end of the young man's report—the better part of an hour—Elliot seemed practically relaxed. By that time, Orson was as drunk as the first time I'd seen him (*Was it only this morning? Oh, to be done with this day!*), yet other than some stray unpredictable hiccups and thicker, sloppier speech, he was not so different drunk than sober.

"May I ask, Mr. Fitz"—Elliot closed his notebook—"what happened with the talks?"

"What talks?"

"David said your trip was to meet with—"

"Because my mortal illness isn't enough reason . . . me take a trip?"

"Of course, I just—"

"There weren't 'talks.' That was . . . keep David busy. 'Progressive!'" Orson scowled. "That whole damn island—"

"You went to an island?"

"Armpit of the Third World. Ended up . . . this witch doctor—"

"You went to a *witch* doctor?"

"What?" Orson stopped. "No. She . . . like a fortune-teller. Tourist thing . . . Listen, I know I'm not allowed to have any *personal* . . . unlike you people 'working' in the office all day . . . or for however many . . . doing whatever it is you do, but shouldn't I at least be allowed to have a little . . . considering I'm the only person who ever generates any *business* for this . . . Anyway I'll be dead before—"

"What did she say?" offered Elliot.

"Who?"

"The . . . fortune-teller."

"Oh. Who remembers? Hocus-pocus . . . This little house, hot as hell . . . Like somebody vomited a spice rack . . . I have to go to bed."

Leaving Elliot with the company credit card, Orson stumbled from the bar, out of the hotel, past his car, and into the Pittsburgh night. By now the streets were deserted, the streetlights were on but the buildings dark, and he made his way around one corner, then another, out onto the avenue, before grabbing hold of a newspaper box and lowering himself to the curb. He leaned back against the box, and in the sudden stillness that followed I was profoundly struck by—silence. Suddenly Orson was silent, and everything around him was silent, and it was surprising, even affecting: a business district after dark. Great waffles of black windows rose up on either side of the avenue, glossy in the moonlight, and I could only imagine that the melancholy feeling it gave me had come over Orson as well, and that this was what had suddenly calmed him. It lasted less than a minute, this feeling, before Orson started grumbling again, that hot-running gurgle of his perpetual disquiet, bubbling up from deep beneath the surface.

But somewhere in that peaceful minute, in the too-short space before Orson's foulness returned, it had finally sunk in for me: I was really and truly stuck in Orson Fitz. I'd *known* it—but somehow, up to then, I'd not believed it. It had all happened so quickly, like a dream or delusion. Of course by then I'd come to see myself as incapable of delusions. Long-suffering soul that I was—practically a whole year dead already!—I imagined myself both world-weary and wise, thus impossible to surprise or confuse. But the truth, I now saw, was the opposite: I was still very far from true weariness, and the trials I had faced so far had not even begun to prepare me for all that was to come.

In other words, in that moment, I finally understood something. Tiny and silent beneath those dark waffled towers, in a sense I understood *everything*. I did not know the particulars of my future, of course, but on a more basic level, I saw my reality in a way I'd not even considered up to then. No matter how large my understanding grew, the world would always be much larger; yet there would also be moments, perhaps no more than two or three I would ever experience, when suddenly and for no particular reason, I would *see myself*. I would recognize and know myself in a way I normally could not. And that silent minute at the newspaper box I will always remember as being one such instant of clarity. I understood my circumstances as clearly as I do right now. I said to myself (it struck me even then as an odd comment, oddly lighthearted at a time when my heart felt anything but light), I said, *Here we go again.*

Here we go again, Samuel Johnson.

5.

If I have trouble telling Orson's story—not just the story of how he became the person he was when I entered his existence but even who he was after that—this is at least partly because I never really understood it myself. I knew he was a grossly negligent, inexplicably successful businessman driven to distraction by the seemingly imaginary belief that he had contracted an unidentified yet assuredly terminal illness. I knew that, under the auspices of "business," he traveled the world seeking new diagnoses—mostly around the u.s., Mexico, and Canada, but with a few trips to South America, and once as far as Finland—by virtue of which I at last saw quite a bit of the world I had sailed past with Christopher, and discovered firsthand that even the most interesting destinations are spoiled by bad company. Ever restless, he seemed never to *arrive* anywhere, but only to escape, over and over, wherever he'd previously been. I knew that at home he was even worse, sinking ever deeper into a personal malaise, a self-administered slough of drinking, ranting, and obsessing, nighttime philandering and television viewing, frequent business neglecting, excessive self-pitying, and other dull, desperate, or degenerate activities, some of which were initially interesting to witness, but all of which grew tiresome soon enough, and none of which seemed to have an actual cause or object of any sort. As months passed, and then years, I tried to follow along as best I could this story with no beginning, which had (for the most part) a single unlikable character, and which did not seem to know where it was headed or how it would possibly stop.

Fortunately, there is a different story from my time with Orson that is perfectly cogent and much easier for me to tell—and that I am going to tell instead of his—because it is mine, my own story. It is the story of what happened to me during my time with Orson Fitz.

It begins four years after that first night with the newspaper box (years, for me, of loneliness and hopelessness, not to mention infuriating powerlessness, the sense of *possibility* I had gotten from the Fortune-Teller having quickly revealed itself to be a curse: somehow, somewhere, there was a way to return to my son, yet I had no idea how to find it, or even where to start!), in the same bar as that first night, around the same late hour, over the same french fries and booze, Elliot, the red booth seat, the music probably different by then—Bee Gees or Donny Osmond, something like that—Orson having just returned from another pointless trip. He'd been performing one of his favorite satirical routines, the one about David's hairdo, when Elliot leaned back and nodded what could only be described as a patronizing nod, a nod that acknowledged without agreeing, a nod that I instantly recognized, and that Orson certainly recognized, as profoundly out of character.

"I don't know, Orson," said Elliot, "certainly you have to admit that David works hard. I mean, he's in the office longer hours than I am, and I'm practically never anywhere else!"

To which Orson fell silent.

I should explain that Orson's relationship with Elliot had grown closer during the intervening years, as Elliot had taken on responsibility for ever larger portions of Orson's daily life, and as his worldview had increasingly shaped itself to the claustrophobic contours of Orson's personality. By now any sort of disagreement was simply inconceivable.

"I mean," Elliot went on, "don't you think?"

"So you think you and David work too hard?" said Orson at last.

"Well, no, of course not . . . I'm only making the point, or rather merely pointing out, that it is possible, you know, that we sometimes underestimate the difficulty of the situation."

"The situation?" said Orson. "What situation is that?"

I should also mention that Orson's business had by now lost perhaps two-thirds of its staff, and though it had also lost at least half of its clients, Orson had managed to generate enough new projects that current staff was handling almost twice the work per person, which was not going well, and which I assumed was the "situation" to which Elliot was referring.

"The situation. The overall situation. I mean . . . Well, after all," Elliot pushed out, "nobody's perfect!"

"Nobody's perfect?"

"Of course not. And I—"

"Not even David? Your good buddy David?"

"What? No, Orson, I didn't say—"

"Not even you? You and your buddy David, even *you two* aren't perfect?"

"Ha ha, I see where this is—"

"Perfection is certainly a hard thing to attain, no question about that," Orson went on. "But if *even you and your fraternal twin David* . . ."

"Orson, come on. I was just—"

"No no, I agree with you. I'm agreeing. You know what I think my problem is?"

"I certainly never said—"

"It's that I've been so fortunate with my employees' incredibly high level of performance for so long that I've come to take it for granted. I've grown so accustomed to *excellence* that I no longer even recognize it sitting right in front of me, and I fail to appreciate all the painstaking hours of daily struggle that got this company to such a fucking high level of perfection in the first place. But as you've now pointed out—"

"O.K., O.K." Elliot hand-signaled surrender. "I've learned my lesson. Can we drop it?"

"You'd like to drop it?"

"I've learned my lesson."

"Shall we call David to see if he also wants to drop it?"

"I've learned my lesson!"

Unfortunately for Elliot, and inexplicably to me, he had not learned his lesson, but over the following days and weeks grew only more awkwardly self-assertive. He posed hypothetical questions. He called for "perspective." He pointed out positive attributes of his fellow employees and pleaded on behalf of "reason," as if all Orson had ever needed to become a more caring employer was Elliot's guiding hand. I might have felt bad for him, had I cared at all. But while I did wonder what had caused Elliot's sudden shift in personality (I assumed some sort of early midlife crisis, that he had woken one night in a panic, had realized he was not getting any younger, that all his old school friends were passing him by, that he needed to "step up to the plate," and so on), mostly I was surprised that something different was happening.

Of course to Orson, who'd once felt betrayed when the mailman accidentally delivered his mail to the wrong address and for months thereafter continued to refer to his "fucking mailman," Elliot's new confidence was an infuriating joke. That he tolerated this new version of Elliot for almost two weeks attests, as much as anything, to real sentiment on his part. Yet as soon as it became clear that the old Elliot was not going to resurface, Orson stopped responding with sarcasm, then stopped responding at all. In an instant, Elliot was out.

When you consider just how many functions Elliot served in Orson's life by this point—not just in business and friendship but also things like grocery shopping and dry cleaning—the speed and totality with which Orson extracted him was frankly impressive, and no doubt possible only because of Orson's latest business strategy, which was simply not to deal with business at all. In the absence of Elliot, however, Orson found himself without an assistant, or for that matter any friends, and so this is where Blossom comes in.

In fact she'd been in Orson's life longer than I had. Short, sturdily built, with cropped black hair, dressing casually if unremarkably in jeans and t-shirts, she hardly ever talked, and what she did say tended to contain a lot of swearing. It was more a habitual than an angry swearing, I always thought, and since she never betrayed the slightest expression, I could never tell her mood or ascertain anything about her. I knew she'd met Orson years ago, under circumstances I assumed had to do with drinking and sex, for that was what they did together—drink and have sex—once every two or three months, when one called up the other for company. That was the extent of their relationship, and as for her life outside, I certainly had no sense of it, nor, I think, did Orson. She was another unexplained piece in the puzzle of his life.

With the extrication of Elliot, however, a position had opened up, in his life if not in his business, for which there were not many viable candidates. And she must have needed the money, because within a matter of days, Orson had hired Blossom as his assistant, with a salary and benefits, after which she would show up most afternoons, doing things or pretending to do them. And with Blossom in place, Orson was able to move on with his usual routine, while Elliot, finding himself suddenly demoted, was left to flop around in a state of perpetual panic, bewildered by his own expendability.

Now, the reader might be forgiven for failing to notice how any of the mundane events I've just rattled off could possibly constitute *my* story, the story of Samuel Johnson. The truth is, even I did not recognize them as such at the time. In fact, three more years would go by, years remarkably similar to the four before them, during which I continued to tune in absently to the Orson Fitz Show, with Blossom now in the role of Elliot, before my story at last announced itself. The celestial dots connected to reveal how strange and fickle Fate can be, how events lead to events, and how consequences reverberate across the ages. For if Elliot had not become unbearable, Orson would never have turned to Blossom. And if Orson had not turned to Blossom, there never would have been any question of Phil. And if it weren't for Phil, if it weren't for Phil . . . Well, I won't get ahead of myself.

Three more years, remarkably similar to the four before them . . . yet as time passed, life started to take a different toll on Orson. He continued to pursue his manic course, but with no enthusiasm whatsoever. Eventually, he began to slow down. He traveled less, spent less time with Blossom. He stayed in more at night. He went to movies in the afternoons. Indeed it was returning home from a Tuesday matinee in the winter of 1973 (with Nixon still in the White House and *Hawaii Five-O* airing at eight thirty on CBS) that Orson found Elliot standing outside his door looking extremely agitated. We'd not seen Elliot for a while by then; whatever business Orson still conducted was either through Blossom or over the phone. He looked older, Elliot. He had a patchy beard now, and none of his youthful exuberance.

"What is it?" said Orson.

"Well, I have some . . . It's actually good news. It's actually *great* news."

I should mention that Orson's company had been in the toilet for a while by this point. He had lost most of his employees, although Elliot and David had for some reason straggled on. Perhaps they could not find other jobs.

"Let us try this again," said Orson. "What . . . is . . . it."

"We received a phone call, is what! A very interesting one! It's . . . Can I come in?"

"No."

"No?"

Orson stared at the door. "I'm not feeling well," he said finally. "Just tell me."

"Well, we've been invited to submit a proposal for a new project, and, Orson, it's a *great deal* of money. David thinks it could bring about a new chapter in the company's future."

"*David* thinks?"

"Well . . . yes. Listen, Orson, I know things have been going badly for . . . it's been a while now. I know. We all know. But this is a *great* opportunity."

"o.k."

"Orson, just hear me out—"

"I said o.k."

"Please don't play games. Not this time."

"Who's playing games? Jesus—"

"Peoples' *lives* are in the balance!"

"Are you even listening? Am I not talking out loud?"

"Don't you even—" Elliot stopped. "You really want to hear about it?"

"Come by again tomorrow and you can tell me what you need."

"I . . . That's great!" Elliot was confused. "Because—oh, that's the other thing. It all needs to be finished and submitted in just one week. The proposal, that is. It seems we weren't the first choice, but . . . well, that doesn't matter, does it? They're sending the specs tomorrow, so—"

"Come by when you have what you need," said Orson, and let himself into the house.

From inside the door, I pictured Elliot outside asking himself if it was a trap or a joke or if, somehow, Orson had turned a corner. I imagined him weighing these possibilities before heading back downtown to the office, where David no doubt awaited his report. I imagined both Elliot and David caught between hope and suspicion, wondering what sort of horrible unforeseeable trick Orson would spring on them the following day. That is what I would have been wondering if I were them.

What I did not imagine, and what Elliot definitely did not imagine, what even Orson could not have imagined, since it was in fact impossible to imagine, was that this new turn in Orson's story would never play out to completion, and that Fate was about to take a far stranger turn.

For although it seems odd to say so, given how fantastical everything I've told you up to now must seem (I assume that so far you've found the story of my journey through this world fantastical or ludicrous since I still feel that way about it myself), still, what I am about to describe is even more bizarre. It is so strange and inexplicable that all I can do is acknowledge its strangeness and assure you, before you accuse me of lying, that I agree you ought to think so. For at this point Orson's fate was hijacked by the least likely of sources. I, Samuel Johnson, a do-nothing in life, and even more hopelessly ineffectual in death . . . I, Samuel Johnson, messed everything up.

It happened that night, after Elliot left, when Orson called up Blossom to keep him company.

Lately she'd seemed frazzled. She was short-tempered and was gaining weight, and it had occurred to me more than once, over the past weeks, that something with Blossom was off. She looked perpetually tired, her usually flat expression now flabbily slack, which at the time I attributed to the accumulated trauma of three years of near-constant exposure to Orson. Only later did I understand that Blossom had her own problems, the nature of which I could never have guessed.

She arrived that night looking particularly exhausted, and when Orson announced there would be no talking this evening, that he wanted only to drink, she sighed thankfulness all the way to the sofa. He put on loud jazz and joined her there with various bottles, and the two of them proceeded with such resolve that before long the evening, still young, seemed soon to be over. Orson was on his back by then, with Blossom draped over him, her face partly mashed into his chest. They were drunker than they had been in a long time and had arrived at the very edge of consciousness, or at least the edge of willfulness, that twilight moment when a mind and its body are preparing to part ways, when suddenly Blossom's face sprang forward, alarmingly awake. She sat up and said, very clearly yet in a voice only slightly like her own, with an accent I had come to know as a local Pittsburgh way of speaking but which sounded no less bizarre, despite being somewhat familiar, when spoken by Blossom's mouth:

"So how long yinz been in there?"

Which of course made no sense to me at all.

"Blossom here I been in just the past month or so, but I figure you's in there longer n'at. Course I only sussed it aht the other day, whenever yer man there told his story about Antigua and so forth, and the herbs and bull's head and so forth."

It was true that a few days earlier Orson had told Blossom that story.

"I sussed it aht right then, though," the voice coming from Blossom went on, "and ever since, I been rill anxious to speak. I never met another soul in this same perdicament. I always did figure it were possble, since what's so special abaht me? That I'd be the one and only? And now, here y'are. Yuh *are* in there, yeah? Phil Williams."

And he held out Blossom's hand as if he wanted me to shake it.

I say "he" and "me" because despite how disorienting this moment obviously was, I did understand at least that I, and not Orson, was the person being addressed, and that the individual addressing me was not named Blossom, but Phil. Of course I could not fathom how this was possible, nor did I know how to respond—by what mechanism, I mean—but since it was the only logical thing to do, I tried speaking.

"I'm Samuel Johnson," I said in Orson's voice. Or rather it was and it wasn't Orson's voice. It was his vocal cords, but through them flowed my own words, in my own manner of speaking, which sounded only distantly familiar, since I'd not heard it in so long. "How are we speaking?"

"How we . . . You mean yuh never been aht before? *Shit.*" Blossom's face fell to a pout. "Yer even more ignorant than me!"

"How are we speaking?" I repeated with urgency—and without quite realizing it, I sat up.

Phil sighed. "It's irregaler for sure. Can't say unnatural, since who can say what's natural? Not Phil Williams, and it seems not Samuel Johnson neither. Seems not one of us can say what is or is not natural, and if not us, who? But one thing I *can* tell yuh is"— he looked hard at me, effecting an air of consequence—"there's a moment. Or more it's a range. Anyways, a *gray area* when a body's not quite awake or asleep, but somewheres between. When the mind's gahn in the house and turned aht the lights, but left the car keys in the ignition out the garage. And *that's* when a soul might take a body for a spin . . ."

Now, as Phil was speaking, I had been looking around Orson's living room, trying to ground myself in physical reality against the sudden swirling volatility of my metaphysical state. Here was the sofa, the lamps, the coffee table, end tables, the chairs, the desk, the television. Here were the rugs, the filing cabinet, all the various stacks of boxed-up stuff. Everything looked the same, I thought—except that *I* was the one looking. And since I do not dream (unless it was all a dream, everything I'd gone through, which had occurred to me, of course, countless times, that all this must be a dream, except that it wasn't, or couldn't be, since how can you dream things you've never seen or imagined?)—since I do not dream, that is, this had to be happening. I'd spoken. I'd sat up. I'd leaned in and looked around. I thought: *I can do things?*

I stood then, and wobbled.

"Whoa there." Phil put a hand to my shoulder.

I sat back down.

Had I been able to do things all along? For how long?

Suddenly I was angry with myself.

Every time Orson drank himself unconscious (which, to be fair, was not *that* often), could I have done things *then?* Had I been this way for years? Had I wasted whole *years* of opportunities? So busy resigning myself to my circumstances, thinking about how lost I was, wallowing in self-pity that I did not even bother to discover the *actual possibilities before me?* No, I assured myself, as great a failure as I had always been, I was not that great a failure . . . and yet, *yes*, I went on to myself, that was precisely the sort of failure I was. The sort who fails not only to act, but even to figure out what actions are possible . . .

I stood again, and this time I wobbled my way across the room, Phil trailing at a close distance. When he tried to assist me, I shooed him away.

I said, "I can feel my hands."

"Yeah, but it's a balance." Phil held up Blossom's hands. "They sober up: yer aht. They pass aht: yer aht. It's tricky, sure, but with some work you can keep them this way a good while." He followed me back to the sofa, where I lowered myself slowly and (I thought) reasonably well. "I once kept hold a body five ahrs straight, and Blossom here I kept tree, tree an a half? Long as yuh feel those fingers, you know you's the one driving."

"Wait," I said, "you *drive?*"

"That's a figure of speech, but sure, pretty regaler."

"So you could—" But here the feeling left my fingers; they became again Orson's fingers, and Orson's eyes closed.

Suddenly sunken into darkness, I panicked. I shouted inaudible shouts, thrashed my incorporeal arms—but calmed down again as Phil's reassuring voice reached out to me.

"Ah, there yuh go. No worries, Blossom's a big drinker. She gives me plenty opportunities, so I'll be back rill soon. Maybe soon as tomorrah, couple-tree days at most, and we'll get back to talking. I imagine yer full of questions. Can't say I have answers, but I do know how flustrating them questions can be. And the loneliness, of course . . . Fact is, I been dead a fairly long span now. In Blossom just a short while but before that were a priest, before that a trucker, and the line runs back. Originally I'm from over in Munhall. Was a bit known, Phil Williams from Munhall? Well, you wouldn't of heard of me. Never spent much time aht the area . . . What else can I tell? These days I do get abaht pretty regaler, which weren't so good for Blossom, owing to the sorts of things I get into, which she wakes up thinking she's done herself only can't remember . . . But there's only so much philandering a soul can desire to do. After a while, yuh get tired of . . . well, yuh get tired of all of it. Say, next time arahnd, what say we take a walk, just a walk and a talk? It's a luxury, a walk and a talk. But also they're easier to handle on foot. Yuh can keep better gauge of which way they're headed, sober or aht, and can try to adjust n'at. Takes some getting used to, but, truth be told, not so much . . . So, well, it's good to finely meet. I'll be by tomorrah, you'll see. But owing as you's already lights-aht there, I figure I mise well head aht. You understand . . . Anyways, au revahr, Samuel Johnson. Till rill soon!"

It wasn't the next night that Phil found me, but the one after, and by then I'd had plenty of time to think. Orson had spent much of the interval in bed, recovering from what must have been a powerful hangover, with Elliot stopping over several times a day to discuss the looming deadline on the critical proposal, which was labyrinthine in terms of paperwork and required Orson at every turn. He was frantic, frenetic—Elliot was. No doubt he expected Orson's ill temper to reappear at any moment and felt great pressure to rush everything through, above and beyond the pressure he felt from how quickly it needed to be done anyway.

Finally on the second night, Blossom arrived, unannounced, carrying several bottles of whiskey and acting nothing like herself. In fact I was a little embarrassed for Phil (*embarrassed* is perhaps not quite the right word) at how poorly he imitated Blossom. Even with his best effort, he sounded nothing like her at all, and if he hadn't been in her body, and that body hadn't clearly drunk a great deal, and if it hadn't been holding forth whiskey on offer, I wonder if even Orson might have figured out something was wrong. In the end, though, Phil knew what he was doing. Soon Orson was staggering around the room, and not much later I stood firmly, or very close to firmly, in his place.

"Welcome back!" Phil slapped my shoulder. "Now I imagine yer full of questions . . ."

But being prepared, I replied: "Only one."

6.

From the beginning of what might be called his conscious life—so from about the age of two—my son was very curious about the world. Always full of questions and, perhaps most impressive to me, never satisfied with the vague or lazy answers I was naturally inclined to give. It was exasperating, in one sense, those endless questions (why is the sky blue? Where does the blue part start? What's behind the blue part? And so on), but I also could not help but admire them in a person so small. I barely remembered my own childhood, yet I was quite sure, in watching my son, that I had never been even half as serious. Oh, I finished the lessons assigned me, and my early interest in television indicates at least a basic curiosity about the world outside. But I was never *serious* in my curiosity, is the difference. I wore curiosity, as I wore everything else, more as a whim than a conviction. But my son—he was not like that. He was not like me at all, but much, much better. Not simply more curious, or serious; he was more driven, less easily distracted, endowed with those qualities of mind a person needs in order to make his own path through this world. And since I was not only a dull person but one with very few answers to his questions, I found I was constantly letting him down.

So it was a great relief to me when, for his third birthday, his grandparents (Emily's parents) bought him the *Reader's Digest Great World Atlas*—the new one, 1964. For hours each day, Samuel would pore over the pictures, or he would make me read him the articles; that, at least, I could do. It wasn't strictly maps, although it included all kinds of those, but there were also pages to teach you about weather, and types of clouds, and gemstones and minerals, and the Earth's geological composition, as well as population, vegetation patterns, the history of global migration, even the ages of the Earth. A half page of this last had been torn out before the book arrived to us, but I could forgive his grandparents some minor religious editing, since there were pages I steered him away from myself. Two pages in particular, maps of the ocean bottoms, triggered my protective impulses: the idea of undersea mountain ranges seemed inexplicably threatening, despite or perhaps because of the fact that I'd never in my life seen a mountain higher than a foothill or a body of water larger than a lake.

But it was a great big colorful book, is the point, filled with learning and ideas, and we plunged into it together, father and son. It was an interest we shared, really the first and only mature interest we were able to share in our too-short time together. Through my son's eyes, the world became a more complicated place, and knowledge a thing I was suddenly happy to have. And this newfound curiosity carried over to life beyond that book as well. We would watch clouds and trace their movements. We would decide their shapes (elephant, tree) and name their types (altocumulus, cirrostratus). Not just clouds, of course, but plants, animals, rock formations. Everything in the world became something new to know about.

Now where this enthusiasm for learning would have led me had Fate not intervened, I truly don't know. So tied was that pleasure to my feelings for Samuel that I doubt it would have lasted long, once he'd outgrown me. For outgrow me he certainly would have, and quickly. The day was not far off when he would graduate from that atlas to other books and ideas, to possibilities beyond any I could provide, and far from ruing that day, I was eager for it. To watch my son grow into the sort of person I had never myself even considered becoming—that was to be life's greatest reward. Then Fate played its hand and I was cheated of that future. I was forced instead to merely imagine my son's progress, to invent for him many hypothetical lives, to dream up all the adventures and occupations I've assigned him over the years. In each of these imagined lives, he does well for himself. He grows rich in ideas and strong in the capacity to pursue them. Nor do I think such dreams are simply the wish fulfillment of a doting father, but instead realistic extensions of the very impressive little person he had already become by the time I was torn away.

Those, at any rate, were some of the thoughts I was having—memories of little Samuel and his atlas—as I sat on the passenger side of Blossom's jangly, clanking orange-brown sedan on that night in 1973, barreling down the Pennsylvania Turnpike through winter darkness, determined to reach Unityville and be with my son, or near my son, despite some incalculably steep odds against it. Cozy in the green glow of the dashboard, amidst the clanks and car hums, under the too-hot heating system, I thought about Samuel, about our afternoons of learning, about the many varieties of clouds and the eeriness of undersea mountains. Probably I did not get as far that night as to imagine Samuel's life trajectory, now that I think about it, since at the time he was still only twelve.

Perhaps I should back up.

At my second meeting with Phil—where I left off at the end of the previous chapter—I'd proposed an expedition and, Phil being instantly amenable, even excited at the prospect of an adventure, we'd made what preparations we could. Phil gave me tips for gauging Orson's drunkenness or sobriety by certain physical indications—feeling in the hands, weakness in the neck—and showed me how, by drinking or pinching myself or stretching my limbs, I could try to keep control of Orson. All of which I waited through, though in truth—which I did not say to Phil—I was feeling very impatient, and rather strongly suspected it was all the sort of thing you just figure out as you go.

But it was over the following two days that Phil did the really important work. While I watched Orson pull himself out of a second hangover and stumble back to Elliot's proposal, Phil stowed a map and cash in Blossom's glove compartment, gassed her car—a Dodge Dart that was both rusty and rust colored, so it looked like the car itself was bubbling up around the wheel wells—stored extra canisters in the trunk, and managed to pack the passenger-side foot space with enough booze to take us to the far side of New Jersey, had booze been our only obstacle. Even his Blossom impression had improved, and when he arrived on the third night with bottles in both hands, it took no time at all before Orson was out of commission and Phil and I down to the car, winding our way through the Pittsburgh streets, our borrowed faces silly with smiling, more full of hope and happiness and more genuinely excited by the adventure before us than two nonliving people had probably ever been.

He'd been jabbering from that first moment—Phil had—but my own mood had quickly shifted, as I started to think about my son. Now in addition to joy and excitement, a great deal of sadness flooded in, along with terror, anticipatory regret, an overwhelming clash of emotions—with the result that I wasn't really listening to Phil. I thought all the thoughts I've just shared with you, those memories of Samuel as well as many others. I remembered and reminisced and no doubt I even wallowed for a while, until finally Phil quit whatever he'd been talking about and started going over our plan.

It was simple: If Phil started to lose feeling and it was beyond anything he could fix, I would dump him. We'd pull to the side of the road and he'd get out and I would drive on from there. "Don't worry abaht me, Samuel, I'll be fine. Blossom'll be fine," Phil assured me. But if I, Samuel Johnson, began to lose feeling, or specifically if I passed out, Phil would take us as far as he could and leave us. Best to get as close as possible, my reasoning ran, and take my chances from there.

This plan had been decided during our second meeting, but it wasn't until Phil rehearsed it again in the car that it occurred to me to mention that I did not actually know how to drive. I'd seen Orson enough to understand the mechanics of it, but I had never, myself, driven. You might imagine this would be a point of concern for Phil; in fact, it was a point of hilarity, apparently the most amusing thing he had ever heard. In general, too, as we rumbled down the turnpike, I could see the deep enjoyment Phil was taking from the "knowledgeable" role he got to play, and it struck me that, following his early disappointment, he had become rather pleased with the idea that he knew more about our circumstances than I did. Ah, were that only the case! Unfortunately, when it came to the real questions that haunted me (*How long will we be stuck in this torturous purgatory?* being the obvious first), Phil's responses were vague and conjectural, and other than his handful of "tips" and a condescending impromptu driving lesson he proceeded to give me right there in the car, I found his "knowledge" both disappointing and irritating. I even started to lose some enthusiasm for our newfound friendship, when fortunately a new question occurred to me that Phil would actually be able to answer.

"Phil," I said, "what did you do?"

In the closeness of our little green-glowing cockpit, Phil squinted.

"I am not one hunnert percent sure I understand that question, Samuel."

"It's just that I've always assumed that being the way we are"—my voice slowed here, and actually I had a melancholy tone throughout this conversation—"that *this* was intended as a punishment for something I'd done."

"Hm." Phil thought. "That I never considered."

"So you never did anything this could be punishment for?"

"I did a helluva lot this *could* be punishment for, I just never considered it were. Why, what did *you* do?"

"Oh," I sighed. "It might have been a few things."

"Such as?"

"I slept with a woman out of wedlock."

"Cheated on the wife." Phil nodded understanding.

"No, she was my wife, we just weren't married yet."

"Hm," said Phil, and he did not seem very impressed.

"I never held much belief in God," I went on. "I never disbelieved either. I wasn't a believing sort of person—or maybe the point is that I wasn't a disbelieving sort. I never challenged my own mind, as far as God was concerned. Or as far as anything else was concerned. I just went along with it."

"Hm," Phil said a third time, and now it was a little annoying. It occurred to me he was not really considering what I said, but was just acting ponderous as a courtesy. "I think," he said finally, "none of that sounds so bad."

"My parents thought otherwise."

"Well, yeah. Parents."

That was true—I did not really care what my parents thought.

"There was one other thing," I said, my voice very purposeful now. "I watched television when I should have been watching my son."

"You watch television?" Phil sat up, and his face—Blossom's— lit with new interest.

"I . . ." The question surprised me. "Well, yes, I have. I mean, I do."

"If one thing bums me aht abaht Blossom," said Phil, "it's she never watches television."

And while I'm sure some part of me was irritated by how blatantly Phil had just changed the subject, when clearly I had been trying to say meaningful things about myself and my sins, or "sins"; nonetheless, given how poorly our conversation had gone up to that point, it came as something of a relief that we then started talking about television.

It turned out that Phil and I shared many favorite programs— the programs of my youth—and quickly found ourselves laughing over memorable episodes and beloved characters and disappointing program cancellations. I expressed sympathy for how long he had been away from television, not just since Blossom but for several years before, and when I offered to tell him about some of the programs he had missed, he said, "Samuel Johnson, that'd please me!" So just like that, our roles in the conversation switched, for now *I* was the one sharing what I knew, experiencing the pleasure of having knowledge and sharing it, if not indeed surprising myself a little by the sheer quantity of information suddenly flowing out of Orson's mouth.

And given how important television was to the formation of my friendship with Phil; and given how greatly television defined my experience of the world during my Orson years, about which I've said almost nothing; in fact, given what an enormous role television has played in my existence in general—on and off, of course, over the years, but overall so significant that it would be fair to say the story of Samuel Johnson is almost as much about television as it is about Samuel Johnson; given, moreover, how careful I am being, in writing this account of my adventures, to skip the dull parts, to merely allude to the boredom and passivity of my existence without actually subjecting you to it, at the risk of giving the wrongful impression that I've spent most of my time tuned in and alive to the world, when in reality I've been almost always tuned out, and for quite a lot of that watching television; for all these reasons, and more generally just to give you a better sense of what television has meant to me, perhaps I will quickly say a few words, here at the spot where I said similar things to Phil, about my television viewing during my Orson years.

Although they had just one year between them—my year at sea with Christopher—the television I'd known in life and the one I came back to with Orson were quite different. It was as if television in the late sixties and early seventies had departed a wholesome childhood to embark upon an awkward adolescence, where half the programs had gotten smarter and half dumber, all at once. For every mature and forward-thinking *Mary Tyler Moore Show*, you had five mindless repackagings of *Let's Make a Deal*. For every brilliant Richard Pryor or Carol Burnett, you suffered a heinously mediocre *Hee Haw*. Between these two extremes were stuffed lawyer and doctor shows, which seemed to have replaced the police and cowboy shows of the early and midsixties, and which at the time struck me as disappointing, rather bland, and boringly formulaic. Yet when I thought about it, I realized those lawyers and doctors were no more formulaic than the police and cowboys before them. Which meant, I supposed, that my own tastes had changed?

In fact I already knew this to be the case. On the day I had died, television had lost much of its "magic" for me (because I held television partly responsible for what had happened—if not television itself, then its effect on me—but also for more complicated reasons, which I intend to describe later on), yet in the year that followed, marooned with Christopher, with no television anywhere around, there'd been no opportunity for this disillusionment to play out. Thus it was only with Orson that I realized how much my feelings toward television had changed—had grown more mature, were less easily impressed or affected. And perhaps this "maturity" also accounts for my increased interest, in returning to television during my Orson years, in *the news*.

That, and the news itself was so urgent, with Vietnam and the Chicago race riots and all kinds of other issues and unrest. There were earthquakes and coups and world-altering assassinations; men first walked on the moon. Documentary-style programs taught me about famine, and the plight of immigrants, and economic crises (though the big one, OPEC, I missed by six months, and only learned about on the History Channel two decades later. I did catch coverage of the Watergate scandal, which broke in the summer of 1972 and dominated the news in the months after, though the hearings weren't scheduled until May of the following year, by which time I was again far away from television).

But it was a socially engaged era for television, is the point—and not just in the news or the more sophisticated programs, but in many of the more general programs as well, with even sitcoms taking on controversial issues (*All in the Family* comes to mind, whose big-mouthed, bigoted Archie was a favorite of Orson's). Of course none of this seriousness would last very long—indeed, television in the years that followed took a very different turn—but at the time it felt important, even exciting. If television could no longer connect me to its imaginary world, for a while at least, I imagined it might show me the *real* one. Things were happening in that world, and through television I could be a part of them, or feel as if I were, or tell myself I felt so, a feeling I'd not known even during my lifetime and that came to mean a great deal to me during these years when everything else was so grim.

Unfortunately, in the midst of this volatile, changing, socially engaged televisual world, or rather not in the midst but five or six feet in front of that world, sat Orson, who was every bit as volatile but not the least bit changing or engaged. Whatever optimism

I mustered, his presence smothered again. His pointless attendance to those very same programs spoiled my vision of social engagement, causing me to admit that my "portal to the real world" idea might be as misguided as the "magic window" before it. For when the televisions were turned off, were not all lives just as isolated and ineffectual as Orson's?

But now—to get back to our story—*now* even my own profoundly isolated existence had taken a distinctly less ineffectual turn, for here I was with my new friend, Phil, speeding along the dark corridor of the Pennsylvania Turnpike, en route to my son—my son!—keeping a weather eye on our intoxication levels as we talked and laughed about television. I could hear in my voice the pleasure I was taking in describing all the programs, and could see that Phil felt this as well, for the smile on Blossom's face grew wider as we went on, until at some point he interrupted to suggest that if we got through this and somehow both ended up in Unityville—who knows?—maybe there would be occasions—why not?—when we might arrange to get together to watch television? I laughed, but he was serious. I told him that would have been wonderful, an idea I would think back upon fondly, but unfortunately it was unlikely to happen, even if all of this *did* work out, since Unityville had no alcohol, let alone any television. But Phil said, simply, "How do yuh know?" And I had to admit he was right: more than seven years had passed since I'd left, and how did I know Unityville hadn't changed? Certainly my son would have changed, grown larger and smarter and better at things, but maybe the town had changed as well? And I began then to tell Phil all about that strange tiny town I was so desperate to get back to, that strip of shabby houses huddled around the solitary church. I told him about the people there, and my life, the life before my son was born and particularly the life after, the things we used to do together, the tedious games he invented, his atlas, everything . . . And these various conversations, all the topics I've recounted here, took us just past the exit for Bedford, Pennsylvania, when suddenly and abruptly we pulled over.

"Come arahnd," said Phil, jumping out of the car and running back to fill the gas tank with the canisters from the trunk. A moment later I was at the wheel and he was leaning in at the window with a pained look and forcing me to take the keys.

"Phil?" I said.

"I know a feeling when I feel a feeling. No point discussing. Stick to the plan."

"But Phil . . ."

"Maybe we meet again, Samuel Johnson. For yinz sake, I sure's hell hope not. Good luck to yuh, though, and I'm sorry not to've made it there myself."

Before I could say another word, Blossom's body was bounding away as fast as possible, leaving the lighted roadside and disappearing into the night. Just like that, Phil was gone.

My sadness at losing Phil—and so suddenly!—was greater than I would have expected. It took me by surprise (I'd naturally assumed Phil would last longer than I would), but mostly I felt bewildered, for I had never before had a friend. Emily, of course, but no male friends. Certainly not Abram, and then, who else? Of course I'd known Phil only a very short while, and our personalities were so different; we had virtually nothing in common, except for the one thing we *did* have in common, this one rather profound thing. Or two, if you count television. Plus we'd both been lonely for a very long time. In short, so inevitable had been our bond, so quickly had it grown in our brief time together, that now that he was gone, perhaps forever, I tragically missed him, this man I'd barely known.

Of course I did not wallow but slammed into gear, jerking and bucking Blossom's abysmal vehicle back onto the road, thinking it was one thing to watch a car being driven by Orson or Phil, quite another to drive one yourself. Yet I am proud to report that after a frighteningly rocky first few minutes, the vehicle did claw its way to top speed (top of what I could manage), after which it was just a matter of holding to the road, which was a wide road, if hilly, and nearly empty of traffic at that hour. There were dangers, of course— hitting a deer, popping a tire—but the greatest obstacle I faced, at that point, was simply panic. I began to imagine Orson creeping back into my fingers—*his* fingers—and then was sure I was wrong, but then right—here he was!—was he? Yet when I took a drink to keep him down, I again panicked, this time that I'd over-compensated. His body would pass out, I told myself, and Blossom's crappy sedan would wrap itself around a tree. I would wake up in some other awful existence, alone in the dark brain space of some backwoods religious fanatic or pregnant rest stop employee, some-one who never touched alcohol and would never afford me the sort of unprecedented opportunity I was currently in danger of wast-ing, if only because I could not seem to calm down . . . How long I continued in this state is hard to say, but when the situation finally resolved itself, it was not by my own effort, but because Orson finally sobered up enough to retake control. There was a dangerously awk-ward moment, during which I fought him with all the power I could muster—which was none, it turned out. He jolted upright at the shock of himself driving, yet managed to pull off at an exit and park us behind a Dumpster before dropping off across the front seat, thus ending ingloriously my second chance at return.

And so I turn back, begrudgingly, to Orson's story.

Though before we do, I might mention how surprised I am to discover the emotional changes mere thinking and remembering can bring about. For I can feel, at this very moment, my own hap-piness extinguishing, utterly extinguishing, as I switch from the memory of that first trip with Phil back to more of the Orson drudg-ery. It's strange, when you consider how long ago all of these things occurred. You would assume that, given enough time, a person's memory would stop carrying around its emotional baggage. Well, and perhaps it eventually does. Perhaps the problem in this case is simply that I hated Orson and his life very deeply, and despite how long it has been, it has still not been long enough.

He awoke early the next morning to find himself in Breezewood, Pennsylvania, a town you may already be familiar with if you have traveled much or are the least bit unlucky. *Town* is perhaps a stretch for a town that is itself little more than a stretch, a single strip of gas stations and restaurants, its citizenry composed not of human beings but of truck stops and burger places, its claim to fame the same as its slogan: "The Town of Motels." (Admittedly, I was predisposed to hate this place, the site of my journey's end, yet I am certain I would have hated it under better circumstances as well.) According to local lore, the town's history of providing rest and refreshment for weary travelers began centuries ago, in the days of the native people, and proceeded via hundreds of years' worth of paths, railroads, and highways that had all for some reason dropped their travelers at precisely this spot. Yet it was only recently—just a few years back, in fact, during the construction of Interstate 70 and simultaneous renovations to the adjacent Pennsylvania Turnpike—that the town had truly come into its own. It seems a loophole in the Federal-Aid Highway Act had left neither the Turnpike Commission nor the u.s. Department of Transportation legally responsible for constructing an interchange, or any way for travelers to move directly from one route to the other. In the ensuing battle of budgets, each had opted out. The result of this bizarre yet strangely believable scenario was that anyone moving between those two major thoroughfares now had to bottleneck through Breezewood, a time-delaying nuisance that overnight had transformed the town from a glorified truck stop of yesteryear into the ludicrous monstrosity one finds today: a transportation mecca, a bustling oasis of in-between-ness, and the ugliest, loudest place Orson had ever woken up.

Not sure how he'd gotten there, he abandoned Blossom's car and stumbled to a Denny's. He ordered a breakfast platter with a ridiculous name, and when it arrived, he learned the extensive history of Breezewood—everything I've just recounted—from Phyllis, his sassy middle-aged waitress who was coming off-shift anyway, who did not have anywhere particular she needed to be, and who always spoke her mind and did not give a fig what others thought about it. To my surprise, Orson sat through the entire story, which far outlasted his pancakes. Phyllis stood beside his booth the whole time, as if this were some sort of civic duty she performed whenever the occasion presented itself. Orson seemed to like it, though, or at least he did not seem to hate it, and even stayed awhile after, talking with Phyllis, before setting off to find a motel.

He slept most of the day. Alone again in the dark prison of his brain space, I had never hated myself so much. When he'd passed out in the car, I had hated myself, all that time in the Denny's, I had hated myself, and now I hated myself for the better part of the morning and the entire afternoon. To have come so close to my son— relative to how un-close I'd come previously—and failed. To have failed again, as I had always failed him! . . . Alone I wallowed, and then, alone, I stopped myself. I sobered myself. I reminded myself that despite this recent failure, which after all had never been very likely to succeed, my overall situation was still far more promising than before. Not only had I regained my sense of possibility, but I knew now what needed to be done. And I began in that moment to plan my next expedition to Unityville, which I would launch immediately upon our return to Pittsburgh. I would reconnect with Phil. He would have a new vehicle, or would find one. We would plan ahead for every sort of contingency. There would be something we could do better, something we'd not thought of this first time around but that in retrospect we'd realize and improve upon. *As soon as Orson wakes up,* I told myself, *it begins.*

Yet when Orson woke after sundown, instead of heading back to Blossom's car—which in fact he never returned to—he showered and dressed (same clothes) and set out to explore the town. O.K., I told myself. *It's late. He's been through a lot. All this must be strange for him. He'll wander around. We'll leave tomorrow.*

At night, Breezewood was not the same garbage-strewn eyesore the daylight revealed, but was transformed into a strange and lovely light show, a melancholic choreography of headlights and taillights and every color of neon cutting patterns in the dark. It was quieter as well, or had a quality of quietude, as if the darkness itself muffled sound. Silent and bone-sober, Orson made his way alongside the slow-moving traffic, on a berm edged with potholes and only occasional slabs of cracked sidewalk, from the turnpike on-ramp to I-70 and back, then the whole loop over again. Four times he lapped the length of that strip in what I took to be melancholic introspection, but which could as easily have been bewildered confusion, or even emptiness, an absence of thought or emotion—the entire walk lasting perhaps an hour and a half before landing him back at the Denny's, where it seemed he was again going to eat.

And the first person he saw as he entered was: Phyllis. They said, at the same time, "You still here?"—and then laughed together at the coincidence. She smiled at him, and I thought: *What the heck is going on?* In fact I momentarily wondered if, while he'd slept, as I had been busy cursing myself and my fortune, I'd unknowingly transported from Orson's body into the body of some more sober, thoughtful, and amiable stranger. And it was only when he went into the bathroom to wash his hands before eating and I faced him in the mirror that I was willing to admit it was still him.

He stayed at the Denny's for several hours that night, drinking coffee and picking at his pancakes and listening to Phyllis when she came around, which was more or less constantly. Eventually he headed back to his motel and sat at the window until midmorning, at which point he again went to sleep, again slept all day, again woke, took his brooding, confused, or emotionally absent laps between the highways, and ended up at the Denny's, to my mounting dismay. This time when he walked in, Phyllis gave a brash laugh and hooted that it was downright peculiar for a gentleman to spend more than a single night in Breezewood, especially a worldly gentleman such as himself, and what on earth was he trying to prove?

"To be honest," said Orson, "I have no idea."

Phyllis smiled slyly, and winked, and brought his coffee, and I could see she did not actually believe that he had no idea. She believed he had a very particular idea. And later, when she told Orson what time she got off work, and still later when they had awkward sex in his motel room, I'm sure she felt confirmed in her suspicions as to why Orson was still there in that town.

As for me: notwithstanding my desperate desire to be gone from "The Town of Motels," I thought his "I have no idea" had sounded rather true. There was something different about Orson in Breezewood, a difference that had started back in Pittsburgh but that here seemed to have taken hold. He wasn't drinking. He wasn't swearing. He just wandered in silence, wandered the strip, wandered into Denny's, not—this was the thing—as if he had no place to be, but as if he specifically wanted to be *here*. Not here with Phyllis, just here in Breezewood. And since I could not fathom why anyone would ever want to spend time in that place, I therefore took his "I have no idea" to mean that he himself did not understand why he was remaining in a place that obviously had nothing to offer, unless it was somehow to punish me, Samuel Johnson, who he did not even know existed, for having briefly disrupted his horrible life.

Nor did the fact that he stayed in that motel for the rest of the week, and continued to see Phyllis, convince me that he had the slightest idea of what he was doing. And when, at the end of that week, he moved into her trailer home at the far edge of town (not a great distance from the near edge of town) and proceeded to enter into what can only be called a "new life" there, a sober life in which he did little more than sleep and eat and walk Phyllis's dog, wear her deceased husband's clothes, run errands in her truck, watch television in the trailer, and wander around; and when this "new life" kept lasting, week after week, until I could again feel myself losing hope, leaking resolve, and seriously doubting that a new return attempt with Phil would ever take place; in other words, during the entire tedious process by which the bizarre awfulness of Breezewood gradually became, for me, my new normal-and-familiar sort of everyday awfulness, still I never once believed, in all that time, that Orson understood what he was doing. Whatever it was—"life"—he was just going along with it.

For three months he went along with it. It was a better life than the one he'd been living, so after a while I assumed we were done.

In fact it had already begun to seem that Elliot and David and Blossom and whatever history had spawned Orson's unending downward spiral all belonged to an irretrievable past, when one night, over sloppy joes in the trailer, Phyllis asked about his life before Breezewood. She had brought it up before, of course, early on, but had received such a gruff response that first time that she'd never tried again. But this evening, for some reason: "You had a job or . . . ?" Orson was already eating his sandwich, but paused, his mouth stalled, sloppy joe stuffing up his cheeks, which must have looked rather weird and made Phyllis uneasy. "Never mind," she said—but Orson, swallowing, said "No, no," meaning yes, it was o.k. to ask.

And then he told her—not all of it, but enough. A lot. He told her things even I didn't know—such as that he'd had a wife (?). About the business he'd built, how successful he'd been, and how after a while he'd let restlessness get the better of him and did things he'd later regretted. How boredom wasn't the word for it, it was something much bigger than boredom, more all-encompassing, and how his wife's leaving left him even more untethered than before. There was an illness—it was all kind of hard to pin down. He talked about his junk-filled house, his stuffy office, how he liked to drive around in his car. His wandering, his drinking. His life alone and the habits he'd fallen into, how one thing led to the next. About traveling but never really enjoying it; in fact how everything supposedly enjoyable eventually isn't, but how you keep doing those things anyway, God knows why. About David, vaguely about Blossom, and eventually about Elliot, whom he went on about for a while. Until finally he arrived at the last thing that had happened, the new project proposal, how Elliot had kept coming over with forms and how surprised he, Orson, had been to find Elliot so concerned about it. That Elliot had actually seemed to care about it. So he'd gone along—he told Phyllis—he'd filled out the forms or whatever, but then life, or Fate, or something intervened. He'd ended up here, ended up doing this, the trailer, the sloppy joes. He hadn't over-thought it. Probably he'd under-thought it. It was hard to know how much thinking was the right amount. At which point Phyllis, who'd been listening intently the whole time, who in fact seemed to have gotten wrapped up in Orson's story as if it were a movie she was thoroughly enjoying rather than the dismal actual life of the person seated across from her, switched for a moment into the sassy Phyllis we'd seen less of lately and said, "You mean ya just *left* him there, with that deadline an everything? Ya just *left?*" Not with contempt, but anticipation, as if waiting for the part where the movie turns and everything is made better. But all Orson had to offer was, "Yeah."

Then he stopped talking, and he must have been going a good two hours without a break, long enough at least that when he finally stopped it was as if the lights came back on (to continue this movie analogy), and they were both startled, bewildered back into real life.

Phyllis cleared the dishes, then cleaned them while Orson walked the dog. Later, they lay silent and fidgety beside each other in bed, pretending to sleep, until the very first light appeared, and they both got up early. Phyllis kept busy through breakfast, then off to work. Orson fussed all morning around the trailer, and shortly after lunch he locked up and walked to one of the truck stops, where he arranged a ride back to Pittsburgh. It happened without warning or ceremony, and in my excitement at the sudden turn of events, I did not spend much time considering what it meant for Orson or what might be transpiring in his mind. Climbing the turnpike on-ramp, we took our last look back at Breezewood, and it was, for me, as if our three-month hiatus there had never even taken place, so gloriously remote did it suddenly appear, so instantly distant.

Which is also, incidentally, how I felt about my entire time with Orson, many pages ago when I first started describing it for you. I felt—as I have always felt gazing back upon my past—as if I were inspecting a scrapbook of someone else's memories, distant and strange. But telling this story, my time with Orson—this has gone on longer than expected. Inhabiting these memories deeply enough to write them down has proven emotionally exhausting, and by this point I am ready to be done.

But I will rally myself one last time for the finale.

The trip back was, for me, unbearable with anticipation. Once in the city (I assured myself) Orson would fall back to his old ways— the *old* old ways, the drinking and carousing—would fall back with a vengeance, and I would be ready, had been ready now for a very long time. I would call Blossom's number and say, "This is Samuel for Phil!" I would name a place to meet, and while realistically I could not expect Phil to be prepared for me, at least he would know I was back in Pittsburgh. Unless Phil himself was not back? It was possible that Blossom had gone off somewhere . . . But no, I told myself, Phil would be back, he would, and would make arrangements—he was good at these things. In the meantime, I would wait. I would plan and prepare. There were things I needed to do. What things? Well, there had to be something I could do. I would figure out what that something was. I would find steps and take them. And Phil would come. He would come. Everything would work out.

As for Orson, he remained, of course, a necessary precondition to my plans, and as we pulled into Pittsburgh and he headed to the office (not his house, as I'd expected, but to the office downtown, where he hardly ever went), I began to pay more attention to him and to wonder what was going on in his mind. And when we entered the office to find it abandoned, with chairs and desks but not a single paper pile or even garbage in the trash—at that point, I became very keen to know what Orson was thinking and how it might affect my own expectations. Given the scene before us, it seemed likely he was thinking about his past, some vast range of previousness I'd never seen or known about that had shaped his behavior during all the time I'd spent with him. Also about the company, the employees, the years invested, the anger accumulated. And when, after ten minutes of standing there, Orson moved to the window, where he stared out for several hours, until the light outside began to dim and the empty office filled with dark contours (because he hadn't turned on the lights), during this time my anxiety only grew, until finally I began to have a *bad feeling*. A premonition, or sense of foreboding. It was the feeling of knowing, or of feeling as if I knew, that the situation I had been stuck in would soon be ending, and everything would change, but not in the way that I wanted. In some ruinous way, some way even more torturously pointless than everything that had happened so far . . .

That was just a feeling, however.

At dusk, he wandered out into the world. He circled the streets of downtown for perhaps an hour, then faced uptown and walked without turning. He walked and walked. We ended up, around eight o'clock, at a jazz club in the Hill District. It was a place Orson used to occasionally lurk but where he hadn't been in a long time, a venue particularly popular with the black community. In fact on this particular night, there were no other white people there. A few customers hung around the bar, and an unusually tall woman sat reading a book beside the stage, where a tenor trio (saxophone, piano, bass) blew through some Ellington standards. Orson headed to the bar and began ordering boilermakers, staring intently at his reflection in the bar mirror.

No, *intently* is not the right word. Intently is too intense. He stared *deadly*, as if dead. He stared deadly and drank boilermaker after boilermaker—and as his blood-alcohol level rose, I allowed myself to feel more optimistic. I told myself that my earlier fearful premonition had been groundless, a bit of fanciful paranoia my mind had picked up from too many years with Orson Fitz. And this nervousness I felt? That was my overwhelming anticipation to be off again to my son. Yet it also occurred to me that the image in the mirror was likely the last look I would have at the living, raging Orson; however this ended, by my hand or his, our time together would soon be over. In fact it could not be over quickly enough!

Until at last he staggered off the barstool and made his way to the tiny stage—which was low, just a couple of feet up from the floor—where he stood and began shouting in a manner completely inappropriate to the mellow music—"Yeah! Yeah! Yeah!"—and rocking back and forth. He bent over to beat the stage front, like a drummer at the red-hot center of a manic swing band, which in his mind is perhaps what he was. The saxophone player blew a loud note squarely into his face to back him off, but Orson leaned into it, shouted into it—"Yeah! Yeah! Yeah!"—so that the saxophone player now stepped back, and the woman seated by the stage shot Orson an alarmed look, and I suddenly knew, with a sunken heart but with utter surety, that the events transpiring were no longer moving me closer to my son, and that the *bad thing* I'd been imagining was in fact about to transpire. I did not know what the bad thing would be, but already I hated it. Then Orson stepped onto the stage and grabbed the back of the upright piano, which I found out later was brand new and had just been delivered that day, and had wheels that the movers had mistakenly failed to lock, and which Orson, a weak man but raging with the terrible force of existential obscurity, was somehow able to single-handedly pull backwards off the stage, where it landed on top of him, crushing his lungs and leaving the most horrible look on his face, bulging eyes and the whole deal, an unforgettably nightmarish expression, which an eyeblink later I found myself staring down upon over the bell of a tenor saxophone.

Thus, in befitting absurdity, ends the story of Orson Fitz.

7.

"Henry Nelson!"

In turning my mind upon the next episode of my tale, I imagine a low rumbling sound, like a herd of animals approaching fast
but still far off in the distance—I seem to be feeling poetic for
some reason—as yet another round of memories travels toward me
across the years. To be honest, I am not eager to dive so quickly
into another period of my past, having not yet managed to recover
from the last one. One memory, however, has already arrived, well
in advance of the others: even before her face, her voice—

"Henry Nelson!"

There were two things I quickly learned about Henry. First, that
he spent afternoons running a shot-and-beer bar (a bare room with
chairs and tables that sold shots of whiskey and cans of beer from a
refrigerator) in the Homewood neighborhood of Pittsburgh, so was
around booze all the time. And second, that he never drank it. He
had a "history" with alcohol, and left to his own devices would likely
have drunk a great deal of it, allowing me, his body's new tenant,
to mount a new expedition to my son. But the devices he was left

to were never his own, in fact he was hardly ever left alone, but was kept always in mind, if not in sight, by Alma.

Alma who had wrested him from a drunken down-spiraling life. Who had saved him from himself and was not about to hand him back to himself any time soon. Alma who had married him, housed him, and given him a job in her bar. Who took him wherever she went, and went with him wherever he needed to go. She was not a bad person, I should say. She was a good person, in fact, a charitable figure and community leader. Only that, where Henry was concerned, she was quite a bit more anxious, suspicious, and possessive than she ever was toward anyone else.

Four and a half years—I'll just tell you—four and a half years is how long I spent in Henry's world, a world that was technically just a few miles east of Orson's, but that might as well have been located on a different planet, in a different dimension of time and space. Homewood in the midseventies was a bustling neighborhood of wood houses and brick tenements, wide avenues and alleys. The sidewalks "hopped," voices filled the streets and shops, and all kinds of music floated out of windows. Everyone was black—which back then was still fairly new to me—and I was unprepared for the sheer amount of friendliness, having come from life with Orson; in fact it was the liveliest place I'd ever been, certainly much livelier than Unityville. I even found myself wondering, when I first arrived with Henry, before I got so used to his life that I forgot it had ever seemed new—I wondered how differently I, Samuel Johnson, might have turned out, how much more personable a person, had I grown up in this livelier place? But the answer soon became obvious. For not everyone in Homewood was equally sociable, and I had landed in the least social of all. Their loner, their mope: Henry was their Samuel Johnson. I would have been Henry Nelson!

Which perhaps explains why, despite our many differences, Henry's life felt familiar to me, and I imagined I understood him, at least better than I'd ever understood Orson. And which perhaps also explains why, in the end, I did not get to know Homewood as well as I might have, since all I ever saw was the view from Henry's fairly adventureless life. And so repetitive was that life, so run together are its particulars in my mind, that the memories I'm left with cannot be actual memories, not individual scenes that occurred in the manner I remember them, but instead must be recycled out of broken-up moments of endlessly repeated events, as the passage of time reduces whole eras to a handful of reconstituted images.

For example:

Here's Henry at work in the bar. It's a summer midafternoon, and the floor fans blow a sound like swarming into the room, but not much air or coolness, I think, since everyone is sweating. "Everyone" in this case meaning the four or five regulars who sit around the place, chiding each other and joking with each other and talking all afternoon about the heat, whether the heat is typical of this time of year or is actually hotter than usual, or whether hotter than usual is itself typical of this time of year, whether anything other than usual can also be typical, or if that's foolish, and so on. Henry doesn't talk much—he never talks much—but pops beer cans and lugs boxes from the basement, runs a wet rag over surfaces, and there's a feeling of goodwill in the room, a lazy calm despite the noisy heat, until the day winds down, the night comes on, time passes, the morning arrives, and the same day starts all over.

Here's Henry on a bench in the hallway outside the multipurpose room in the church basement. It's the same bench where Alma waits for him during his Monday night AA meetings, but where more often he waits for her to finish up her various committee meetings. A wooden bench with a back. This hallway is strictly municipal, cinder block painted over in a shade between tan and yellow, with floor tiles that vaguely resemble marble but seem more in imitation of a splattered stone that never naturally existed. And though I cannot smell, I imagine this place smells of paint. It is full of tiny echoes, this hallway. Of muffled other-room voices and pockets of dead air and these tiny echoes caused by the slightest movement atop the bench—and there could not be a more boring place to sit in all the world.

Here's Alma driving Henry home from a gig.

"And what would've happened, you think, Henry, if I hadn't been there tonight? With all that gallivanting and alcohol?"

"Nothing," says Henry, staring absently into nighttime traffic. In fact this may be the defining characteristic of Henry, if I had to pick a defining characteristic, that although he was constantly surrounded by people, or by *person*, still he seemed so often in his own head that it was as if he were always alone. Not how Orson was almost constantly alone, or how for the longest time Christopher had tried to be—but alone nonetheless.

"*Nothing?*" says Alma.

"Not nothing?" says Henry, his mind at last entering the conversation.

"With all that gallivanting and alcohol?"

"Well," says Henry, "I do work in a bar."

"In *my* bar," says Alma.

"Well," says Henry, "your bar does serve alcohol."

"It serves what I *say* it serves," says Alma—and Henry cannot disagree with that; in fact, I do not know why he has given Alma a hard time in the first place. "And I *supervise* everything in it."

"True," says Henry, who from here on simply agrees.

"Everything and every*one*."

"Well, that's just true."

And when they get home, after he's gone off to his bedroom (they slept in separate rooms because Henry was a terrible snorer, a fact that brought me no small amount of irritation during our time together), after she's closed up the house and stopped in to say good night, she gives him a kiss and a shy smile, and I think that she is feeling a little sorry about the spat in the car. That she wishes to convey without quite saying so that she knows she can get a little fiery. He is not a hooligan, after all. Not a playboy or a schemer. He is just Henry, her Henry—Henry Nelson. A thought that surely comforts Alma and that she can tell herself with confidence, since she has no way of knowing the truth. She has no way of knowing that below the surface, in a hidden compartment of his existence, Henry is a different person altogether.

For you see, Henry Nelson had a secret that only he and I knew about. It was not the sort of secret a person gets into trouble over, but he kept it hidden nonetheless, and waited each night until long after Alma had seen him off to bed before he would escape to it. He would lie perfectly still while the neighborhood outside grew calm and the house went quiet. Then he would reach down from the bed (climbing down caused the floor to creak) and slide out the long low box he kept tucked beneath the dresser. An ordinary cardboard shirt box, yet it contained, for Henry, an entirely different life, a life in which he could be the person he wanted to be, remaking his personality to match his self-imagining, under the bedsheet, with a penlight, in a notebook. *The Saga of Henry Nelson*. Strictly speaking, he had only one chapter of it, which he reread so often that even now, all these years later, I can remember the whole thing by heart.

And given that, other than Henry and myself, only two other people ever read his one chapter; and given that his writing was not at all bad (I thought) and probably deserves to be read; and given that I was not, in the end, very good to Henry, and regret what happened to him, not that I was entirely responsible, but still . . . Given all of that, I hope it seems reasonable that before I begin the story of what happened to Henry Nelson—because obviously I have such a story—but before we move on to that, I will first set down here from memory the entirety of Henry's chapter, beginning with what

I think must be the most elaborate title in the history of titles. For it was not simply *The Saga of Henry Nelson*, it was:

The Saga of Henry Nelson

or

a tale a little taller than some
about a man a little shorter than most,
who some called a washed-out has-been
and others a might-have-been never-was,
how he was born on a porch swing
and raised in the Hill
and never got farther than Homewood,
how he drove all his life in the wrong direction
because he couldn't find a place to turn around,
how he hooked left when he should've run right
and jumped low when he should've ducked high,
how he lost his path, skipped the tracks,
and landed smack in a cul-de-sac,
and how despite all his wrongful inclinations
he one day found himself in the light,
having learned a few things
and seen things and known some characters,
and having now and for a good while since
thought upon his missteps and prepared his own
sober, sound advice to young people
struggling along that same road,
all this being written down here by that selfsame
Henry Nelson,
the least likely man to say a word about himself to anybody,
who for reasons even he can't understand
one day sat and scribbled out what follows

Chapter 1
I'm Born and Grow

One . . . Two . . . Three . . . Hooooo!

I was born on a porch swing, and if you don't believe that, you might as well skip the rest and forget it. My mother'd gone to see Fletcher Henderson's band the night before and got in her head I was to be a great musician, and got also in her head that since rich people are born chewing on silver spoons, and smart people are born doing algebra on their toes and fingers, great musicians must be born swinging. Oh, I remember *that* day. (I was there, after all.) The swingchains jangle and the whole seat's shaking and the doctor's doing the count-off when I jump the beat and shoot out an eighth note early (never quite learned to lay back), quick as a slippery rocket past the old doc's catcher's mitt and up over the big wide world of the porch. That's me traveling light through the troposphere, taking my first fine look at the world: handsome houses . . . nice warm sun . . . great big marshmallowy clouds . . . *So this is living?* I say to myself. *Why, it's not half bad!* I figure to keep on going this way awhile, a crazy naked baby-rocket on a solo flight through the universe, but then something starts yanking from below, something invisible's got ahold of me. (Nobody'd hipped me to gravity, see?) It's powerful, it's *unshak-*able, and before you know I'm falling fast, bouncing off a porch rail and landing in a prickle bush out the sideyard. Henry Nelson, welcome to the world!

See the first lesson life taught me was *physics*, and I learned it the hard way, which was good practice for later on.

That particular prickle bush was in a neighborhood called the Hill in a town called Pittsburgh in a state called Pennsylvania. In case you don't know those places, I'll describe them for you: the Hill looks like a hill, Pittsburgh looks like a wedge, and

Pennsylvania looks like a clog, which is a big Dutch wooden shoe. I hope I do not seem to be putting on educated airs, mentioning that Dutch shoe. Truth is, my education was of the narrow sort, and I have never once in my life seen a real wooden shoe, only in pictures. Nor have I ever so much as set foot outside the Pennsylvania clog, or hardly left the Pittsburgh wedge, in fact for my first fifteen years I never even climbed down the Hill's hill. And needless to say, never have nor will these feet ever come close to the continent called *Europe*, nor the country called *Netherlands*, which is where Dutch people live with their wooden shoes.

But let's get me out of that prickle bush before I start to bleed. I'm a small boy, who's soon enough grown to a small youngster. I keep growing and growing but no matter how big my body makes itself, compared to everybody else I'm still small. Can't say I loved that. My mother never worried about my size, in fact the only part of me she seemed to mind at all were the ears, which were stubborn or maybe just dull, but were no ways hip to the sundry varieties of music she was always trying to pack into them. Oh, I loved when she sang to me, but other than my mother, there was nobody I'd stand to listen to at all. "Don't worry," say the neighbors. "Henry's young. Musical feeling don't start till eight, nine. Let the boy be a boy for a while!" So my mother, being a good mother, let me be a boy.

And the Hill back then was a fine place to be one, and I have nothing but fine memories. It was a real community and people knew how to have a good time together. The men worked down the Hill and the women watched over the Hill and the kids crawled like ants all over it. Weekends folks spent out on porches and stoops, or visiting round the houses, and everybody knew everybody, and for the most part everybody got along. It was like growing up on a desert island, but filled with kids and grown-ups. You didn't think about the future, until one day you did, and then you didn't think about much else. For me, that day came earlier than most, just two weeks before my eighth birthday, when it came time to pick an instrument.

For having waited so long for her musician, my mother was much choosier than you'd expect. I guess all that waiting *somewhat elevated* her expectations, because now it turns out trumpets cause head pains and pianos don't grow on trees. My eight-year-old arms couldn't reach the end of a trombone slide, and my eight-year-old fingers didn't span the fingerboard on a bass. Drums were too boomy, flutes too fruity, and let us not so much as *discuss* the violin. All seemed just about lost till finally along came the saxophone. Now *there* was an instrument my mother could countenance, by far and without question the least wrong instrument of all. So, quick as St. Nick, I'm a sax man in training, and boy what a training it was.

You ever hear a tale how Charlie Parker stepped into a woodshed and stepped out a short while later the greatest sax man ever lived? Well, Henry Nelson climbed up to an attic (with dusty low light, squinty eyeballs, sweat-dripping T-shirt, the whole bag) and came out *a whole lot* later barely holding his own. If that makes no sense, then perhaps now's the time for me to mention the first of many *mis*concepts I mean to speak to in these pages.

See there was around that time a belief widely held to (or at least my mother held to it) that a true musician never set foot in school. Musical talent came natural, and school just messed you up. If you were even halfway serious, you'd hole up in a shack with a horn for the long side of childhood and musical talent just magically *happened*, or so people thought, and for all I know they still think it. Well, if you ask me, this is *un*true. This is a *mis*concept. *Something* happens when you hole up in that room, but that something will not always resemble music. Oh, for Charlie Parker maybe it did (or maybe he snuck some lessons and just never told anybody). But not for Henry Nelson! See, for all my *in*spiration and *de*dication and *per*spiration, I suffered a shortage of the most important –*ation* of them all: *education* . . .

Here Henry leaves off from his own life's story to lecture (essentially it was a lecture) for several pages about youth education, starting with music lessons but quickly expanding to the importance of education more generally: how education leads to opportunity, how parents need to play an active part, how young people are the future, and so on. The style shifts—long paragraphs of earnest, heartfelt advice. And while I know I said I was going to include the entirety of Henry's chapter here, the truth is, I do not have that part memorized. In fact, my memory had forgotten these pages even existed until I arrived at them just now. This is not because Henry's chapter suddenly became, in these pages, quite boring, but because it became *so* boring that most nights, when he reread his chapter, he skipped over these pages himself. He would pick up with:

And that's why, if there's one thing I mean to convey to young people setting out to play music, or whatever else you might do, it's to take it from an old washed-out has-been might-have-been never-was and *get yourself some lessons.*

But let's get back to me. By now I'd come down out the attic, a skinny *de*hydrated fourteen-year-old with no natural talent or instruction and well on my way to setting a *new world record.* I mean a record that never even existed before I came along to set it: the world record for *lack of progress.* I started gigging around the Hill, and at first, no surprise, things did not go too well. But you know, stick with it long enough, even a lack of progress progresses, and by the time I hit mid teens, my badness had become a kind of talent. I was so bad I was almost good. Or, I was so bad it confused folks, they didn't know what to do with my no-good talentless noises, and some started calling it a "style," while others just called it *baloney* or worse. But I got work, then more work, and before long even my mother could squint and convince herself I was on my way to becoming the great musician she always imagined. It seems strange to say now, but no less true for seeming strange, that for a brief shining moment, Henry Nelson's lowdown life appeared to be full of promise. And that was when I first stood up and looked around, and when I finally decided it was time to head on down the Hill, but I'll be darned if I'm going to pack all that happened next into the same chapter with all this I've said already.

Unfortunately, that was all. He never wrote a second chapter. Now, one thing I should have mentioned earlier, but did not mention earlier because that would have spoiled the effect of mentioning it now, was that during the entire time I spent with Henry, while he was working on his saga, he was still just in his midthirties. Not his seventies, not his sixties, not even his fifties or forties. In fact, he was just about the same age I would have been, had I lived as long. If he nonetheless wrote as if he'd reached the end of a long life that had left him sage and world-weary, that is not because he was an insincere person, but simply because this was how he'd decided to feel about himself. He had a romantic vision of life that he strongly held to, even if no one around him would ever have guessed. In this vision, he was the Henry Nelson who had lived a lifetime's worth of trials and tribulations, and whose existence continued on, now, primarily for the purpose of writing it all down.

All the more odd, then, that night after night he failed to. Frankly, I could never understand it. He kept a second notebook, a "scratch" one, or rather he kept a series of these in which he would write things down then scratch them out, sometimes letting them sit a day or two first. These were anecdotes or bits of stories of his past exploits, and many were exceptionally funny or surprising, I thought, but none was ever copied into his primary notebook. Oh, I had my theories: (1) that he admired his first chapter too much and felt he could not regain the "spirit" of it; (2) that secretly he did not *want* to proceed, but only to stay in his made-up universe, fiddling forever and ever; (3) that he simply lacked confidence in his writing, just as more generally he lacked confidence in himself.

Whatever it was, it was frustrating. I felt frustrated for Henry, and even more for myself, for it seemed to me that once he finally *did* push forward, he would finish his saga in no time. And if he finished his saga, he would at that point wake up to the fact that he was still essentially a young man, with a life very much in progress. He would live his life rather than eulogizing it, and perhaps—who knows?— start drinking again (a circumstance I, Samuel Johnson, selfishly longed for, since no matter how involved I became in Henry's life, still somewhere in my mind's heart I always held out hope for a new return to my son). Yet stuck as he was in his saga, he was stuck also in the "self" composing it, the sagely world-weary self, who moved through his own private world as if through the hallways of a nursing home, vaguely aware that life outside still persisted but seeing no opportunity or reason to take an active part.

That, then, was the situation Henry found himself in—or the situation he had placed himself in and that I, Samuel Johnson, found myself in—for the first three and a half years we were together, and up until the day when he volunteered at the local library, where his life at long last took an eventful turn.

A program was being organized to provide free music lessons to people in the community, and Henry had been asked to teach saxophone. The opportunity to teach strongly appealed to him, to the sagely part of him, but I suspect even more appealing was that the Saturday morning sessions overlapped with Alma's committee activities, when he would normally sit out in the hall. And since the lessons were for charity, to help out people in the community, she had no choice but to let him go.

From the start, Henry loved this program, loved being a teacher and sharing what he knew. When Saturdays rolled around, he now woke full of vitality, and fixed and ate breakfast with a cheerfulness that clearly concerned Alma—not simply, I think, because she did not recognize this Henry, but also because she suspected there was more to his new vitality than he was letting on. Before long, the program's organizer asked if he would also run a small swing band with the other teachers. They would rehearse Saturdays after lessons and would perform for charity events around town, maybe pick up some paying gigs on the side. Thus Henry became leader of the Teachers Band, and it was through the Teachers Band that he came to know Benjamin, an undergraduate English major at a local university who'd seen a flyer for the program, had called to volunteer, and now drove up from Oakland each Saturday morning to teach music theory and piano.

They could not have been more different, Henry and Benjamin. They had the Teachers Band in common but demographically, dispositionally, and in just about every other way, they were worlds apart. You might say their friendship was based on these differences: they were not just friends but a particular kind of friends, the kind who know nothing about each other's lives outside of the one situation in which they see each other, and so allow each other to be whoever they wish to be within that one situation, without having to answer for whoever they are everywhere else. To Henry, Benjamin might as well have been from outer space, and this distance freed Henry to be his energetic, playful, smart-alecky self— the self from his saga—rather than the mopey recluse everyone else expected of him.

"Jewish people ain't exactly white people," was one of the first things Henry ever said to Benjamin (who was Jewish), and he meant it as both an endearment and a joke. In fact, Henry rarely said anything to Benjamin in earnest, but would constantly gibe about how Benjamin's feet flailed around when he played, or how badly he cluttered his chord voicings, his music *theory* that could use more music *practice*, and so on. The fact that Benjamin really was not a very talented musician might have added sting to these gibes had Benjamin been the sort to take offense, or had Henry been anything more than a mediocre musician himself. Which I suppose was another thing they had in common.

And when the Teachers Band started performing in the community, if a performance happened to conflict with one of Alma's church activities, it was Benjamin who gave Henry a ride. And after such events—which did not happen often, or at least did not conflict with Alma's schedule as often as Henry might have liked—Henry and Benjamin would stop afterwards at Ritter's (a beloved Pittsburgh diner with a pebbled exterior and booth radios and wood paneling that I had previously been to several times with Orson) for burgers and fries. Henry would tell Benjamin his stories, those slightly tall tales he was always writing in his extra notebooks, which were really very entertaining and which would have made excellent chapters—*I* thought—in his saga, and Benjamin would laugh and smile and egg him on.

Until one day, on one such occasion, following a local charity fashion-show fundraiser, after they'd ordered food and Henry had just told Benjamin about how once, for a few months, he'd juggled three girlfriends all living within two blocks of each other, how he'd had to stick to a strict schedule like in the military and take vitamin supplements to keep his cock up and it was like holding a full-time job plus overtime and weekends . . . As he was wrapping up this story, his voice full of energy and humor, with Benjamin saying how crazy that must have been, Henry suddenly, in a zealous burst, blurted out to Benjamin that he was writing a book. Actually what he said was that he *had written* a book. And seeing as Benjamin studied *English* ("Though my book's in *American*," was his joke), he asked if Benjamin might want to read the first chapter.

"Of course!" Benjamin smiled with such natural enthusiasm that it was as if he'd been waiting to be asked. "I absolutely want to read your book!"

That was their entire discussion, or the entire portion of their discussion that mentioned Henry's writing. A tiny discussion, an inconsequential moment in the history of human discussions, yet for Henry Nelson nothing was ever the same again.

The following week he spent shifting between anxieties high and low, faced for the first time with the possibility that someone else, an actual living person, was going to read what he had written. Those late-night hours he would normally spend writing, or trying to write, or thinking about trying to write, he spent instead copying out his chapter into a separate notebook for Benjamin. And meanwhile he did his best to avoid Alma, who had grown increasingly suspicious, and increasingly everything else she was in addition to being suspicious, and had for the past few weeks been following Henry more closely than ever, and particularly now, with him acting so strange.

"Henry," she said to him finally. This was at the dinner table. "What are you up to?"

Henry did not stop eating or look up.

"Nothing," he said. "I'm up to just exactly nothing."

"I *know* you're up to something. It better not be what I *think* it is."

"Can't be what you think it is"—Henry chewed—"since you seem to think it's something, and if you're thinking anything at all, it's not that, because it's nothing."

"It better not be what I think."

"There's no 'it,' even. Not even an 'it' to keep the 'nothing' company. There's just nothing, all by itself."

"You wouldn't even be *talking* so much if it weren't something."

"I wouldn't be talking if you didn't keep asking."

"*Excuse* me?"

And here Henry looked up, and on Alma's face, in addition to anger, there were other emotions, less aggressive, more fretful emotions, and I felt bad for her then.

"Well"—she finally broke off—"it just better not be what I think."

Finally Saturday arrived. Henry stowed his second notebook in his saxophone case and headed off to the library. Alma had offered that morning to cancel her church activities and go along with him for the day, and Henry had praised the idea highly, encouraging her as sincerely as he could, no doubt reasoning (correctly, as it turned out) that it was the best way to convince her not to.

It was a longer walk than usual because he stopped so often along the way—because he had started out too early—yet eventually he arrived at the library entrance, then in the big wooden foyer, then downstairs to the basement, where by that time he was already late.

His first student sat bored, a young man who could not yet hold a whole note, so they spent the lesson making sounds through their mouthpieces.

Second came a pretty young woman entering high school who did not sound particularly good to me, but who was already far better, Henry assured her, than he'd been at her age.

Third was a new student, a man who had played many years ago and had recently found his old horn in the basement. It turned out he wasn't there for lessons but only to ask Henry how much he could get for it, and finally he offered to sell it to Henry right there.

The fourth student I do not remember. In fact I only remember any of these because it was such an anxious day for Henry, and I suppose for me as well. For I was tuned in to Henry's life rather intently, by then. I had come to feel myself a part of his life, with a stake, if only imaginary, in what was about to happen—and each of these lessons seemed to last an entire lifetime.

Fifth was the man who ran the program, who'd originally asked Henry to volunteer. He was a decent saxophone player, not better than Henry but not much worse, and the two sat talking for most of the session until it was time for the Teachers Band to rehearse.

"Henry, hello!" said Benjamin when he saw him.

"I brought it," said Henry, not joking or jovial or teasing in the least.

"Brought what?" said Benjamin, which obviously was not the response Henry expected.

"The . . ." Half the band was sitting down already. "What we talked about."

But Benjamin only looked puzzled, and there wasn't time, right then, to talk.

Then rehearsal happened, a languorous rehearsal. Henry was quiet the whole time, as quiet as he could be while still leading the band, and I assumed he was thinking about their brief exchange, about the surprising and frustrating fact that Benjamin seemed not to have given much thought to Henry's book this past week, or any thought at all. In fact, he seemed to have forgotten entirely that Henry had a book he was planning to share, which must have caused Henry a sour feeling. And this sour feeling, which I imagined as composed of a variety of specific emotions, such as irritation and disappointment and self-doubt, this was the feeling Henry carried with him back to the piano, when rehearsal was over and others were packing up, which no doubt accounted for the gruffness in his voice when he said—

"I don't guess the grammar and punctuation and all that is up to college standards. I never got to college. It's no college story, so . . . You'll let me know what you think."

—and he handed the notebook to Benjamin.

"Oh, your thing!" said Benjamin. "This is great. This is . . . I can't wait to read this. Thanks for this!"

"Hopefully you can make out the handwriting," said Henry.

"Sure I can!"

"It still needs to be typed."

"Oh, this is totally fine . . ."

"So . . . you'll tell me what you think?"

"I will!"

"And don't hold back about it, right?"

"Hold back?"

"With what you think."

The confusion on Benjamin's face I took to mean that holding back had not actually occurred to him, nor that Henry's story might contain anything to hold back about.

"I'm sure I'll love it!" he said.

"o.k., good. Thanks," said Henry, who by now seemed to have forgiven Benjamin's earlier forgetfulness. In fact he sounded pleased.

And that was it.

It is frankly painful to remember Henry walking home that day, practically skipping over the sidewalk. It was his finest hour, though in true Henry fashion, his finest hour lasted fifteen minutes. *Someone's reading my book,* I imagined him thinking, *Benjamin's reading my book, and next week Benjamin will report back what he thought. Maybe he'll want to see more of it, and I'll have to write some more, which I'll be able to do, then, with that encouragement . . .* When he came through the kitchen door, however, expecting to find the house empty, as it was most Saturdays at that time, he instead found Alma at the table in a fit of hideous laughter. It was a snorting, gurgling laughter such as I had never heard from Alma before, and I am happy never to have heard it again. Tears on her cheeks, body quivering, and there on the table sat Henry's notebook number one.

"Is this . . . ?" She turned to him, awestruck. "I can't . . . It's . . . Here in my own . . ." At this point you could tell that what followed was going to be simply awful. "The *world-famous* Mr. Washed-Out Has-Been Might-Have-Been Never-Was? Leading expert in *early childhood education*? Right here in my own . . ." And so on. You can imagine the rest. Or, if you cannot imagine, simply flip back a few pages and reread Henry's chapter, inserting boisterous mockery between the sentences, and you will have as good a sense of this scene as I can give you. It went on for a long time.

"Henry!" she finally shouted, because by then Henry was gone, up to his room, cursing Alma behind the door.

"Henry, come back down here!"

Cursing Alma and also his notebook, and himself for having that notebook, or for not having hidden it well enough.

"Henry Nelson!"

No doubt asking himself, as he began to cool down, *Well, what the hell's she know?* Telling himself, *Not a damn thing.* And next Saturday he would see Benjamin, who studied English and knew a whole lot more about writing and how to get stories to come out in a way people want to read them than Alma ever would. In fact that was one topic about which Alma, for all her talk, knew exactly *shit.*

All week he was cold to her, and avoided her, to the extent that was possible, and I think Alma, too, felt she had gone too far. The revelation of Henry's utterly tame secret must have come as a great relief to her, and she had overcompensated for her insecurities. She had let her relief come out as mockery, a joyful mockery that was neither Christian nor kind. Unfortunately, her apologies were, if anything, worse. "If writing crazy jive and imagining yourself some kind of broke-down wise-man saint of young people is how you keep to the Christian path, why, you go on ahead and"—is the kind of apology she tried several times to make, and she seemed surprised each time when Henry did not instantly pull out of his funk.

Her mistake, it seemed to me, was to assume that Henry's attitude was nothing more than a funk, one she herself had caused. She failed to see that the real change in Henry's attitude had nothing to do with her, or very little. The real change was: he had lost his secret. Both by accident (Alma) and on purpose (Benjamin), his secret life was laid bare. And while Alma was perhaps right to think that Henry the man was changeable and ought to come around, still, some changes are irrevocable, and the loss of a secret most of all.

Saturday arrived, and while I suppose we might note, on Benjamin's behalf, that he could not have known the importance Henry had placed on his opinion, nor realistically said or done anything that would have stood up to Henry's expectations, still, his response was fairly inane. The moment Henry approached him, he called out: "I read your chapter!" This was before the Teachers Band rehearsal, before the onset of the sinking feeling and all the extraordinary events that followed, when Benjamin had just sat down at the piano with the notebook set on top.

"And?" said Henry.

"I thought it was great!"

"Well, great is good." Henry picked up the notebook. "Great is real good. But what'd you *think*?"

"I just really liked it!"

"*All* of it?" said Henry.

"Sure!"

"So no parts were better than others?"

Here Henry was flipping through the notebook, as if to locate passages that might be particularly questionable or need special attention.

Benjamin took a moment, either to consider his answer or simply to figure out how best to state an answer he had already formulated but was perhaps hoping he would not be pressed to give.

"Well," he said finally, "I suppose if I'm going to really push myself to think about it in *that* way, rather than just enjoying it, as I think probably anybody reading it normally would—"

"Yeah?"

"I suppose in that case . . ."

By now the other musicians were sitting down.

". . . I'd say that I think it's strongest when you're telling funny stories and being lighthearted, and like that. The stuff about education and the advice to young people part is probably a little less . . . I mean, obviously it's *supposed* to be. Those are important issues and obviously it wouldn't make sense to be as jokey in that part."

"Right," said Henry.

"Sure, of course," Benjamin went on, not really looking at Henry at this point. "I guess it's more that when you move into this long part about education, which is really interesting by itself and says important things people definitely need to hear . . . But as part of the overall *flow* and everything, that part does drift away a little from what's so . . . Henry-like about this." And now he looked up—Benjamin—and brightened, pleased to have discovered the right phrase. "Yeah, I think that's what I'm getting at," he said. "It's all *really* interesting, I just found that part a little less . . . *Henry-like.*"

"o.k.," said Henry.

"Does that make sense?" said Benjamin.

"So you'd get rid of that part," said Henry.

"What? No! Don't do that! I'm just talking about the . . . how it fits . . ."

By now the other musicians were waiting.

"That's the part you're supposed to learn from," said Henry, and you could hear the irritation.

"Yeah, I mean . . . Yeah, you're absolutely right."

"Without that part—"

"Yeah, no," said Benjamin. "Forget everything I just said. I completely overstated it."

"You have other suggestions?"

"No, I just really enjoyed the whole thing. It's great and not like anything I've read before! It feels *real*, you know?"

"It is real," said Henry.

Though of course quite a lot of it wasn't.

"O.K.," said Henry finally. "Thanks for reading it"—and he took the notebook back to his saxophone case, and rehearsal finally got under way.

Now, probably Henry was already, at that point, thoroughly disappointed and angry. Most likely he felt the same unchanging sourness the whole way through rehearsal, even if personally I chose to imagine him fighting those feelings, for a while at least. He might have struggled (for example) to reconcile the actual conversation they'd had with the more successful conversation he'd anticipated. He might have tried to convince himself that it had all gone better than he thought, and, failing that, might have attempted to stay afloat, at least, of the ugliness pulling him under. Whatever the case, and however his thoughts actually unfolded, by the time he left the library that day, Henry had clearly decided things had not gone well at all. And I know I am not wrong in saying that this realization struck his ego a terrible blow, and struck a terrible blow to the imaginary future he had consciously or otherwise been constructing over the previous week, if not over the previous years. I know I am not wrong in saying this, because I remember very well what happened next.

8.

It was around two in the afternoon when Henry arrived at a bar. Not his bar, not Alma's, just *a* bar, one a few blocks from the library in the direction away from his house. It was dark inside despite the day; there was a pinball machine, and booths and tables. Rotating fans hung at various spots around the ceiling, and the man standing behind the bar, and another on a stool across from him, watched basketball on a bar-top television. Henry ordered a beer. "Beer." He took his beer to the back and sat flipping through his notebook, or rather he *flicked* through, as if disgusted by its pages. Not just by the words but by the pages themselves. As if he wanted nothing more than to tear them out, those pages, the way a hero of Greek tragedy (allow me this seemingly heavy-handed comparison, since surely no life in ancient Greece was inherently more tragic than a modern life like Henry's), the way an aggrieved hero of Greek tragedy might tear at his own eyeballs. To have them gone, to be done with them forever . . . except that destroying those pages would not have mattered. Nothing for Henry would have changed or changed back; plus there was another copy back at home anyway. Soon he switched to whiskey, after which he stopped looking at his note-book at all.

And it was then that Samuel Johnson, who up to that moment had been rooting for Henry, in his way, and feeling sorry for Henry, suddenly woke up and remembered himself, Samuel Johnson. Remembered he had a goal that was entirely separate from Henry's. I was me again. I shook off years of stupefaction—shook off, too, any thoughts or concerns about Henry—as my mind sprang back to an earlier time, to the feeling I had left four and a half years ago, in another bar, in another part of the city, inhabiting a very different human being, when I had last found myself facing, or on the verge of once again facing, some extremely narrow—but not nonexistent!—chances of returning to my son.

No time to prepare, now that Henry had switched to whiskey, but I did not need time—surely I had waited too long already! I knew the best course to follow, had known it since before I'd even landed with Henry, and I knew, too, that it wouldn't work. How could it work? There were too many steps, and no Phil Williams, and what were the chances I would reach Blossom after all these years?

After all these years, a new attempt! Exhilaration wrestled with despair in the face of so much unlikelihood. As if I had already failed, my chances had failed me, and what I was about to embark upon was nothing more than the tragic performance of that failure, which would leave me even more miserable than before. Yet when the time came—around four in the afternoon—when Henry's head drooped drunkenly toward the tabletop, another feeling took hold of me, a no-nonsense feeling, a resolve. My resolve forced aside my despair, where it could wallow—my despair—and sardonically comment all it wanted upon the series of impossible steps that my resolve was unquestionably going to proceed with, no matter what my other feelings thought.

Cash on the table, fast from the bar, a convenience store, a pay phone, and that number I remembered perfectly well, Orson having dialed it so often.

"Whadda you want?" barked the voice, and this was my first surprise, for it was better than I could have hoped and precisely as I had always imagined. The voice fulfilled not just one but *both* criteria of my best-case scenario: that it was hers, and that it sounded practically drunk already. And what a pleasure to finally use (a slight variation of) the statement I'd so long ago prepared!

"This is Samuel for Phil who should meet me in front of the Homewood Library on Hamilton between Fifth and Braddock as soon as possible!"

"Wrong number"—and she hung up. Just as I had imagined!

Now, you might think such early good fortune would have made my outlook more optimistic, but if anything, as I got off the phone, I found myself falling deeper into disillusionment. Having reached the far side of those initial improbabilities, a vast field of impossibilities now came into view. How long would I keep hold of Henry's body, after all? What were the chances that Phil would find me in that time? That after four and a half years he would be ready, with a vehicle and everything we'd need? And even if he was—and it seemed absurd to add more ifs to such a list—even if my luck held and I managed to solve problems I had not yet even imagined, it would have taken so long, by then, to get us on the road, how far could we possibly travel?

In the shadow of the steps of the Homewood Library, nursing a bottle I'd brought from the bar, I stewed, my thoughts scattering.

Time passed, probably not as much as seemed to.

And as my mind grew thinner—I mean as my hopes grew more remote—I began to think again of Henry's life, of what would happen to Henry once my failure had played out. That he could simply return to his life seemed impossible. He could return to his *situation,* of course, but his life, his secret life, was already gone. *Probably for the best*, I told myself. Perhaps all that had happened would give Henry the push he needed, would force him back into the world, and there were still things out there for him—we'd seen it with his teaching—things better than the rut he'd been stuck in. Yes, it was definitely for the best. I almost hoped it all worked out for him. Or rather, I *did*; I began right then to hope that things would work out for Henry, and to picture the life he would move on to . . . when suddenly and unbelievably a decrepit white van pulled up, driven by a familiar stocky, expressionless woman who called out:

"Samuel Johnson!"

"I'm here!" I cried, and ran over.

"It's you?" Phil laughed, seeing Henry.

"It's me!" I laughed, and I jumped into the van.

Penn Avenue to Parkway East to the turnpike, a quick and unencumbered escape, all green lights and effortless passing (even at the turnpike you just grab a ticket)—in short, a more perfect exodus than anyone could have planned, Phil and I ecstatically jabbering all the while over wind through the open windows:

"It's rilly you?"

"Who else!"

"Yuh look different!"

"Obviously!"

"Yer a black dude!"

"And you have a van!"

"Rill piece of shit, though!"

"I've never ridden in one!"

"Blossom got her in a bet if yuh believe it!"

"I believe everything today!"

"This dude tried to . . . Ah, listen to me, already gahn on about Blossom and all her nunsense and bullcrap, when you been away more than four yers now doing who knows what and—"

And so on: a hugely enthusiastic reunion. Yet we had hardly started onto the turnpike and rolled up the windows when already I was souring the mood with my worries and doubts.

"No worries," said Phil, having brought us up to cruising speed. "I've thought everything yer saying a hunnert times aleast. We got all we need right there"—he indicated the passenger foot space, which was packed with bottles of liquor. "Most important, I got *a plan.*"

However, he would hold off telling me his plan for just a minute, Phil said, because he was very anxious to share with me all that had happened since we'd parted.

Thus I learned that following our last trip, Blossom had hitch-hiked back to Pittsburgh and returned to her life as if it were all perfectly normal. Phil, thinking I was long gone and that he was once more alone in the world, had returned to his own philandering ways—yet nothing felt the same. Nothing satisfied him. Having at last connected with another stranded soul, and having felt again the wholesomeness (his word) of human camaraderie, he was no longer able to take pleasure in the empty pastimes he had previously enjoyed. He found himself staying in at night, or taking Blossom home after she had taken them out. And when, after some months had passed, he did begin to venture out again, it was only to a bar to watch television.

Indeed, Phil told me (facing out the windshield as he spoke, the distant waft of his voice making clear that he had rehearsed this long explanation many times in his solitude, and had many times imagined performing it for me), television had taken on a new importance for him during the years since our parting. He had tried to watch as much as he could. And when I told him that during that same period I had watched none at all, he seemed very disappointed—for apparently Phil had often thought of me while watching television. He had pictured me off somewhere seated before a television myself.

He would imagine us watching the same program, and this had been a great comfort to him. In fact, he said, he had come to believe, during this time, that the very best thing about television, the best and most important thing, was not the programs it showed but the fact that they aired everywhere simultaneously, for everyone all the same; so that, if a person watching in Pittsburgh had a friend way off in Unityville who happened to like the same sorts of programs, the Pittsburgh person could tune in knowing there was a sizeable chance he was not watching alone, that he and his friend were enjoying it together, even if not right there beside. So there was really nothing closer or more personal you could do with another person than watch television together, even two hundred miles apart. You were seeing the exact same things, thinking pretty much the exact same thoughts, or not really thinking any thoughts at all but having the same pictures and words run through your head—you were practically the same person during that time! And this realization had been a comfort, and had made watching television the only thing he ever really wanted to do any longer.

"Then abaht a yer ago, or maybe less than a yer, but a while ago anyways, I thought something else. It was that maybe I'd see yuh again after all. Never went so far as me imagining all the things might of happened to yuh, which you'll tell me abaht in just a minute . . . But what I *did* think was, the more I missed yuh, Samuel, the more it seemed you'd somehow or other end up calling one day. Blossom'd pick up the phone and there you'd be. It was all wishful imagining, of course, and most of me was sure nothing like that'd ever happen and I was just embarrassing myself thinking it . . . but then I *did* go so far as to start making *plans*, on the off chance someday you'd call—just the way *you did*—and I'd need to be perparced— just the way *I was*—which, even while I was building this booze stash and keeping the van gassed and with extra fuel cans I got back there by the spare, even then, seemed a fool's hope at best. But what the hell, I figured, since the only other thing I had to do was watch television. Anyways, probably yer anxious to hear the plan . . ."

At which point Phil finally began telling me his plan, which I will hold off recounting, since we eventually went through with it, so you will see what it was in a page or two anyway. But as I listened to his plan, I found myself growing uncomfortable, morally if not in other ways as well. Certain aspects of Phil's plan struck me as rather disrespectful toward Henry, and for that matter toward Blossom, and I was surprised Phil could be so cavalier. I even felt a little disappointed in Phil, who for all his loose talk I still wished to believe was a decent, well-meaning soul. Yet when I interrupted him to express my concerns, Phil only laughed, and rather than set my mind at ease, he pointed out that my own plan—returning to my son—would inevitably involve acts far worse for Henry than anything *he* had proposed, a fact I was of course aware of but had somehow managed to push to the very back of my mind, and so far had safely avoided. Nor did Phil's reminder cause me suddenly to confront this fact; I simply grew irritated, as if he had missed my point or changed the subject. "Fine, fine," I said, "tell me the rest of your plan."

By now the sun was going down, though it was not yet dark outside. I put it around six thirty. The trees along the roadside flew past in a blur, while the trees far ahead on the horizon seemed to approach much more slowly. Then the approaching trees became the ones that flew past, as new slow ones appeared up ahead, and on and on that way while Phil was talking. I was listening but thinking also about my situation more generally. We had traveled only about an hour down the turnpike, but more than two hours had passed since I had first taken control of Henry's body, and considering that I had no way of gauging how long that control might last, it struck me as odd that I felt so unconcerned about it. If anything, I felt rather confident, unreasonably confident. Why? It was not the reassurance of having a plan (not *Phil's* plan, at any rate), nor that I had grown better at controlling a body (though surely one does, and probably I had). No, as I listened to Phil and watched the trees pass and the sky and so forth, I decided my inexplicable confidence had little to do with either Phil or me. It seemed, oddly enough, to have something to do with Henry.

And this was when I finally noticed something missing from Henry. Something that in Orson I had constantly fought to suppress, in Henry, it seemed, was simply not there. If I had failed to notice the presence of this thing in Orson, that was because the last time I had ridden this turnpike, the entire experience was new to me, and I had no point of comparison. No, it was only in being here with Henry that I understood, in retrospect, what a struggle inhabiting Orson had been, and felt the absence of this thing, this feeling. Put simply, I felt that whatever part of Henry was still Henry, and wherever that part was currently residing, it did not seem in any hurry to get his body back. I could have it, his body, for all he cared. And while under other circumstances this realization might have saddened me for Henry's sake, under these circumstances I could not have been more relieved, nor considered it anything other than a fortunate turn, which I supposed I was due, all things considered.

After Phil had finished going over his plan, I told him these thoughts I'd just had about Henry, about this difference I'd noticed between Henry and Orson. Phil seemed very moved. He said that on occasion he had noticed such differences himself over the years, in the different lives he'd known, but that he had never been able to put such a thing into words. He said he appreciated my sharing that with him, and that these were the sorts of moments that friendships were for.

Now, all this must have taken longer than it seems in my memory, for by this time the sky had grown dark, or dark enough for headlights. The van's cockpit, though cavernous compared to the front of Blossom's old sedan, still felt quite cozy in the dashboard light, as if we were gathered around a campfire telling each other our tales. *Phil's* tales, I should say, for by now he seemed to have forgotten his earlier wish to hear about *my* past several years, and instead spoke more about his own life: his actual life and how he had lived it, how it had ended, and the various lives he had landed in since. All of which I found quite fascinating (it had never actually occurred to me what entertaining tales might be made of our unabated suffering), and I would happily here digress into a few of Phil's sordid adventures, were I not busy trying to get us through my own.

It was well after the sun had gone down, but only a short time after I had at last begun sharing with Phil a few of my own adventures, when a pained expression suddenly came over Blossom's face. I put it around eight, but the truth is I have no idea. I knew what the expression meant, though. And sure enough, Phil pulled us into an empty rest stop (not the shopping-mall sort where you get gasoline but the unattended ones with just a few picnic tables and portable toilets) and called out, as if to a legion of participants, "Time to do the plan!" Upon which he popped the hood and went to fiddle with the wires while I refilled the gas tank from the containers by the spare. Then we both climbed into the back of the van—it was spacious in back, a cargo van—each with a full bottle of liquor. We removed our clothing (this was the part that had made me uncomfortable), then lay down under some blankets Phil had stored there. We drank very rapidly and deeply all at once, and put our heads down to pass out.

There was a bit of an awkward moment before we fell asleep, when Phil suggested that I might at that point engage Blossom physically, and I quickly snapped: "I do not remember that being part of the plan!"

"All I mean's cuddle," said Phil. "Cuddle or it won't be convincing."

So we cuddled and passed out together, thus successfully completing the first part of Phil's plan.

In the darkness of Henry's brain space, I waited.

I thought of Phil waiting so close beside me, unreachable in the darkness of Blossom's brain space. Mere inches separated us, yet for all we were able to do for one another, we might as well have been a million miles apart.

Melancholy gave way to worry. I began to think that the next phase of Phil's plan would not play out as he had imagined it, and that we had made a grave mistake.

Too late for regrets! Too soon to despair!

Until at last, around three in the morning, or at any rate still predawn, the next phase of Phil's plan was propelled into motion by a sudden, disorienting, van-rattling shout in the darkness:

"What the fuck!"

"Henry Nelson!" yelled Henry, thrust back into his waking life.

"Get off! Get off!"

Followed by a full minute of banging and swearing, and something that sounded like tearing, and something that sounded like slapping, until finally the two of them managed to climb through the front of the van and spill out next to each other, naked in the light of the empty rest stop parking lot. Henry stood baffled, disoriented, but Blossom, now that she could see the situation, became calm, if not cool, if not frankly irritated, as if this sort of thing happened to her all the time.

"Jesus, calm down!" she ordered. It must have triggered Henry's highly active passivity response, because he immediately did.

The rest area was no darker or less dark than when we had first pulled into it, but it felt very different at this hour. It felt early rather than late, waking rather than sleep-bound. Mostly it was louder, because of bugs. There were two streetlamps, one on either end of the long but narrow lot. The lamp we were parked under cast light over a trash can and a pay phone, and the other over some portable toilets, and everything else, whatever was out there, was dark.

Blossom and Henry got back in the van, turned on the interior light, and dressed. They had something like a conversation. They had no idea where they were, but Phil had staged the scene well enough that at least they did not particularly question how they had gotten there. In fact, now that he had taken it all in, I thought Henry seemed rather proud of himself, that he had managed to have such a memorable experience, all the more memorable for not remembering any of it. His expression in the rearview mirror—for some reason he kept looking at himself in the rearview mirror—was one I had never seen. Mischievous, a bit devilish. I thought of all his past exploits, the ones he had described in the notes to his saga or to Benjamin, and for the first time, it occurred to me that he might not have made them all up, that he might actually have done some of those things in his life before Alma.

As for Blossom, she was in a sour mood, particularly when the van failed to start.

"Fucking A."

"Seems you and me had a time," said Henry, in the passenger seat now and sifting through empty bottles with his foot.

"Yeah yeah," said Blossom. "You got coins?"

"I got *what?*"

"To call a tow, dumbshit."

"Nope." He settled back in his seat as Blossom searched the various small compartments of the driver's side for change. "Nope, I got no coins . . . Not in any hurry, either . . . Just taking my time, enjoying the view"—by which he must have meant his view of the back of Blossom's head, as she was at that moment leaning over his lap to check the compartments on the passenger's side.

"Huh?" Blossom sat up.

"I was saying—"

"Fuck you."

Then she tried the key again, and when the van still wouldn't start, she stepped outside and kicked the door.

"Guess we'll have to wait till somebody comes," said Henry.

"Fucking A," continued Blossom, and she began to walk around the van, every few seconds kicking a tire or door.

"Could be a while, I suppose," called Henry.

Blossom kicked the driver's side.

"Much more comfortable here in the van."

She rattled the back door.

"Phew! Can't imagine all the booze we must have drunk."

She kicked the passenger side.

"A lot left, too, looks like."

"Yeah?" came Blossom's voice.

"Whole lot," said Henry.

"Well, huh," said Blossom. Then: "Fuck, whatever"—and she came back around to the driver's side and climbed in.

Upon which more booze was consumed, more conversation attempted, back to the booze, and before we knew it, Phil was reconnecting the wire under the hood while I sat dumbfounded by the success of his plan. Thirty seconds after that, we were back on the road.

Since we had no way of knowing what lay ahead or who would last longest this time around, it seemed prudent, despite how bad I was at it, that I be the one to drive. There passed a tremendously rocky first few minutes, which Phil found very entertaining and which you can imagine well enough—but when at last we settled into the next leg of our journey, Phil began:

"So you were telling yer story. Yer death story? The story of how yuh died."

In fact I had *not* been telling that story before Phil's plan had interrupted me. Rather, I assumed this was Phil's awkward way of asking me to tell it. But it was too personal, that story. Too depressing. So instead I started talking about my childhood. Then about Abram and Emily. Then about my son and what an impressive young person he had been from the start, how I had struggled to be a good father to him, and how more often than not I had failed. In other words, I told Phil many of the things I have already told you, some of which I had already told *him* on our previous trip down this same road. And it was only after I had spoken my way through a great deal of this history that I realized I had in fact been easing myself into the deeper waters of memory, and that I'd arrived, as if unknowingly, at the story Phil wanted to hear.

"It was after Samuel had gone to bed," I said, my voice grown waxy and distant, as it seems to whenever I speak of the past, "and I was watching *The Andy Griffith Show*. If you know that program, you know it stars a friendly sheriff, Andy, in the funny small town of Mayberry. A sweet program, but this particular episode was strange. An article about Andy had been published in a national magazine, 'The Sheriff without a Gun'—because Andy never carried a gun— and a television producer who'd read the article had brought his film crew to Mayberry to make a documentary about Andy's life. Throughout the episode they talked a lot about guns, a topic more serious and ominous than I expected from Mayberry, and which gave the episode a surprisingly threatening tone. On top of which, it turned out the television producer was not even a real producer, but a con man planning to rob the local bank by pretending to film a robbery scene. And since I had always thought of Mayberry as a sort of television version of Unityville, innocently tucked away from everywhere, this ominous tone of guns and crime unsettled me and made me question for the first time whether Unityville itself was safe, and whether anyone in town kept a gun, questions that in hindsight were eerie premonitions of what followed . . .

"Well, but it was more than that," I went on, staring out at the illuminated portion of road, which disappeared beneath us as the car sped forward and new road rolled into the headlights, but which looked so similar from moment to moment that it might have been the same road over and over, spinning beneath us on a giant wheel. "Over the years, thinking back to the events of that night, including the events of that television program, I've come to question whether the guns and violence were only the *obvious* threat, the *apparent* source of my ominous feeling, but not the only source, or even the most profound. Because there was something larger going on in that episode of *Andy Griffith*, something I was unable to fully articulate for myself at the time. The idea of making television *on television*, of making fake television on real television—or, technically, faking making fake television on real television—and in Mayberry, the last place you'd imagine television being made . . . for some reason this idea caused a great disruption in my sense of normalcy. I started to have thoughts, strange disorienting thoughts, though they were soon interrupted by the tragedy that followed, and by all the chaos that followed that, and I didn't think back to them, the thoughts, for a long time after . . .

"But later, much later, I *did* think back to them—not once but many thousands of times. Indeed, over the years I've thought about that night in extraordinary detail, about the tragedy, but also about my feelings during that television program. And among the many things I've noticed . . . I was going to say 'about that episode of *Andy Griffith*,' but of course it's not the episode I've noticed anything new about, only the feeling it gave me, the disturbance it stirred inside me. And yes, it's possible that in reality I did not feel *all* the feelings or think *all* the thoughts I've remembered, or any of them for that matter, but only invented memories in light of what came after, planting in my past not just my *understanding* of my feelings, but even the feelings themselves. For when you look at the sheer amount of detail I've 'remembered' from that evening, the breadth of what I've 'discovered' in my memories, it does start to seem improbable that, for example, in the midst of watching *Andy Griffith* and wondering about guns and so forth, my mind would also stop to consider the more theoretical issue that any program produced by characters on my television program (such as the con man claimed to be producing on that episode) was presumably also *viewed* by characters on that program (that is, by Andy and his friends), yet this is exactly the sort of thing I 'remember' thinking. It would be *their* program to watch, but also still mine, since my reality contained their reality, and my television their television. This thought leading, then, to an obvious follow-up, that if a program could be produced and watched in Mayberry that reflected Mayberry's reality as fictionally yet faithfully as Mayberry reflected mine, it further followed that there could be, or in theory undoubtedly *would* be, television producers inside *that* television program producing their own shows, perhaps set in other small secluded towns. Such a program's reality being contained within Mayberry's, of course, which was still, for the same reasons as before, contained in mine. And wouldn't the people on *that* program—that is, on the program inside the program inside the episode I was watching— wouldn't those people, too, be perfectly capable of watching a program inside the program inside the program inside my own? And so on, a potentially endless sequence, programs inside programs all the way down, an improbable image that for some reason has taken hold of me more often than any other, over the countless hours I've spent reliving the events of that evening, and looms largest in my memory, regardless of whether I thought it then or only invented it after the fact. Larger and more recurring than the actual scene of my actual death is this image of me sitting before that episode of *Andy Griffith*, my mind spiraling out from my sofa-bound body, chasing a chain of strange logic forward or inward through an endless tunnel of television programs, one after another, each taking me farther from reality, but actually taking me nowhere at all. There

I am falling forward through generations of programs, or variations of programs, through version after slightly different version of essentially the same thing. Until finally—as I picture it—I stop and look around. I look back through this enormous line of television screens, this endless corridor of programs, only to see, at the far end, a tiny face staring into the first screen way back at the beginning, which is now the last screen from where I've arrived. And that face is mine, of course. I left it only moments ago, despite how many screens and programs have passed between us in that time. It's my face, it looks just like me, I'm there and I'm here and I'm no different at all, except for one difference, there's one decisive difference, that back there playing beside me on the sofa is—"

"This is the story of how yuh died?" interrupted Phil, at the height of my reverie.

He was right, of course. I had fallen into this memory too intensely, and the point of the story was getting lost in the process.

So I told the rest more directly: about hearing shouts outside—"Samuel Johnson!"—and running out to the crazed long-haired man with the gun in one hand and my son in the other. About the struggle, the shot, the instant darkness. About looking down upon my own dead body before my soul flew toward the town, not knowing, at that point, that I had transferred into my killer's body. About the pickup truck and seeing the lights on in the houses, and the voice in my head shouting, "Samuel Johnson! Samuel Johnson!" About the highway and the Susquehanna and veering into my second death, and how looking down upon the dark Pennsylvanian landscape, I had thought I was finally done. I had said goodbye and told myself that Samuel would be safe. And how, no sooner had I made my peace than I turned and saw I was not bound for heaven at all, but had simply been transported to an airplane passing overhead. How, once I had realized I was *not* departing this world, my belief in Samuel's safety had vanished, and I have never been able to regain it. How I have long felt that if I could just die, I mean die in a real and lasting way, if I could just move on somehow from this unending slog of ineffectual attendance, I was sure everything would be fine for my boy. Which meant that on some level my constant worrying about him was more for my own sake than his—which at any rate was entirely obvious—that my worrying did not help him and that nothing I could do would ever save him from anything at all. That it was essentially a self-serving desire, my desire to return to him. That I was essentially a self-serving person. That surely a self-serving person was not a good father—was, in fact, the precise opposite of a good father. That—

"Slow down," said Phil, and I took a breath. "Nah," he said, "I mean the car."

Frazzled, I did as he said, and only when we'd gotten down under twenty miles per hour did I bother to wonder why we were slowing. Before I could ask, though, Phil cried out, "Once more unta the breach!" in a very dramatic voice. He laid his hand upon my arm.

"What?"

"Once more unta the breach!" He had the look on his face, the pained warning look. "From a movie. Aleast I think it's a movie. Something I always imagined saying. And I'm afraid, friend Samuel, it's finely time for me to say it."

"Phil . . ."

"Yer a good dude, Samuel. Far as I can tell, yer even an o.k. dad. Worrying must count for something. Anyways, au revahr!"

"Phil . . ."

And then my friend Phil Williams, the only real friend I have ever known, smiled the largest smile I have ever seen, and hollered, as fearlessly as I have ever heard, while casting himself and Blossom out of our slow-moving vehicle into the predawn darkness: "Once more unta the breach!"—and rolled away.

The line is from Shakespeare, in fact. *Henry V.* I just looked it up on the internet. The "breach" is literally a breach, a break in a wall, and some soldiers are being called upon to attack this breach, which is equivalent to throwing themselves in harm's way. In other words, there is futility in attacking the breach, an unspoken understanding that the act, though heroic, is essentially pointless. But Phil's act was not pointless. It was an act of friendship. He was trying to help me return to my son.

Once more unto the breach, Phil Williams!

And then Phil was gone, and I was alone with the road.

It was either right before or right after I ran the tollbooth at the turnpike exit for Route 11 that the sun made its official entrance on the horizon. Well, it must have been before, while I was still traveling east, before I turned north, because I hold in my memory an image of orange smears swelling up into the predawn lavender. My head was swirling, had been swirling for some unknowable span of time, the present and past colliding in a confusion of thoughts and images and emotions. North up Route 11 . . . the river to my right . . . fields and forests and small towns . . . Phil gone . . . Unityville ahead . . . Samuel was sixteen!

Twelve years I had been away. Twelve years since the night my name was shouted and I ran outside to save my son. For I had saved him, hadn't I? I did not usually think of it that way, but that was obviously one way it could be thought of. I had seen the gun and had acted. I had saved him. Yet my actions had not been rewarded; we had both been made to suffer for what that lunatic had done, his reasons even now utterly unknown to . . . But at this point my mind landed upon a very unsettling thought.

There in that van speeding toward Unityville, where I would presumably need to cause something bad to happen to Henry (with Phil gone I found I could no longer ignore this fact, could no longer tell myself I was just going along with Phil, which, I now realized, was precisely the lie I'd been telling myself), it occurred to me that I was at that moment in the same position the drunken, crazed long-haired man had been, all those years ago: steering toward my son with the intention of doing something terrible. Nor had I even begun to grasp the ugly coincidence of this thought when another, far worse thought, among the top three most horrific my mind has ever managed to conceive, suddenly struck me with the force of revelation.

It was the voice. The voice of the killer not when he had been yelling outside my house but later, when I was inside the killer's body and we were speeding away and the voice *inside* was still calling, "Samuel Johnson!" I had forgotten that voice, or lost it in the commotion, but now suddenly I remembered it, and knew it, or felt I knew it, was convinced I had known it all along. It was Emily. It was my wife's voice.

And then it all poured out at once, out of whatever vessel of repression or unknowing I'd stored it in all those years and into my hyper-awake, hyper-aware, suddenly mortified consciousness. The events of that night replayed for me as they had many times before, but entirely transformed, this time, by a new understanding.

She would have driven this same road, taken the very same journey I was taking . . . She was not trying to hurt Samuel, only to return to us . . . Four years she would have worked to return to us and at last there she was, calling to me, to bring me close . . . to get me close enough so that she could . . . and I had stopped her! Forced the gun from her hand and shot myself in the process. *Saved* Samuel? Why, I'd ruined everything!

But wouldn't I have recognized Emily? I went on. Even in that body, was it possible I had not known my own wife? And why would she have been holding Samuel but calling out to me? Unless she was calling to our son? Perhaps she had only just managed to grab him as I appeared at the door? What was her plan? Was her plan like *my* plan? Would she really have killed a man to see that happen?

Or was that why the lunatic had simply stood there, why he had not fired but simply stood as I rushed toward him and grabbed for the gun? Because it was Emily—could it really have been Emily?—not a lunatic but Emily, and when the time came she could not go through with it?

Am I *going to go through with it?* I finally asked myself directly. To kill Henry? *Henry Nelson?* Earlier, when I had told myself he no longer cared to be in his body, was that true? Or was I already trying to justify an act I had barely allowed myself to contemplate, for fear I might fail to see it through? Had Emily failed to see it through? Was *she* the one who had failed? Or would *seeing it through* have been the failure, a purely selfish act? An unworthy act? Unworthy of Samuel? Was *that* the point to all of this? *Was* there a point to all of this? What was the point to all of this? To choose correctly?

And why now? Why was I asking these questions now? Couldn't I ask them some other time, when I was not so close to achieving my goal? Couldn't I set aside any thoughts about Henry and Emily and parenting and morality for another hour or so, before I over-analyzed myself into a horrible mistake? Before my thoughts or my conscience or my weakness or my sense of futility and despair ruined everything I had waited so long to realize? Was this not precisely what must have happened to Emily that day? That having gone through it all, whatever terrible experiences she must have gone through, her own Christopher Plumes and Henry Nelsons if not—dear God!—her own Orson Fitz, having survived them all and finally returned to us, she had allowed doubt into her mind?

She would have driven this very road, passed this very spot, the river to her right, this town coming up on her left. Twelve years ago she was where I am now and did what I am doing and thought and felt these same things, and she made a choice. Was it doubt that stopped her? It was not me who made a choice that day, but she.

She chose humanity. She chose responsibility.

What did I do? I messed it up.

And now I am beside myself, aside of myself, as if I can see my own soul from inside this same body. A new failure rises up before me, a terrible storm cloud racing toward me across a clear morning. I cannot kill Henry Nelson! Why had I ever thought I could? For my son? For love? What sort of monster calls his selfishness *love*? What sort of father suffers such *love* upon his son? Suddenly, it is all very clear, yet how long I've gone on in this illusion! Through Christopher, Orson—would I have even killed Orson? Only now in the final moment recognizing the reality of the situation I have been in all along. For I was never anything other than a weak-willed man. A pointless being who, though blessed with a wife and son much finer than himself, has never managed to make himself any—

9.

The late seventies through the early eighties was a strange time for television. There were the same three networks (NBC, ABC, and CBS; the Fox network still a few years off), but they had changed in at least one significant way while I was with Henry; they had given up on social relevance. True, M*A*S*H was still around, and a few other early seventies' holdovers, some hard-line journalistic programs, but the new prime-time programs were all fantastical melodramas (*The Love Boat, Fantasy Island*), nighttime soap operas (*Knots Landing, Dallas*), and lighthearted crash-'em-ups (*Magnum, P.I.; Charlie's Angels*), things like that. I am sure there was an interesting sociological explanation for this move toward escapist, simple-minded programming, perhaps having to do with the political or cultural climate at the time. But since I had very little exposure then to news or current events, I had no idea what that explanation might be.

Now, you might imagine that this mindless fare would come as a disappointment to me after the relative sophistication I had come to expect from television in the early seventies. The sophistication

I had come to expect of *myself*, I should say, since my finer tastes in television back then had meant, to me, that my own mind had matured and grown more interesting. We had grown smarter together, television and I, or so it seemed to me, and this was an optimistic feeling. So you would think these new programs would disappoint me, and at first they certainly did. I was disappointed, or at the very least surprised. Yet left with no choice in the matter, my expectations rather quickly lowered, and I learned to love these dumber programs just as much.

Love, yes, love. This is what I wish to make clear. For in scrolling back through all I have written so far, which I took some time to do after ending the previous chapter, I saw that I have described several times my negative feelings over the years about television's hold on me, but have been less clear that this anger was never really toward television, but only toward myself. And post-living, my relationship with television has clearly been something else. With no choice but to attend upon lives that have nothing to do with me, tediously sprawling lives infinitely uninteresting to watch, television has been a blessing and respite. And guiltless—since stripped of the ability to act, one loses one's guilt at not doing so. Television becomes a faultless pleasure, if not a welcome friend. And this is the sense in which I can say without compunction that 1978 to 1985 (actually to 1989, but I don't want to get ahead of myself) was one of the better periods of my post-life existence—because I watched more television than at any other time—though the rest of that era is almost entirely a blur.

Following the inadvertent catastrophic death of Henry (though I should back up to explain that I did not kill Henry Nelson, or certainly I tried not to, or *chose* not to but then messed it up. I was driving, my thoughts scattering, panic escalating. I was overwhelmed with emotion, overrun by thoughts and doubts, and I lost control of myself—so, also, of Henry. Who unfortunately was not very quick to regain himself, and unlike Orson, did not handle the transition back into consciousness well at all. Waking to a straight road with no obstacles or traffic, he slammed down on the gas pedal, presumably mistaking it for the brake, veered sharply to the right for no apparent reason—like flinching—and flipped the van into the river. I had made the "right" decision, but had failed to see it through, and was suddenly and forever burdened with this failure, and with regret for putting Henry in such a dangerous position in the first place. In my defense—since whenever these events return to haunt me, and I again hold this discussion with myself, I at some point always come to my own defense—I did not exactly ask to be put in *my* position either, and surely intentions matter as much, from a moral perspective, as whether one succeeds or fails. Which does not, however, change anything for Henry, of course, and the truth is I will always suffer the knowledge that, though I did not intentionally kill Henry, my intentions did kill him—my *failed* intentions—which, whatever else you might say about them, are still mine and not his, even if he was made to suffer them, on that emotional morning all those years ago); following, that is, the tragic end to my time with Henry, I found myself standing at an upstairs window, staring down across Route 11 at the underside of Blossom's van, now stuck half-sunk in the river. I was bewildered, overwhelmed. Around me were cats, what seemed liked hundreds of cats—actually there were five—yet before I could think about cats or could process in any other way the particulars of my surroundings, I was thrust into rude sobriety. It was not drunkenness I was suddenly sobered of, but idiocy, the idiocy that moments earlier had sent me into paranoid hysterics and caused me to lose control, and that I now—too late!—recognized as complete nonsense.

Emily's cries? How would that even make sense? How could Emily and I have been in the same body? If more than one soul could be in a body, wouldn't other dead people be here with me now? Where are those

*voices? If that day I heard Emily, why not others right now? Wouldn't
every body in the world be filled up with souls from the beginning of time,
legions of voices stuck listening to each other forever, and . . .* and I went
on this way, unraveling the logic I had spun for myself moments
earlier on the highway, convincing myself now that it had not been
Emily's voice I'd heard, nor even a woman's voice at all, that it was
perhaps my own voice, though that theory had its own holes and
landed me, as every theory seems to land me, in yet another cloud
of doubt. And trying to lift that cloud with additional speculations
left me, as usual, awash in self-loathing. How I wished to be rid of
myself once and for all! Yet having just died my fifth death, I could
not help but notice I was as intolerably present as ever.

Since that particular spot along the Susquehanna was not deep
enough for the van to sink from sight, we stood watching a long time
as police and ambulances arrived. We did not stay long enough to
see Henry pulled from the river, but long enough for the light outside to become fully a daytime light, until the cats became irascible
for breakfast. We turned then, and I saw that I had landed in a
very old house, in a room stuffy with old and weathered things: a
rag rug and a shadeless lamp, another lamp with a beaded shade,
an antique dresser, a glass cabinet of figurines and trinkets, and a
rocking chair draped with what looked like it could very well be
an original Colonial-era quilt. The air around me held visible dust.
There was dust on the lamps and furniture. There were cracks in
the walls, but just the hairline sort that occur naturally in old plas-
ter, and other than the dust, I did not find the room particularly
dingy or unclean or ill kept. Beside me, beneath the window, stood
an enormous old television console, while across the room, beside
the door, a tall dressing mirror revealed to me at last the new form I
had found: tiny, wiry Lillian Rudge.

She was ancient even then, her spine already bowing. She would
grow older, and older still, and all the while her body would continue

to fold inward, year after year, as if packing itself up like luggage for a trip it kept refusing to take—but of course I did not know that at the time. No, in the early days of our time together, she seemed a perfectly doomed elderly person, and certainly in many ways she was. Always depressed, she spoke only of wanting to die. Nor did I blame her, with all her friends long dead, living alone in her empty house with her cats and her presumably very painful degenerative osteoarthritis. It was Catholicism that kept her from suicide, and for that she resented Catholicism quite a lot. To her daughter, Elizabeth, practically an old woman herself, who stopped by every lunchtime to play cards and deliver groceries, Lillian would describe at length the various ways she might have committed suicide by now, had she been gifted with a less Catholic soul. Elizabeth, for her part, seemed not to take this talk very seriously, perhaps because, like me, she expected Lillian to die at any moment anyway, hopefully peacefully and in her sleep.

She drank no alcohol; it bothered her esophagus. Each day she swallowed an assortment of pills—painkillers and others, in various shapes and colors—which made her loopy but did not cause her mind to vacate her body in any significant way. In short, I was once again stuck. Which you might think I would find very frustrating, but the truth was, after what had happened with Henry— his death but also my realizations about myself, who I was, how selfish I'd been, and what I was capable or not capable of doing— I had no stomach for more "adventures." In fact I felt rather empty right then. Much like Lillian, I no longer had the heart or saw the point. And since she continued not to die—or her body couldn't, or wouldn't—we spent 1978 to 1985 in her upstairs room watching television.

She liked Tom Selleck. As a matter of fact, so did I. He was known for his remarkable mustache, but I always thought his voice was his most charismatic feature, raspy and intelligent sounding.

His voice gave his Thomas Magnum character a kind of dignity that I found lacking in similar characters on similar shows, of which there were plenty back then. That, and the program's exotic Hawaiian setting (it brought to mind Antigua, that hour spent with Christopher hiking into the green hills, under the red sky, now so many years in the past); his voice and the setting made *Magnum, P.I.* the program I loved best and best remember from that period. And programs are all I *do* remember, the programs and almost nothing else.

There was Johnny Fever and Venus Flytrap and the bald boss and the blond secretary and the uptight younger man with the feathered brown hair. Fast-talking Arnold with his "Whatchu talkin' 'bout, Willis?" and a big bar full of people shouting "Norm!" A talking black Trans Am that fights crime and an orange Confederate sports car that for some reason had its doors welded shut. There were a lot of programs featuring characters with complementary hair colors, not just *The Dukes of Hazzard* and *Charlie's Angels* but *Three's Company, CHiPs, Cagney and Lacey,* even *Simon and Simon,* although the brown-haired brother (they were sibling private investigators) always wore a hat. *Bosom Buddies. The Facts of Life.* There was Buck Rogers, whose sidekick was a stuttering robot, and there was a truck driver whose name escapes me but whose sidekick was a chimpanzee, and there was the Incredible Hulk, doomed to walk the Earth with no sidekick at all. That one was oddly serious for a comic-book show, with some very somber music at the end. Like *Mork and Mindy,* a silly sitcom that always tried to end on a thoughtful note, with Mork (a space alien in rainbow suspenders) stepping into his egg-shaped spaceship to report back to his commander, Orson (Orson!), on how odd yet lovable humanity turns out to be. B. J.—that was the truck driver's name. And the program was *B. J. and the Bear.* There was *Airwolf,* which was about a super helicopter. And *MacGyver,* which for some reason I am getting confused with *Airwolf. Hardcastle and McCormick.*

Scarecrow and Mrs. King. 60 Minutes and *20/20*. These are all just off the top of my head.

Of course, for me they name more than programs, more than characters with story lines in exotic or familiar locations. For me these titles name the categories into which my existence during those years was divided.

The words "Magnum, P.I.," for example, describe a nonsequential period of time (a regularly scheduled series of pieces of time) and the manner in which I spent that time as meaningfully as (probably more meaningfully than) the words "my late twenties," for example—a category just as specific as regards chronology but far less so as regards the manner in which that time was actually spent. In other words, my memory, which clearly has its own criteria for judging the value of each moment spent, has determined to store away Tom Selleck and his raspy intelligent voice in much finer detail than it has stored away "my late twenties," by which time I admittedly was already dead. But my memory has its criteria, is the point, and since my memory is mine, its criteria must be mine as well.

In fact it is even more than that. (I should say that I am not having all these thoughts about television just now. I have been pondering this subject since at least the Orson chapters, but have saved up my thoughts, having decided this would be the right place to share them, since it was during my time with Lillian that my relationship with television reached its most tumultuous pitch, leading to the end, not of television, of course, but of everything television has ever meant to me.) It is more than the meaningfulness of what my memory chooses to remember—for of course "entertainment" was never television's greatest value for me, not in those days and not ever. It was perhaps the most immediate value, the most obvious, but the *real* value had changed over time: a magical window . . . a portal to reality . . . and now? Now when I looked back upon my relationship with television, upon the various eras during which I'd watched television, and asked myself what those experiences had truly meant; and granting that they must have meant *something*, that the time I'd spent with television could not have been merely a giant waste of my already utterly wasted existence, but in fact must have contributed in some way to the formation of my soul (since I seem to have a soul, and what else could have contributed to it?) such that I could actually say about my time watching television, "That was meaningful"; in *that* case, the most meaningful thing about television must be (and I am not suggesting that this would be true for an actually living person, though I don't see any reason why it would not be), it must be that watching television made me feel *nearly alive*, and a part of things. Not because it reminded me of my life, not because it transported me to one place or another, but because it was the one experience that was no different for me than for anyone else. Because seated in front of the television, I was, practically speaking, no less alive than Lillian. Or than Orson had been. Or anyone. During those moments, our experiences of existence were precisely the same.

Phil had said as much, or something like it, on our final journey together, but I had not been paying much attention at the time. He'd described how television allowed him to feel near to me during our time apart, that it provided a connection between us—but busy with my own thoughts, I'd patronized him and then turned melodramatic about an episode of *Andy Griffith*. So it was only now, with Phil gone, with our peculiar, miraculous friendship lost, probably forever, that I finally made sense of what he'd said. That for people like us, watching television was a way of being in the world, not a portal but the connection itself, and not just with each other, but with the thousands if not millions of others who were watching that program at that time, that legion of breathing humanity tuned in to whatever comedy or drama or game show or news program happened to be on, their minds simultaneously engaged with the same characters, proceeding through the same story lines at precisely the same speed. When J. R. Ewing was shot (on the nighttime soap opera *Dallas*), I was among the millions who gasped, then spent the off-season trying to guess the shooter's identity. When all of America was laughing at "Where's the beef?" I too laughed, and was as self-consciously curious as anyone as to why exactly I found it funny. When Luke and Laura on *General Hospital* finally got married, and when later they broke up before Laura was kidnapped and Luke just barely survived an avalanche, I too was riveted and flustered—nor am I being anything other than *perfectly serious* right now, despite how dumb I am sure all of this sounds, for it mattered to me, my participation in this shared human adventure of viewing. It must have mattered, or else my mind would not have chosen these moments to store away while tossing into memory's trash can almost everything else that made up my existence during this time.

Yes, it was only with Lillian that I realized television's true value, its value all along. And this was me maturing, I thought. This was wisdom, the payoff for passing years: things don't change, but your understanding of them changes. Through Phil and Lillian I had at last come to understand how television truly connects us: not a portal, but the connection itself! And I had acquired this knowledge (unless it was merely a higher form of foolishness, as part of me already suspected) just in time to enjoy it for a few years, before that knowledge and that value were lost forever, to me and to everyone else, in the greatest, quietest cultural catastrophe of our time, which we will get to in just a minute.

Years passed, and seasons—the seasons that froze and thawed the river outside the window, and the seasons that aired on the television just below. Old programs were canceled and new programs debuted. Lillian, however, stayed largely the same. She grew older, more infirm—while I, Samuel Johnson, had gradually come to see the situation with Lillian in a different light. My failure with Henry felt distant to me now, and of course Lillian *wanted* to die. Helping her would be a kindness. And given how close we were to Unityville, my chances were much better than before; in fact they were practically good. In short, I felt again the blood-pulse of purpose, the thrill of possibility, feelings that were unfortunately still pointless and frustrating, since as long as Lillian remained sober, neither of us was going anywhere.

Finally one day her bones were too brittle, and her curvature too debilitating, and her pain too great. In the spring of 1985, Elizabeth moved her into a nursing facility. Lillian had refused this move for years because she did not wish to be around other people; yet having waited so long for life to end, she now found herself burdened with a new beginning. By this time she lacked the energy to make a fuss.

Riverfront Senior Living, which was not on or even close to the riverfront, was an ugly facility, understaffed and poorly managed, and was all that Lillian's pension could afford. It consisted of a large common room just inside the entryway, a dining room to the immediate left, a television room to the immediate right, with two hallways of residential suites extending back on either side. The fixtures were cheap and poorly mounted, the carpeting threadbare, the windows heavily draped. The furniture was mismatched living room sets likely purchased at one or more estate sales, with lacquered end tables that reflected too brightly the overhead lights. The air was stale. The food lacked color. The tenants, though technically alive, were not lively, and the employees were neither attentive nor kind, with the exception of Tanya, Lillian's primary caregiver, who was not truly kind but simply young, too young to have yet gained the confidence or worldliness to be entirely indifferent.

Although, no, to be fair, when we first arrived, Tanya was kind.

Also pale—a pale girl, a little chubby, a little pimply, but pretty. She was not a nurse, and possibly was not even old enough back then to legally hold a job, but she took care of Lillian and kept straight her medications. She brought Lillian to the television room, checked in on her regularly, and occasionally staged a card game, playing both hands. They did not talk much (in fact, Lillian did not talk at all any longer), but Tanya at least attempted to comfort her, which I found very sweet. In picturing her now as she was back then— Tanya—I see a naïve, ill-fated young woman whom I liked, whom I even felt something like parental fondness for, having plenty of parental fondness to spare. She was a child from the wrong side of the tracks, or so I imagined, doing her best against terrible odds and the world's unlimited indifference.

Now, the fact that I've begun describing Tanya might lead you to believe she was the instigator of an important change in Lillian's circumstances. She was, but not until later. At the time, she was simply a new face, a pleasant smile; and other than meeting Tanya, Lillian's transplant to Riverfront Senior Living quickly revealed itself to be mostly inconsequential. Elizabeth continued to visit, if less often. Lillian continued to not die, but now in a different location. We continued to watch television.

Indeed it is for television, more than anything having to do with Lillian herself, that 1985 became for me a benchmark year. You see, as essentially unlivable as Riverfront Senior Living was in every other way, its one amenity, and as far as I could tell its only selling point, was a large communal television set that stayed on all day and well, well into the evening, and that contained not just the normal network programs Lillian and I were used to but a whole host of new ones, in a format unlike anything I'd seen. For it turned out that in departing Lillian's dusty hermit cave and rejoining the world of people, we had unwittingly entered a new age of television, an age that had actually started years before and been spreading across the nation while Lillian and I had sat clueless before her old-fashioned antenna-fed set.

The Age of Cable had arrived.

Here it was, new (if only to us), and looking like television, sounding like television, but seeming in other ways completely unlike the television I'd known. Where before you would tune in for a particular program at a particular time, now whole channels featured a *kind* of program at *any* time: a news channel, a sports channel, movie channels, and so on. Two channels for shopping. One entirely in Spanish. Two just for women. An entire channel running nothing but congressional proceedings! Much of it not even resembling entertainment, yet we watched as if it were. And people had made short movies out of pop songs? And someone had decided the weather was worth a channel unto itself? Even just the clutter of faces—of Budget Bob and Bobbi Ray, Pat Robertson and Downtown Julie Brown, and all those generic ones on CNN . . . Well, it was just too much. I was accustomed to television's seasonal migrations, its annual unveilings, occasional upheavals, and the land-swell shifting of the culture over time. But I was not prepared to handle so much newness all at once. I felt, in the face it, for the first time ever, old. Unexpectedly old. Unpleasantly old. Though forty-two in human years—more or less "midway"—I had come to assume for myself a sort of agelessness: there is no getting older than dead. But there is, it turns out; there is an oldness of the soul.

This "old" feeling only compounded, then, by the other great change cable wrought, which for me was even more emotionally complicated than these other changes, though it will not seem complicated when I say it to you, it will seem very simple, the simplest thing in the world, at least in the world of television, for the change I am referring to is nothing more or less than *reruns*. Television in the Age of Cable had expanded not just *outward* but *back*, toward not just new programs but old ones, and while certainly there had been reruns before this, the Age of Cable brought back not just *some* old programs but *all* of them, every program that had ever aired.

Stations stretched into the stillest hours of night, the wee-est hours of morning, rehashing the entire life of television to that point, from *The Honeymooners* to *Mister Ed* to *Happy Days* to *Moonlighting* (which at that time ran new episodes and reruns simultaneously on competing channels). Here was the past made present, and not only the past I'd known but also a whole host of programs I'd missed, whose entire runs had aired either during years I was away from television or in time slots opposite some other program I'd regularly watched. Nor do I mean only the obscure outliers, for it turned out I had in fact missed whole continents of televisual experience and had simply not known. *The Twilight Zone, Gilligan's Island, Star Trek* . . . I only now discovered *Star Trek!* Yet it was not a "new" discovery, is the point. It was already old. The production values were old. The sets looked old. The actors, on the other hand, were off-puttingly young. William Shatner had aged backwards, or rather—since Captain Kirk was already T. J. Hooker to me—T. J. Hooker looked shabby, suddenly, compared to his younger self. And if the arrival of the past aged the present, the present made this new past depressingly irrelevant, the Starship Enterprise long since canceled and boldly going nowhere for all eternity. And "old" and "irrelevant" was how I felt, as well. As if I'd discovered new facts about a life-long friend, facts that did not alter my opinion of my friend so much as make me conscious, unhappily conscious, of how much life that friend had been living apart from me all along, how large a portion of that friend's world back then had nothing to do with me, and, by extension, how little I had meant to anyone, or had actually known or understood about anyone for all of my life.

In short, hunkered there in the television room of Riverfront Senior Living, stuck inside Lillian who was stuck inside herself, who wanted to be done with herself as much as I did, the two of us like squatters in a bomb shelter waiting out a war, feeling old and disconnected, day after day, then year after year, I found myself sinking into a long bout of melancholy and the most unpalatable nostalgia. Or not *sinking* so much as *being sunk*, since of course it was television's past that was being remembered, and the television doing the remembering. Although in a sense it was my past and my nostalgia as well. For forty-two is an age when a person might look back upon his youth, and were I still alive, and capable of making real choices and so forth, I would probably have sunk just as deeply into my own memories, only to discover that most of them were of television anyway.

But this sickeningly sweet melancholy—well, it made me disgusted with myself. It's torture enough to be alone in the world, but worse to be a stereotype on top of it, and a "midlife crisis" was something I could not countenance. Yet I was unable to shake my melancholy, no matter how foolish it felt. As time went on, I even began to pity myself for my foolishness, then feel even more foolish about my self-pity, and back and forth, or down and down, with at every step more disgust.

Later, I would come to understand what had really happened. I would see the future that cable wrought, a future where people stopped meeting on the common ground of television, but cordoned themselves off in the comfort of whatever tiny worlds they already felt they knew: where women watched women's programs and men watched men's; where family programs "streamed" to individual family members cloistered in their separate rooms; where "choice" had exploded into infinitely esoteric sports options, segregated movie channels, and news programs catering to each person's preferred politics; where the idea that in tuning in you shared something, you participated in something—where this idea had been lost without anyone other than Phil Williams and myself having noticed how important it was in the first place . . . Yes, later I would look back on my time in Riverfront Senior Living and see there the beginning of an end. I would understand that the unpalatable self-pity I felt was not a form of oldness at all, but simply a new (to me) form of loneliness, which was not unlike Lillian's loneliness, for like Lillian I had lost, or was in the process of losing, my available means of participating in the world. At the time, however, I only intuited this future. I felt its weight, but had no way to understand it. And of course in another sense I was not yet truly "like" Lillian, for whatever my emotional state, the fact was I had not yet resigned my own future. I had not given up my own hopes and desires. I was still planning to return to my son.

My chance finally came—and I was at last able to put this long period of geriatric television viewing behind me—one fateful day in 1989, when the television broke down. By then, a few important changes had occurred.

Lillian was still Lillian, a shell of her former shell, but Tanya had grown, during those years, slender and quite pretty. Also *disappointing*—for age had made her restless, and proximity to lazy people had made her lazy, and long hours of debilitatingly boring labor for indifferent employers had taught her that any attitude or action she put forth into the world would yield the same indifferent result. Whatever effort she made would not be rewarded, whatever kindness she mustered would not be reciprocated, and so why not retreat into adolescent narcissism and let everyone else fend for themselves? It filled me with sadness to see it, a sadness that was never entirely absent from my feelings toward Tanya then or later. Yet my sadness was also rather strongly tempered, both then and later, by the disappointment, irritation, and anger I often felt at her incorrigible behavior, including—at this point—when she began using Lillian's room as a place to have sex with her hairy loser of a boyfriend, Donald.

I might as well describe him since he features later on. He was older than Tanya, though not by much. He had hair everywhere, long and greasy on his head, thick and wooly on his limbs and torso.

His black leather jacket was so cracked it looked like it was peeling paint, and he lumbered about in the stupidest of boots. In general he was filthy and (one assumed) smelly, and in either case not at all the sort of person you would want to have sex with, or watch having sex. And yet here was Tanya, my once-innocent Tanya, locking Lillian's door and sneaking this gorilla in from the patio, even though the rest of the staff were so disinterested I'm sure he could as easily have walked in through the main entrance. Lillian would be lying in bed, or turned in her wheelchair to face the corner, or just as often not turned away at all. Thus around three every afternoon I was made to witness their ugly, boring sex—and this was only one of the significant changes in our situation.

The other important change, which I suppose technically was first, since it was this change that made Tanya's illicit sexcapades possible, was that Lillian's medications (which of course Tanya administered) had increased in dosage to where Lillian herself was far beyond woozy, was in fact very close to catatonic. So medicated was her brain, by this time, that it was as if she no longer resided there at all. And perhaps you will not be entirely surprised when I tell you that one day I, Samuel Johnson, felt some feeling. I managed to make noises, to wiggle some fingers and toes. For a moment, it appeared I was back in business! Time to return to my son! And so on. If I only now mention this remarkable development, and even now am not making a big deal of it, that is because it quickly became clear that Lillian's body was too physically decrepit to be able to do much with, regardless of whatever control my mind could muster. Standing up was out of the question, for example, or even dialing a telephone. And so what after many years of waiting ought to have been cause for great excitement became instead yet another variety of frustration (being so close to Unityville, and at long last technically capable, yet stranded in a body unfit for the trip!), just when I thought I had exhausted every variety there could be.

All this was the situation then—Lillian's subdued but broken body, Tanya's exhibitionist sex, my own feelings of age and isolation—when one day in 1989 the television broke down.

It broke down and it was not a very big deal. Lillian was the only one in the television room that morning, but Tanya checked in shortly after and discovered the problem. I wasn't even disappointed, to be honest, since we had been watching so much television for so long—really we had done little more than sit before the television console for years by then. So when Tanya wheeled us over to the window to stare at average weather and an entirely ordinary lawn, I experienced this as a pleasant change. Plus, I had heard a nurse in the common room on the phone with a television repairman, so I knew it would be fixed soon. And sure enough, I had barely grown bored of the window before this repairman arrived.

I heard him before I saw him, huffing and puffing and doing things with his tools back behind me in the room. He struck me as a curious person, based on just his noises. I pictured him fat and sweaty, damping his brow on his shirtsleeve as he cursed, under heavy breath, in what sounded like pidgin German. In fact I had worked up a rather specific image of him based on just his noises, before Tanya returned to the community room to check on us and swiveled Lillian around to watch the repairman at his work. She left, he stood up from behind the television, and I saw: a very large man in overalls, with a gray mop of hair and a tackle box of tools, moving noisily through his routine, smirking in our direction without quite looking, speaking only in those Germanic puffs and mumbles. He was almost exactly as I had pictured! Yet my pleasure at the accuracy of my prediction was cut short as I realized—first as a question mark, then a double take, and finally as a rush of surety—that I knew this man. I had seen him before. He was older now, of course, and saggy; but having known so few people during my time on this planet, I would hardly be able to mistake him, whatever damage the decades had done. It was Abram. He looked awful. Probably I should have recognized him from his noises alone.

He had not gotten very far in his travels, I noticed. Indeed, I felt a little disappointed seeing him there, even though up until that instant Abram's fate had never caused me even a moment's concern. *I suppose he at least pursued his passion,* I thought, for he had found a life with television. *In fact,* I went on, *he's ended up better off than I would have guessed*—had I even once bothered to guess how Abram had ended up. And as I watched him move through the motions of his trade, you will not be surprised to hear that I felt a great desire to speak to him. That is, before I even recognized the true opportunity his presence represented, I was seized by a strong desire to speak.

And the extraordinary thing was: It was possible. It was possible I *could* speak to Abram, with Lillian a medicated lump. This body that was mechanically capable of almost nothing still might be capable of making words, or the sounds of words, in the direction of Abram, and so: What does one say? Does one say: Hello, Abram?

"Hello, Abram."

Except that of course I spoke these words out of lungs and through a throat and mouth so weak that they emerged hardly like words at all, but only indecipherable sounds. I mustered my strength (I mean my strength of will) and pushed them out a second time, dropping the superfluous hello and trying now with just:

"Abram."

Which came out more like "Errrbrm."

But was close enough, apparently, for him to look up.

"Pardon?"

"Erbrm," I said. "Er Smmmmml Jrrnshn!"

Which obviously he did not understand at all.

"Samml Jrhnshn, Erbram! Frm Ooonertybrl!"

Now, I understand that this whole scene will seem a little ridiculous to anyone reading it. Suffice it to say that for me, at the time, it was the most serious thing in the world. And I went on this way, struggling to form vowels and coming slightly closer each time, until finally, after what seemed far longer than it should have taken (but then Abram never was the quickest), he did seem to comprehend at least that it was to *him* that Lillian was speaking, that she was even using his *name*, which caused him to look down in confusion at his shirtfront, as if to discover a name badge he had forgotten he was wearing. And when he saw no badge, this seemed only to confuse him more.

But it was not until I spoke of Emily and of the letter that Abram had written to us—"*Yungins,* yer wrert," I quoted him. "*Merny a nert-an-day haf Ah pert merserf a herdfer a thernkerns erbert thers terlerferssin, an vher gerd Cherstern merms an derds gert ercheyberry an knerckertwerst . . .*"—it was only then that an anxious awareness crept into Abram's befuddled expression, and his eyes passed through the various stages of incredulity as slowly but inescapably a tiny flicker of concern grew into a bonfire of understanding. Summoning all my strength, then, I bellowed:

"Er Samml Jhnshn, Erbrm! Frm Ooonityberl!"

The sudden flush of blood from his ruddy cheeks and forehead, the stupor, the slackened jaws of disbelief—all this I can picture perfectly. I immediately understood: *He thinks he is facing a ghost!* A natural response I had for some reason not anticipated, and which for an instant, I have to admit, I found amusing. Of course, he was essentially correct. I had called myself many names over the years, but *ghost* was for some reason never one of them. It was true, though: I was a ghost! It was true, but meant nothing. *Ghost* is merely a word, after all, and I knew well enough what I was, and how harmless I was, how utterly ineffectual, even if Abram, unfortunately for him, did not.

Yet if my mind had been slow to anticipate Abram's initial shock, it was rather despicably quick to register the power his fear gave me, which it (my mind) instantly decided to capitalize upon, and promptly and unabashedly concocted a means of exploiting. His body was preparing to run, after all—I could see it—and if he ran, I felt sure I would never get him back. There was little time to be reasonable or to attempt to explain to Abram the logistics of my circumstances, and thus appeal to his understanding and goodwill. There was only time to scare him into staying put.

"Dnnt go, Aabrm! Erf yer lerv heer I . . . I wll *haunt youu frrrver!*"

No doubt, too, my mind had by now sorted through its own initial surprises and come to realize the real reason I had reached out to Abram in the first place—a reason you, Reader, must have recognized right away. It was not nostalgia or the novelty of the situation. It was, obviously, that his presence reopened the possibility of returning to my son.

"Abrmmmm!" I strained.

"Shush you, Samuel Johnson," pleaded Abram, "shush you!" in a shaky whisper. "A blaspheming demon I once were, and led you youngins astray the good Christian path, yay, but punished for these sins I have been *ever since*, with perpetual pains and tribulation! Moresohowever, in my heart I weren't nary but a brother to *you*, Samuel, and vhen I learned me of your passing, and how it come about and how you'd left a *son*, vhy, thought me: *poor Samuel.* For long have I known tales of parents too soon from their children torneth, who boundeth theirselves to this vorld—"

"Srrrlence, Abrrm!"

"But Samuel, you must—"

"I serd *srlence!*" I bellowed (well, "bellowed"), having forgotten how irritating Abram's voice and manner could be. "Yer herv been jerdged ber Gerd an fern wrrnting! Yer muss lissern vry crfully erf you wunt to suv yer mertl soul frm *etrnal fers of herl!*"

All this came out with quite a lot of spittle, and the fervency with which I delivered it caused Abram to cower and go silent and listen dumbly to the plan I began formulating right there before him.

My first thought was to have Abram go to Unityville and bring Samuel back here to me. Given Lillian's condition, that struck me as the most obvious course of action. What I did not know, but which Abram now sheepishly informed me, was that he could no longer show his face in that town, under pain of an unspecified (by him—I assume the townspeople had specified it), apparently gruesome punishment. It seems that some years earlier, during a period of particularly bad luck, Abram had attempted to move back into the now-vacant "haus," and some aspects of his plan had not gone precisely as intended. He was unforthcoming with details, which at any rate did not matter to me; what mattered was only that Abram was officially unwelcome in that place, and untrusted, so that even if he did return against the town's prohibition, the chances of convincing Samuel to return here with him were prohibitively slim. Which meant we would need to get Lillian to Unityville. Which meant we were taking his truck.

So now the plan became:

There was an emergency exit from the television room to the front parking lot. I had never seen it opened but felt at least 75 percent certain it was not wired to an alarm. We would wait until we were alone in the television room (Lillian was very often left alone in the television room), at which point he would wheel Lillian out, strap her in, and off we go! Abram would drop her in Unityville, at the steps of the church, after which, as far as I was concerned, he could go about the rest of his time on the mortal plane free of demonic visitations or any other impositions from the spirit world.

"But Samuel," Abram pleaded, "twould be kindernapping!"

"Rerther this," I spat, "er else burn frvr in *erternl herlfer!*"

Why Abram would believe that I, even as a ghost, had control over eternal hellfire, I truly have no idea. Yet believe me he apparently did, and do as I bid, I had to assume he would. Unfortunately, as he now explained, the passenger side of his truck's front seat was a disaster of tools, fast-food garbage, broken glass, and dangerous spring coils that had broken through the fabric, while the back bed was at that moment piled with old televisions, and, it being already late in the afternoon, it seemed best to just wait until morning. Borrowing a trick from Phil Williams, I instructed Abram to leave the nursing home's television unfixed and to inform the nurses that he would come back the following day with a replacement tube or gadget.

The rest of that day and all of that night, I found myself in a state I'd known countless times before (or felt as if I had—in fact, it was only on those few previous return attempts I have told you about) as I peered forward across the short hours, picturing the events to come. This time around, I found myself less nervous than on previous occasions, perhaps even less enthusiastic—was I?—and I wondered why this would be. Had my earlier failures turned me cynical, world-weary? They had, of course, but this was only one aspect of my feelings. Nor was I worried about the slimness of my chances. In fact, as the hours passed, I began to worry things were going too *well*, that my calm was an ill omen, or worse, some punishable form of hubris . . . Thus it came as a great relief, when morning arrived, and Abram with his truck and tools, to rediscover my ordinary panic and to feel my ordinary anxieties return.

He arrived with a blanket, which he seemed to think he was going to toss over Lillian's body, as if an enormous object being wheeled away would be somehow less conspicuous under a blanket. Tanya was a busybody that morning—she was irritatingly present—and there were others in the television room, so Abram had to continue tinkering or pretending to tinker with the television longer than seemed natural. He grew nervous and drew attention, and in general it was an arduous couple of hours before "games time" arrived, when everyone else left to play bingo in the cafeteria, and Abram and I were at last left alone.

He took up the blanket then, but I grunt-spitted at him to put it down, that eternal hellfire awaited anyone who tried to cover me with a blanket. He objected that an old woman in a wheelchair strapped into the bed of a truck barreling up Route 11 was bound to attract unwanted attention, which to be honest I had not considered, having in my mind pictured us only as far as the parking lot. I told him he could cover me with the blanket only after I was safely secured in the truck. Then there was no reason to wait, so we went.

What followed was a ludicrous action sequence, like some pathetic spoof of *Magnum, P.I.*, and I think Lillian would have enjoyed it very much.

Up onto the truck bed and Abram roped us down, on went the blanket, and we were already backing out of his parking space— so, not yet moving forward toward the road—when I heard Tanya (which truly I wished I could have seen) yelling in a kind of hush-yell, a whisper-yell, and running toward us—too late! And Abram "kicked" into gear, he "peeled out," we "hung a left" out of the parking lot, the blanket now slipping off Lillian's head and gathering around her chin so I could see Tanya there in the lot, her gawping maw of disbelief, not screaming just standing there, even better than I had pictured with the blanket over my head . . . But then, *then*, when any normally panicked person would have run back into the building to call the police, Tanya, who was experiencing a very different sort of panic (I understood later that her response to this situation was entirely self-serving; that despite her shock and confusion, some preconscious reptilian lobe of her brain had quickly calculated the possibility that Lillian, under these circumstances, might sober up enough to reveal, upon her rescue, Tanya's illicit sexcapades with Donald)—*Tanya*, that is, jumped into a tiny car and started after us: and the chase was on! . . . Although I do not think Abram realized she was back there, or he might have driven faster. In fact he was driving unadventurously slowly—no Tom Selleck, our Abram!

Of course he had delicate cargo . . . But meanwhile, Lillian's blanket had fallen all the way to her shoulders, allowing me to experience every aspect of this very exciting sequence, the wind rushing over Lillian's ears, and Tanya's tiny bedraggled car puttering up to us, eventually overtaking us, screeching around the side to shout at Abram out her window (I could not turn to actually see her shouting nor make out individual words, but surely it was something like, "Pull over!"), and Abram, who (I was suddenly reminded) had never been anything but a disappointment, almost instantly gave up and pulled over and stopped there on the roadside, the blanket having now dropped to Lillian's lap . . . A moment later they were both back behind the truck, where I could see them arguing, Tanya screaming and Abram crying giant baby tears and explaining himself indiscernibly, and . . . and this was the moment when Lillian died.

Either it was all the stress on her body, or simply a coincidence, that after all these years of not dying, she finally did.

She died, and I suddenly found myself six feet closer to blubbering Abram than I had been the moment before. From deep down in my new darkness, I cried out. I was crushed. I began throwing the most horrible fit. My adventure again thwarted, my hopes once more mocked, and my life with Tanya about to begin.

10.

It lasted many hours, that fit, and was the last I ever threw, because after that I stopped caring. I surrendered myself to Fate. I let go of all anger as well as any residual hope. My existence became wholly Tanya's existence, and from then on, I went back to being nothing but a watcher, a viewer, an audience member. As I'd been from the start. As I'd always been and would always be.

Or that was what, for the longest time, I told myself. In reality, that day Lillian died was simply the fiery prequel to a period of deep-simmering self-loathing, during which I said to existence: *I do not care any longer!* Not because I truly did not care, but because I was too angry and embarrassed to admit to caring. I sulked, essentially. I spent the next several years in a sulk.

How Tanya spent those years, and the years after those, and the years after *those*, is a story that takes us through many unsavory places, under the influence of assorted substances and the tutelage of various hooligans, in a long parade of mostly degrading situations. It is a much more elaborate tale than I have time here to tell, but I will do my best to summarize at least its essential events, since twenty years is not an insignificant span; and since in the end this period proved important for me after all, for my feelings about myself and my place in this world; and since my relationship with Tanya was—well, it was complicated.

Following the roadside debacle, Tanya and Abram managed together—it being in both of their best interests—to discreetly return Lillian's body to the nursing facility, where it spent a final afternoon in front of the television and was discovered sometime after Tanya went home. Claiming sick, she'd left early, and so it was from Donald, of all people, who had come by Riverfront later that day looking for Tanya, that we learned Lillian had been returned to her room, either to await the coroner or possibly because her death had still not been discovered by the staff there. He'd snuck in from the patio as usual, had found her sitting in her wheelchair as usual, and had failed to realize she was dead. He had failed to realize he was waiting for Tanya in a room with a dead person, and that night he became far more disturbed than the situation called for, indeed practically hysterical, hyperventilating and needing to breathe into a bag for several minutes when Tanya finally explained it to him.

Nor was Donald's cowardliness my greatest discovery that day, for within moments of arriving home with Tanya, I saw how many illusions I had built around her, illusions I had not even known I was building. For years my mind had gone out of its way to cast Tanya, first, in the role of an angel, then later of a victim, no doubt of a broken home; and this was because—I saw it clearly now—she had come to stand for me as a sort of surrogate child. The daughter I'd never had in place of the son I'd barely known. Even when Donald had arrived on the scene and Tanya's behavior turned despicable, even then some part of me was sure that Donald was at fault for all of it, Donald and the abusive parents I had concocted for Tanya the moment I'd learned she still lived with them.

Now faced with the reality of her home life, however, I saw it was nothing like I'd imagined. Expecting cracked tile and boarded windows, I found instead coffee-table doilies and woven baskets of soap. Expecting boozy arguments with bottles sent crashing into patchy drywall, I sat instead through microwaved dinners with dull conversation. Far from abusive, her parents turned out to be rather simple folk, unassertive, permissive, perhaps a bit too often occupied with other things. In fact they reminded me of my own parents. In light of which realities, I was forced to entertain the possibility that Tanya was not much of a victim, unless of her own freedom. But as I was about to learn, freedom in the hands of a young person can be a very dangerous thing.

To wit: our time with her parents proved brief, for following Lillian's death, Tanya quit her job at Riverfront, and this led—when her parents finally discovered it, after several weeks lazing about Donald's trailer during the day, playing video games and watching daytime television—to an unexpectedly heated argument with her otherwise placid father, and to another sudden shift in her circumstances. To be fair to Tanya's father, his reaction was understandable, if not frankly understated, not really even anger but more a blustery exasperation, and having less to do with her quitting Riverfront per se than with her dropping out of high school the year before. And Tanya was so quick to turn this one disagreement into justification for moving with Donald to Colorado, where his cousin had found him a job as a ski-lift operator, that I rather strongly suspected she had decided to leave before their argument even started, and simply preferred to hold her father responsible for it.

So it came to pass, one bright spring morning in 1989 or '90, or more likely it was early afternoon since they tended to sleep in, that Tanya and Donald found themselves bumping along in Donald's hand-me-down Volkswagen Rabbit through the woodsy vales and turnpike tunnels of central to western Pennsylvania, the surrounding hills already gone green. A fine but not glorious day. A so-so day trying to pretend it is other than ordinary. Tanya's window is rolled down and she leans her head out to let the rushing air smother her, to be swallowed by velocity and the open road as she races toward the future, toward freedom without responsibility and adventure without common sense. She has left behind all she had previously been, is set upon discovering whatever she will become—and she is *happy*. She is so happy that I, Samuel Johnson, thick in my sulk and willfully numb to the world, nonetheless find myself hopeful for her. Even as we pass Breezewood, a place I'd promised myself I would never see again, and as my mind inevitably recalls its cautionary tales, replays its several decades' worth of sobering experiences and weighs Tanya's prospects in light of everything I'd seen and learned, even then, some part of me still feels hopeful. Because in her happiness I sense the sweet young woman she had been when I first encountered her, the young woman I tell myself must still be inside her somewhere, inside here with me, intending to save her from the hideous mess her surface self is almost certainly going to make of her future.

And then we were in Colorado.

They lived in a mountain resort town of lodge-hotels and timeshares where everything was made out of logs. Log benches, log lampposts. The town itself, like a stump, expanded outward in rings: at center a pedestrian mall of clothing shops and ice cream parlors; farther out the gift shops, the pizza place; farther still the one grocery store, the gas station; and out beyond the town proper, a knotty cluster of old buildings where Tanya and Donald shared an apartment with Donald's cousin, Todd.

They'd arrived in the off-season, when hippies and burnouts loitered all day outside the shops, drifting among the benches in their dusty denim and tie-dyes, giving the mall more the appearance of a sixties music festival than of the alpine hamlet it affected later in the season. Donald did not like them—thus rose my opinion of Donald.

In fact he had taken a surprisingly serious attitude toward his new life. In addition to operating a ski lift, he was part of a crew responsible for grounds work, facilities upkeep, janitorial, and refuse. This was the list he would recite whenever Tanya complained about his hours—lift operation, grounds work, facilities upkeep, janitorial, refuse—while Tanya, for her part, just wandered around. She wandered in among the hippies, and by the following spring had become a bit of a hippie herself, frequenting the town's one head shop in long skirts and bracelets, smoking marijuana. Before we knew it, a year had passed since that hopeful day she and Donald had set out west in search of their futures, yet somehow Tanya's future seemed farther away than before.

Another year (was it 1991? '92? Tanya hardly kept track of the years, let alone the days; nor did she ever follow the news or seemingly care to know anything at all about the outside world); about another year later, then, she was working at this same head shop and having sex with the manager, Barry. He was around Donald's age and almost as physically repulsive, but lazier, less poor (his uncle owned the shop), and able to boast an even more off-putting personality. In fact, Tanya had grown indiscriminate about sex in general, having all types of relations with every variety of local deadbeat, rich and poor deadbeats, male and female deadbeats, invariably while smoking marijuana, usually in the back of the shop. Had we lost, already, the hopeful feeling? No—or as Tanya would say, "Nah." But I, at least, had lost any confidence that Tanya's better future was something she personally intended to bring about, and as the months passed, I found myself increasingly bothered by her floundering.

It bothered Donald as well, who bothered Tanya about it, and Tanya, who seemed to pride herself in having absolutely no strong feelings about anything, nonetheless strongly disliked being bothered. Now they avoided each other. Now, when not avoiding each other, they argued all the time. Yet it wasn't until Donald began studying for his GED in order to go to school for some sort of electrical training that Tanya finally dumped him, and then only because Barry's uncle had "promoted" him to managing an adult shop in Denver, and he'd offered to take her along. How strange for me to hear Donald and Barry speaking, separately but in near-identical phrases ("get my *shit* together" and "keep my options open" and, oddest of all, "my career") to describe their vastly different prospects! As for Tanya's own prospects, she seemed not to require any, content to choose between Donald's and Barry's. She chose Barry's prospects because—I can think of no other possible reason—they were far and away the worse of the two.

So off we go to Denver.

Though before we do I should say that I do not mean to be glib—it occurs to me I might be coming off as glib—whisking through Tanya's life like this. As if it were just another episode, another pointless situation to be stuck in, like all the others. At the time I might have felt that way about it, some part of me certainly felt that way, but it was also true that my relationship with Tanya was different from any before. Even in my remoteness, I never disappeared into Tanya. There was always an unbridgeable distance, accompanied by a contradictory feeling of closeness that I'd also not previously felt. Both farther and closer, always conscious of myself as someone other than Tanya, but never indifferent as a result. Perhaps part of this feeling was physical, or that was what I told myself at the time, a young woman's body being so dissimilar even from an old woman's body, and certainly from the various male bodies I'd known (the most remarkable difference being Tanya's menstrual periods, which did not appall or surprise me but which caused me, once monthly, to contemplate her life-creating capacity, her miraculous potential to beget small humans, a possibility that I'd never given much thought to as a young person myself and that

Tanya, still a young person, did not seem to find nearly as extraordinary and wonderful as I did). But there was this distant closeness, is all I mean to say, a feeling I recognized even from the depths of my existential sulk but which would remain a mystery to me, a point of perplexity, an inexplicable fission in my illusion of indifference, and would only resolve itself much later, when I finally retook responsibility for myself and saw the situation for what it had been all along.

But for now we are just in Denver.

Or rather Colfax Avenue, which is the worst part of Denver, if not of Colorado, if not of everywhere else—or was back then, and I can't imagine it has changed much. On any given heat-stroked afternoon, this endless strip of airless pavement conjured more a lawless desert town than a modern American city. By night, it attracted only the roughest elements and stank of all the worst odors, the odors attached to all the worst vices, festering in the crevices, and so on. Mornings, too, brought no fresh beginnings, but only again the punishing sun, to bake the pavement, to dry up the piss puddles by the bus stops. Nor is this description at all unfair or exaggerated or unduly colored by the fact that this horrible soulless place was where Tanya—my once-innocent Tanya—now began "working," dancing naked behind smeary glass for incorrigible perverts.

Barry ran the "shop," and they lived together in a bungalow just north of downtown. Despite his pimpish posturing (and his actual pimping, for even if Tanya's "work" stopped short of literal prostitution, surely in spirit it was the same), Barry in daily life was more idiotic than abusive. And Tanya's own posturing, the "professional" posturing she seemed perfectly content to pursue, was itself more tedious than "exotic," and in general theirs was a hazy, listless life. A life like a noontime nap in a stuffy room with no blinds or curtains, a nap that never quite happens, never quite arrives at rest, yet somehow lasts the entire afternoon. In addition to marijuana and alcohol they now occasionally smoked heroin—or "did" heroin, as they would say, though in fact they smoked it—and no doubt this increased substance abuse contributed to the sense I have, looking back at this time, that Tanya's previously scattered attention span had disappeared altogether. In fact, having just racked my mind for a full minute, the only memory I can conjure from that entire period is of O. J. Simpson's white Bronco speeding away from the police while Barry yells, "Go O. J.! Go O. J.!" before Tanya's gaze drifts from the television back up to the ceiling.

By 1993 or '94 (so, our second or third year in Denver) she'd returned to her earlier habit of wandering during the day, though now through different streets, a larger and busier downtown, placing herself in the path of a much wider array of weirdos. She had a gift for meeting strangers, an openness—she always had. Part of me admired her for it. Most of me worried about her because of it. But the part that admired her would often point out, to the part that worried, that I had never known someone so at ease with herself and others, when she chose to be. In such moments I would even swell with pride, like a father watching his child excel at something he himself has never managed to be any good at. If she were only able or willing to pair this gift with a modicum of common sense, I told myself, she would accomplish, if not great things, at least passably good ones. But instead her gift almost always got her into trouble. And even when it didn't (such as this next episode I am about to recount, which is actually the only time I can think of when her openness did not get her into trouble), it was only because Fate tricked her, and the trouble she thought she was getting into turned out not so bad.

Of course the moment I use the word *cult* you will naturally assume that the life situation it describes must be horrendous. Actually, a rather fine line divides what we call a *cult* from any other group of relatively isolated, like-minded individuals. By certain standards, Unityville might be considered a cult, and Unityville, despite my grumbling about it, is one of the most reasonable places I have ever been. So too with Reverend Ryan's Congregation of the Land, which, all things considered, was not a bad life at all.

He'd approached her in a diner, and then over months regularly sought her out there to talk and drink coffee. He was an intelligent man, and not unkind, not unhandsome, which put him far ahead of Barry in all respects. Of course Tanya—being Tanya—was quick to trust him, but I—being me—remained skeptical, in particular of certain liberties he took with biblical passages I happened to remember rather well, liberties that steered these passages toward some very dubious conclusions as pertained to submission, sacrifice, and the supremacy of collective over individual worth. Yet it is a testament to the stupidity of Barry and the degrading horribleness of Tanya's life in Denver that when the day finally came, when Tanya climbed into a van to join Ryan's congregation farming marijuana in the mountain wilderness, I found myself wondering if it wasn't for the best after all. And in fact it turned out considerably better than that.

This I know was in 1996, so Tanya was now twenty-five.

Which is not, as far as I can tell, particularly old for performing in peep shows, but which turned out to be rather on the high side for joining a cult, where the typical age was more like teens to early twenties. It was hard work, actual farm work, and regimented. They would rise in the morning and labor through the day, subsisting on a simple diet of healthy foods and steering clear of drugs, even the homegrown marijuana. They had no television or radio, but talked together in the evenings, and slept well. There was a Ryan-centered religious component and some nontraditional sex, though nothing far afield of Tanya's previous experience. In short, it was the healthiest situation we had landed in since leaving Pennsylvania, and if Tanya rather quickly came to hate this place, all the hard work and hard living she hadn't known she was signing on for and never would have agreed to; if she spoke constantly of wanting to leave and stopped only because her whining was making her the target of widespread scorn; if, that is, even after *months* of acclimation Tanya still wanted only to get away from the Congregation of the Land and back to Denver and Barry, nonetheless I, Samuel Johnson, had become something of a convert (not of the stupid stuff, obviously), convinced that joining a cult was the best decision Tanya had ever made.

But then, *then* Barry came to "save" her. Somehow he'd managed to track her down and arrived with some brutes to steal her back to Denver. He was surprisingly emotional about it, had worked himself into a tizzy, but had difficulty remaining angry when he saw how thrilled she was to go back. Nor did Reverend Ryan make any show of resistance; in fact I think Barry may have purchased marijuana from him on the way out. All told, we'd been in the mountains less than ten months, yet we were not even out of the driveway before I missed it.

And the Denver and the Barry we returned to were worse than before, for Barry had turned abusive, not of Tanya but of heroin, and everything was more serious, suddenly, and more ominous, even if Tanya tried to float along as if she were still young, as if her future were still far off in the distance, too far away (still!) to be able to see what sort of future it might be.

But now she was twenty-six. In youth, perhaps, but no longer blooming. Cult life had made her body strong, and her mind might continue to fool itself, but something in her soul was going sour. Whatever innocence remained buried inside she was clearly on the verge of losing, and in response to this mounting crisis, not my own but another's crisis, I at last faced up to the responsibility that was not actually mine but that some part of me felt regardless. I would never manage to do anything for Samuel, but *Tanya* I could help. I would do what I could, because I could, and because no one else— obviously!—was going to.

My first thought was to return her to the congregation. It was the easiest and best plan. I would pick one of any number of highly intoxicated evenings and leave Barry a note: "Gone home to parents." He would have no reason to question this note, nor any way to pursue it, since "parents" was not a topic Tanya ever broached. I would steal his truck, and he would have no reason to search for it in the mountains. Everything would go smoothly and well.

And so I picked my evening and I did, we did—we escaped! In the early hours, as the sun rose up the mountainside and the congregation set about their morning ablutions, I left us unconscious on their doorstep, only to find, when they finally managed to wake her, that Ryan did not want her back. He wished "no further hassles" from Barry and his goons. Unrestrained, in fact flatly rejected, Tanya jumped back into Barry's truck and happily drove home. Where Barry threw another fit, and Tanya sobbed—"I didn't mean to!"—swearing she didn't remember a thing or even understand how all that could've happened. After which they cried together, and everything went back to normal, or "normal," except that I suddenly found myself feeling even more responsible for her than before. I had taken on the task of Tanya, it seemed. I would need to see it through.

The next time I stole Barry's truck, I took her south instead of west. I drove almost to the Mexican border and left her outside a McDonald's. She woke up around lunchtime, ate a two-cheeseburger meal, and drove back. What she thought had happened, I cannot even imagine.

For a long time I considered writing a letter to her parents, and only hesitated because each time I played the scenario out in my head, it always went badly. Her father would arrive and confront her, and confrontation would only make her angry. Being imposed upon would only discourage her. But it was too obvious a possibility not to try, so finally, yes, I sent them a postcard. And they came, not immediately but as soon as her father could get vacation time. They checked into a hotel and arrived on her doorstep, and it all happened more or less as I had imagined, except that they did not try as hard as I had expected they would, in fact they did not try very hard at all. To be fair, the last time they had attempted to be firm with her, Tanya had taken the opportunity to move to Colorado, and no doubt this made them wary of summoning even the small amount of strictness the situation called for. Finally, I don't imagine handling the situation differently would have caused any different result.

The third time we fled—in one of Barry's friend's cars, since Barry now kept his keys hidden—was more successful, though not due to any planning on my part. Which is not to say I lacked a plan: I drove east as far as Kansas, had run the car out of gas, rolled it into a ditch, and thrown away all her money. By now I had decided that my best hope was simply to fill her life with difficulty, to strand her in strange places and place her in uncomfortable situations so that she might be forced into self-reliance, or just grow so tired of her reckless life that she'd decide she'd had enough. Instead, she hiked to the nearest truck stop and called collect from a pay phone to ask Barry to come get her, and Barry told her not to come back. That *he* was fed up. Actually what he said was more off-putting than that, a blubbering garble of infantile neediness and accusations, like: "Bitch, you crazy . . . Yeah but what about *my* feelings? *Barry's* feelings? . . . Well joke's on you, cuz the Barry train's *leavin*. Uncle Bernard *promoted* me. I'm movin to *Tampa* . . . Nah, it's been planned for *weeks* now, but no way'm I tellin *you*, no way'm I bringin *you* along, you're Cocoa Puffs, you're Fruity Pebbles, I'm *done* with you, get it? Done. Barry is *done*. Get it? . . . How I *treat* you? How *I* treat *you*? . . . Because you never *understood* me, 'swhy. You don't think *I* got feelings? You think *I* got no feelings?"—and on and on this way in what was certainly the dumbest, most expensive phone call I have ever overheard, ending with Barry's friend grabbing the phone to demand his car back.

Then Tanya fell apart. She sat crying in the truck-stop diner until a sympathetic waitress gave her eggs. Over eggs she wept, over eggs she fretted about having no money, no way to move the car, needing desperately to get back to Denver, to "my Barry," and so on. And I, Samuel Johnson, having finally managed to bring about my hoped-for scenario, felt nothing but sorrow watching her go on that way, crying to no one—to no one but me! Until finally she dried her eyes, forced a smile, stepped out onto the pavement, and managed—without much effort as it turned out—to solicit an exceedingly slow ride back to Denver, or rather a series of rides: the first taking her too far south, and the second, which brought her north, backtracking unfortunately east, and the third ride not to Denver but Boulder, which wasted another two days, by which time Barry had already taken off to Tampa.

Since by this point in the story you will likely have become, with regard to Tanya's perennially poor judgment, as incapable of surprise as I was, therefore I will not waste anyone's time attempting to make sense of her next catastrophically bad decision, and will simply tell you that hitchhiking to Tampa took several weeks.

These were sober weeks, and, in their way, quite extraordinary. Difficult, of course—they were "hard-living" weeks—but weeks during which Tanya nonetheless performed a particularly amiable version of herself; not only, I thought, to obtain rides, but because the life itself, life on the road, despite its burdens, was quite agreeable . . . Days chatting in truck stops or traveling, evenings lying out under the stars in cool weather, toasty on the warm ventilation grate at the back of a Denny's or Waffle House, the bag of clothes I'd originally packed for her doubling now as a pillow . . . Meeting people, showing ease with people, placing people at their ease . . . Days that passed like breezes, and as they passed, my spirits lifted.

It seemed to me this version of Tanya, this healthier version, was as true as any other, perhaps more true than all the others. Many times I thought, *There is no reason this Tanya could not be the all-the-time Tanya. No reason at all! There is nothing to keep her from using these excellent social skills in more responsible situations, for example applying herself to a job and a lifestyle that might actually be worth having . . .* After which I would imagine for her any number of better scenarios and would wonder what we were doing here instead of there.

Then one night, stretched out on a ventilation grate behind a Waffle House in—Kentucky? Tennessee? Alabama? Wherever it was, it was swampy, thick with insects, and mysterious in a way only the South has ever seemed to me. The dark mossy magical South, I mean; not Tampa. Stretched, though, under the black dome of night, the stars in all their seemingly meaningful patterns, the Milky Way's galactic smudge, the twinkling bottomless black that makes everything suddenly small, that makes already-small things—such as my own existence—seem even smaller . . . Stretched out and staring for hours, thinking mostly about myself (no idea what Tanya was thinking about), contemplating the long course of my time on this planet, my thoughts unexpectedly turned to that first night with Orson in Pittsburgh so many years ago, that minute spent leaning up against the newspaper box, staring down the dark empty avenue. That moment of self-knowledge, which I suddenly realized I must be having again—now, here—another such moment of seeing and knowing myself, as if I could nod across the ages, call out to my former self: *You saw this coming, not this but something like it . . . You knew I'd be here, just as I know you'll always be there, forever in that moment, seeing all you're seeing, feeling all you're feeling,* and suddenly, or eventually, as this experience of existential largeness began to fade, as I came back into my smaller self, I realized I had reached a conclusion. Or rather, I saw at last the conclusion some part of me had clearly come to long before.

For so many years had I tortured myself over Samuel, trying to return to my son as if there were something I could do for him, even while knowing full well there was nothing. Four times I'd tried and failed. Three times I'd tried again, only in the final instance accepting the situation for what it was. And then I had sulked; I had wallowed. Years had passed, during which I had watched, as if they were staged for my personal entertainment, the terrible decisions this young woman was making or failing to make, the situations in which she placed herself. I had watched and done nothing when all the while right before me was someone I *could* help, because she was naturally passive, near-constantly intoxicated, and because help was something she actually needed. Tanya, I could help.

And then I had helped her, or tried to, but out of a sense of obligation. Imagining myself some sort of begrudging Samaritan, I had stepped in as a stopgap, but pretending it was all a task that would soon be over, after which I would return to my self, my own purpose, as if I had one any longer.

But here, under the stars behind the Waffle House, I know that I have no purpose of my own. And while so far my efforts to help Tanya have not aided her at all, I see that I have not truly devoted myself to the task. Under the stars behind the Waffle House, I am tired of lacking a reason for being and am ready to accept the reason Tanya has been offering all long. If in my time on this planet I have played many roles—a friend, a ghost, a nuisance, an absent father; mostly an audience member, or nothing at all—to Tanya I will be something else. A guardian angel, a parent more attentive than any real parent could feasibly be. And if she is not precisely the daughter I would have chosen, well, we do not choose our children, and in that sense she more closely resembles the daughter I might have had. And she is not yet thirty (I was not yet sixty); it is not too late! So: I will plan and prepare where she squanders and flails. I will think long-term where she, when she thinks, thinks short. I will compensate for her self-destructive impulses and if need be erect elaborate artifices of circumstance, pursuing every imaginable sacrifice, until I have created for her a better life, whether or not she wants it, and this, *this* will be my purpose.

Of course, every parent in the world will immediately recognize the foolishness of this resolution and will laugh at the inevitability of my failure to come. No doubt some part of me was scoffing even then. But the point to having a goal is not always to reach it, and no matter how inevitable my failure might have seemed—or how inevitable it in fact turned out to be—I would like to think I was at least somewhat original in how I brought it about.

In Tampa, Barry still did not want her ("Like seriously, bitch, what the fuck?"), but Bernard, his fat uncle, uglier and scarier than Barry, was happy to give her a job.

Do I need to describe Tampa? It is like the worst parts of Denver spread more evenly around. Plus humidity and palm trees and so on. Salsa music, cigar making, a barn-like building you drive through to buy beer. The truth is I never saw much of Tampa. I occasionally saw the ocean, but mostly what I saw were the cruise ships, those lumbering behemoths that daily puked their passengers into the touristy zones of the city, including the zone home to Gentlemen's Choice, the club where Tanya waitressed and spent all her time. From the club's back lot you could see them in the distance, a long, low cityscape of ships, while a few blocks farther out, from the kitchenette window of Tanya's apartment, they were the horizon itself, a jagged white line that marked the limits of our new life.

And perhaps it is not surprising, with those ships always in sight, that in those days my mind often turned to Christopher Plume, back at the start of my ill-fated journey, and at times I felt almost near to him—ah, Christopher! Forever back there in his cabin, reading his impenetrable books, on the far side of a great chasm of time and space. And it's true that thinking of Christopher often led me to think about myself—as what does not!—about the unbelievable distance I had traveled across those years, all my extraordinary and my extremely ordinary experiences. But mostly I tried *not* to think about myself or anyone else. I existed now for Tanya, I was focused on Tanya, and the situation with Tanya was—complicated.

Though Bernard paid her poorly, he did pay for her apartment, where they "partied" together a few times a week. And it wasn't long before she and Barry were back to "partying" together as well, or "hanging out," or whatever they called their countless pointless hours together. So that, between the nephew and the uncle, Tanya rarely paid for substances of any sort. Plus, she kept her tips. And since she was a popular waitress, not just physically attractive but friendly as well, she brought home quite a lot of money—more than anyone realized, more than even *Tanya* realized, for whenever she was debilitatingly drunk, stoned, or otherwise unsober, I was stealing and hiding away as much of it as I could.

I was stealing and hiding her money because, after careful consideration, I had come to the same conclusion her parents must have reached years before, that *education* was Tanya's best hope. Not only would education provide her with better career opportunities, it would also address the larger problem, that of Tanya herself. Earlier, I had hoped that if I simply altered her circumstances, Tanya would decide on her own to do the rest, but that had not gone well. Gradually I had come to realize that change could only arrive from *inside* Tanya, but before this could happen, first her insides would need to change! Only through education would her worldview expand, would she come to care about worthwhile things, would she no longer settle for the worst possible circumstances but seek out something better.

So I hid her money to save up for school. I stole, to make her a better person. Nor was this the worst hypocrisy I embraced since I had also to condone her self-destructive drug and alcohol consumption, without which I would have been stuck, unable to help her at all. I told myself that these moral ambiguities were a burden I would bear in the short-term so that someday I would no longer need to, because I would no longer be needed at all.

Unfortunately, moral ambiguities were far from the worst of my obstacles (would that moral ambiguities were the worst of my obstacles!); my real problems, both the short- and the long-term, were much more mundane.

My short-term problem was myself.

By this point in my existence I could handle a body as adeptly as I ever would, yet when it came to direct personal interaction, to speaking with sober living people in a normal social situation—for instance, to open a bank account—*that* I considered, and would surely continue to consider, an extremely awkward prospect. This is an aspect of my existential predicament I've not described up to now, because *up to now* it had little bearing upon the situations I'd encountered. Abram was a special circumstance. Stumbling into bars to watch television might have been fun for Phil Williams, but even that was not something I would normally attempt. In short, trying to control a body involved such physical peculiarity, and resulted in such an unruly outward presentation, that were I to engage a normal citizen in sober conversation I would surely be thought (or Tanya would be thought) to be drunk, struck with a severe nervous disorder, or else dangerously insane, none of which had I ever considered a particularly good idea.

Now, however, I had a purpose, and this purpose would require me to do things in the world, things I had avoided up to then. There were sacrifices I would have to make, risks I would take if need be! Or so I told myself. As it turned out, I did not have to take any risks at all—for during all these years Tanya had bummed around in an unwavering state of stagnation, the world had changed a great deal, and now we had computers and the internet.

I'd not had much to do with them, though I certainly knew what they were. The year before, there had been all that hoopla about the Y2K virus, and even though Tanya did not follow the news or actively participate in any form of cultural awareness, it was almost impossible not to know quite a lot about computers in general by the time it was done. In fact, the whole world was more or less "online" by now, even if I, as usual, was late to the party. This all changed, however, in Tampa, as computers finally reached me in the person of Ken, the awkward potbellied computer technician in the apartment next to Tanya's who was clearly in love with her, or in lust, or obsessed over—I could not determine the exact nature of his feelings, only the fact of them.

He was constantly doing things for her, fixing things for her. And Tanya, still capable of sweetness (despite everything!), treated Ken kindly as well, if less like a man than like a large stuffed animal. He was a friendly presence, a cuddly harmlessness occasionally popping its head into her universe of booze and drugs and hooligans. They would drink beers out on the balcony. She borrowed things and never brought them back. Once, she gave him a houseplant. He would tell her he was worried about her, that she should take better care. She called him sweetie and patted his bald patch. And when neither Bernard nor Barry was around, she occasionally allowed him to show her *his computers.* He showed her the internet and how you could buy things, look things up, and "chat." He showed her e-mail and created her first account. He even gave her a set of keys to his apartment so she could use his computers when he was out, which Tanya never did, but which I, Samuel Johnson, did whenever circumstances allowed.

For you see, I had all this tip money—to get back to our story—by now quite a lot of it, which at first I'd zippered into couch pillows, then stowed in plastic bags in the storage basement. But this was a precarious system, and if our money was eventually to pay for an education, what I really needed was a bank account. I could not simply walk into a bank and open one, but on *the computer*, to my amazement and delight, there existed semireputable financial institutions that in exchange for charging grotesquely high fees would allow an account to be opened entirely online, with only a street address, an e-mail address, and a social security number. Already, I had two out of three!

To get the social security number, I would need to write again to Tanya's parents, but for this, too, I had a new expedient means— e-mail! By e-mail, I could quickly obtain from them the information I needed to open an internet bank account, into which I could deposit cash to save for school, even the courses for which—I had done research!—could be taken online. And none of this required me to interact with a single living person. It required only that I continue to steal Tanya's money, and technically her identity, and that Tanya remain indolent and regularly inebriated long enough for me to see it all through.

Having thus found solutions to my short-term problems, I spent the next year pouring all my energies into this plan. Communicating with her father, through a second "Tanya" e-mail address I created, produced a more rhetorically complicated string of correspondence than I had anticipated, but was not difficult in any logistical way. No, the greater difficulty by far was simply getting computer time at all, since this could only occur in those moments when Tanya was (1) alone and (2) sufficiently intoxicated, and when (3) Ken was also out at work. Sometimes weeks passed without such an opportunity. And even when I *did* get computer time, I struggled with distractions of my own, for the internet presented an enormous world of new possibilities to me, the same possibilities it provided everyone else, though for me they were even more tempting. Each time I faced the computer screen, I fought against my desire to participate, to "sit in" the chat rooms, to visit the listservs or "surf" the communal waves of that virtual ocean, where I might for a moment imagine myself a full-fledged member of democratic society. And while I am proud to say that for the most part I successfully restrained myself and kept my focus on Tanya intact, still there remained one possibility I could not ignore.

A search for "Unityville" unfortunately turned up almost nothing. It still does—I just tried it. A search for "Samuel Johnson," on the other hand, turned up so many items I did not know where to begin. Beyond the famous eighteenth-century English writer (who wrote essays and books, created the first English dictionary, annotated Shakespeare, and had a famously large, domineering personality that even now stretches over pages and pages of search results), there lay a vast wilderness of lesser Samuel Johnsons with their various affiliations and accomplishments. "Johnson" turning out to be the second-most-common last name in English, and "Samuel" being, among first names, the ninth. For weeks I clicked through every link I could, whenever I could: frantically at first, then more slowly as the task's pointlessness became apparent. Eventually, I had to concede that I was wasting valuable time. I was not going to find my son. I needed to reapply myself to the problem of Tanya, where I had begun to face new worries.

Her "thing" with Barry was utterly erratic, constantly on again, off again, while Uncle Bernard's favor was beginning to wane. We had amassed quite a lot of money, but I had not yet found a solution to my long-term problem—which I have yet to explain—and with things growing unstable on the Barry/Bernard front, it occurred to me I needed a backup plan, for which the obvious (and only) option was Ken.

I began sending him e-mails from Tanya revealing her truest, most secret self. She was being held captive by Bernard and Barry, I wrote, who had planted secret microphones around their entire building so that she could not, she could *never* speak to him—to

Ken—about her real feelings. Her real feelings were: passion, tremendous passion and longing for Ken, the hope that Ken would steal her away, would take her, at the right time and at a moment's notice (but not before!) as far away as possible, perhaps even marry her—if he wanted that; she wasn't insisting—simply for the two of them to start a new life together, very far away and preferably someplace nicer, but not Denver, or Pittsburgh—possibly central Pennsylvania? She had aspirations: she wanted an education, to make something of herself. And she wanted to support *him*, Ken, because she thought he was just so smart, and talented, she loved listening to him talk about computers and was even frankly attracted by it—"turned on," I probably wrote—and she knew he had aspirations as well. Together, I wrote, they could make a life that would be better than either of them was capable of making alone. Perhaps have children—if he wanted that; she wasn't insisting—and so on. Ken was shocked, no doubt, but willing, or eager, and in the silence of cyberspace, we planned our escape.

So now I had two plans and no more time to internet-search for my son, an activity that had proven fruitless and heartbreaking. Two plans were better than one, but this left me still facing my long-term problem, which all this time I had hoped would somehow miraculously resolve itself, but which I could not afford to ignore any longer.

My long-term problem was, of course, how to get Tanya to go along with any of it.

I will not catalog the various overly complicated plans I devised and discarded, but will simply tell you that in the end it was not Samuel Johnson but Barry and Bernard who found a solution. It came about suddenly and took effect quickly; in fact it all happened in a single day:

1. Barry came over to tell Tanya he was getting married (to someone else).

2. A few hours later, Bernard arrived to announce she had exactly twelve hours to clear out of the apartment.

3. By that time, Tanya was already "shitfaced" (Bernard's word).

4. As soon as Bernard left and Tanya had made her way from shitfaced to incapacitated, I wrote a note and slipped it under Ken's door: Barry was raving! Bernard had threatened to kill her! And so on.

5. Around four in the morning, Ken crept into her apartment to save her.

Of course Tanya did not actually understand why Ken woke her in the early hours, whispering, and hurried her out to his car. She did not understand why she had to bring her things, why his car was packed with his own things, or why they were driving north, then west, then north again. Mostly she did not understand why he seemed to think she should understand all of this. But she was still half drunk, and dealing with a terrible headache, and was used to strange occurrences in her life. She understood well enough the overall gist of what was happening, and Barry and Bernard had made clear the alternative—in fact in some ways she understood the situation better than Ken did—and two days later she was living in St. Louis.

Small downtown, large parks. More Tampa than Denver for humidity, more Pittsburgh than Breezewood for traffic, more swamp than mountains for vegetation and bugs. Popular pastimes include baseball and barbecue. Gated neighborhoods you drive past but never enter. A great deal of red brick and those white-with-crossbeams houses called "mock Tudor," though where I learned that term I have no idea. A free zoo, museums. Host to a world's fair over a century ago that it continues to tout as if it happened last year. Long waits at the traffic lights. Something called "frozen custard." That is everything about St. Louis I can think of right now.

The apartment above Ken's mother's garage, though meant to be temporary, proved hard to move out of once they'd moved in. Ken worked long irregular hours and when home, he was, if anything, too attentive. He had decided that part of his role in their new life together was to save her from her substance abuse, and to this end he employed his mother, a horrible old woman in a fluffy purple robe who hardly ever spoke to Tanya—and never nicely—to "keep tabs" on her while he was away. Most days, therefore, Tanya found herself in the off-putting situation of being alone but under constant semihostile surveillance—harassed with muteness, henpecked with boredom—and I, Samuel Johnson, came rather quickly to regret the role I had played in creating this new, unforeseeably terrible life. I hoped that Tanya would soon revolt against it, as she had revolted against her parents, and against Donald, and against life in the congregation years before. But in St. Louis, Tanya was in no mood to revolt. The events of Tampa, in particular the shock of Barry's marriage, had drained her of all confidence. She plummeted into a debilitating depression that left her wallowing in self-pity and crying for days on end.

And of course there was nothing I could do for a sober Tanya, no means by which I could affect her fate. In vain, I watched her deteriorate. I watched her walk the neighborhoods, shrinking further from the mindful world. And when she stopped walking, stopped shrinking, then, and for quite a while after, I watched her watch a lot of television.

Gilmore Girls and *Grey's Anatomy*, *The Office* and *24*. *Family Guy*, *King of the Hill*, and *Malcolm in the Middle*. It really doesn't seem that long ago. *Law & Order*, *Law & Order: Special Victims Unit*, *Law & Order: Criminal Intent*, *Law & Order: Trial by Jury*, *CSI: Crime Scene Investigation*, *CSI: Miami*—a preponderance of law procedurals and adult cartoons, but many of them quite clever, I thought. The low end, on the other hand, brought a bottomless pit of tediously identical contests and reality programs, all of which Tanya watched, none of which Tanya missed, from *Supernanny* to *Nanny 911*, from *Wife Swap* to *Trading Spouses*, from *Extreme Makeover* to *Extreme Makeover: Home Edition*, not to mention *The Apprentice*, *The Contender*, *The Bachelor*, *The Biggest Loser*, *My Big Fat Obnoxious Boss*, *American Idol*, *America's Next Top Model*, *Project Runway*, *Survivor*, *Fear Factor*, and one I found particularly offensive titled *Who's Your Daddy?*, which placed an attractive young woman in a room full of older men, one of whom, she was told, was the biological father she'd never met. By asking a series of questions, the young woman was meant to identify her father correctly, for which she would receive $100,000. In fairness to America, I should add that this program aired only once and was instantly canceled, suggesting that the pit of reality television was not truly bottomless, as I claimed a moment ago, since in fact this program found its bottom, the bedrock of human degradation below which even reality television could not go.

Also world events: it felt good, I suppose, to be aware of them again (Tanya being perhaps the only person in the world who failed to notice the events on and after September 11, 2001), yet even the news was not what it once had been. The events were serious enough— gay rights, Katrina, George W. Bush—but the programming style was more sensational than before, and even the subject matter had acquired a perversely "celebrity" bent: Janet Jackson flashes at the Super Bowl; Martha Stewart goes to jail. It was news of entertainment, or news as entertainment, which did not surprise me as much as it should have, I think, since by then even the most serious programs had come to seem merely entertaining, that and nothing more. In fact, on most days television did not even entertain me any longer, because it was *Tanya* watching. Tanya who ought to have been getting her education by then, on her way to a more meaningful life.

Is it any wonder she grew fat? Over two years, she grew quite fat. And Ken, who was fat to begin with, grew even fatter, although this did not temper the disgust he now felt looking at Tanya, or the blatancy with which he and his hideous mother allowed their scorn to fester on their thoughtless faces. *Of course* this environment only caused Tanya to feel worse about herself. *Of course* she only sunk lower into depression and started eating even more, compensating for the hollowness of her life and the love and support that no one was giving her.

Now in those moments when my mind turned to Samuel (because of course even then my thoughts often turned to Samuel), I wondered: if I had stayed with him, had remained his father and watched him grow and attempted to guide him, would I have had any more success than I was having with Tanya? He would have made better choices, because he was such a smart and curious person to begin with—although wasn't Tanya promising to begin with? What if he had grown into a bored, disaffected adolescent? What if he had come to be something less than his potential? Something more *like me*? And isn't this, in the end, the true plight of the parent (allow me to reveal to you the true plight of the parent), that even when you can do things, there's nothing you can do?

So this was it, the finale. I had reached it. I could now look back upon my own trajectory and make a fair assessment. I would never know Samuel, or help him. I had taken on Tanya instead. I had adopted Tanya if only to discover how I *might have done* as a father, and I had gotten my answer, disappointing if not surprising. I would never help Tanya. She was miserable, and I was stuck. I would never help anyone. In the end, a sober, depressed, overweight Tanya flopped in front of a television was the best I would ever do.

So now what?

Now Tanya saved herself.

Or "saved" herself—so confused had I become as to what con-stituted a *good life* for Tanya that my mind could no longer decide whether to put "saved" in quotation marks.

One day she took to the computer and began searching for Barry. There was nothing about him in Tampa or anywhere else. For days she searched, eventually landing at an online catalog of mug shots. State by state, county by county—the catalog being organized by state and by county—she scanned for Barry's stupid face. Until at last she found him, right there and recently: a DUI in Peoria, Illinois. That very day she packed a bag, stole some money, said a silent *So long* to St. Louis, a silent *Fuck you!* to Ken and his maternal gargoyle, and boarded a bus to Peoria. Which is not a large city and has relatively few establishments of the sort Barry might frequent, so she found him in no time at all.

This move to Peoria—this was the final stop for Tanya. Quite a bit more happens in this story, but she never moved anywhere else.

I'll skip what Barry had been doing in the meantime (except per-haps to mention that central Illinois turns out to be one of the inter-net pornography capitals of the world). I'll skip describing Peoria (other than what I just said about it). I'll start by saying that, given Tanya's new girth, I could not imagine how their reunion would go. Or rather, I could imagine it perfectly, and was bracing myself—but in fact it went much better than I had guessed. Barry, though no longer married, had no interest in Tanya romantically, and this probably accounted for much of the depression she suffered over the next few years. (And yes, it has occurred to me that Tanya may have actually *loved* Barry. The evidence was there, and certainly it explains a number of her more horrendous decisions over the years. He may even have loved her back, in his way. Personally, I could never see it, could never understand what she saw there—but then that is the cliché of love, isn't it? Of romantic love or any other? That we do not choose it, it is not reasonable, it comes to us in whatever form it wants to and often makes no sense at all.) So, yes, he rejected her romantically, but he also had a new venture going, and at least he offered her a job. It was a job that took advantage of her talents and did not exclude her on the basis of being overweight. It was even a *decent* job, in the sense that its particular indecencies were slightly less indecent—or simply more anonymous—than the sort in which she'd previously participated. Her new job was to have sexual conversations on the phone and in computer "chats." He set her up in an apartment with a phone and a computer, and she settled into yet another new life.

In which her first order of business was to return to her substance abuse—heroin in particular—with a vengeance, a literal one, since abusing her body was a means of rejecting the sober life she'd so recently escaped. Fleeing St. Louis had at last released in Tanya a long-dormant instinct for *self-reliance*, or so I told myself, while her drug use I chose to see as an extension of this instinct, a counterattack against dullness and despair. Obviously I would have preferred her self-reliance take a less self-destructive form, but I held out hope that this new spirit might eventually turn more productive. And of course her drug use also meant that I was no longer helpless to help her! With Tanya now splitting her time about evenly between pornography and substance abuse, we were finally again in a position to pursue her education, and meanwhile I had come up with a new and better plan for getting Tanya herself involved.

I created a long-lost uncle who, after many years of searching at no small cost and effort, had finally tracked Tanya down. Uncle Samuel had no children of his own, he opined (by e-mail—I did this by e-mail), and was getting old. He had no wish to impose himself personally upon Tanya; he understood she had her own life and did not need some nosy uncle hanging around, but he did wish to help her, even though he did not know her, because he was lonely, had been alone for almost his entire time on this planet, and had no one else to help. He understood from her parents that she had never completed her high school education, and on the off chance she wished to address this shortfall, he had taken the liberty of enrolling her in a set of online continuing education courses, for which he'd pay the tuition, and also—importantly!—place money to support her in a bank account in her name. It was admittedly not a large amount (of course I did not trust Tanya with the full amount of her actual savings), but there would be more added to the account if she took the courses as I recommended, and a bonus if she did well in her first semester. In short, my plan was to purchase not only her education, but also her willingness to participate in it.

And she tried. She did. For the first several weeks, she signed into the class websites and did the work. Whether it was the incentives I had given her, or her newfound self-reliance, or the fact that she had no one in her life now and no other way to spend her time, or simply that she was finally old enough (thirty-six going on eighty) to see that the future had arrived and nothing particularly good was waiting to reveal itself . . . whatever it was, all that mattered was it was working. And as she became more involved with the course work, her substance abuse went down. I felt, for a moment, a swell of pride, in Tanya and perhaps even more so in myself. Yet as she *lost* interest in the course work, which happened the moment the lessons became just the slightest bit challenging, her substance abuse went back up again. Which caused me, not anger, but frustration, yes. We were halfway through her first semester—already she was giving up!

When Uncle Samuel e-mailed to ask how things were going, Tanya wrote back, "Fine!" She wrote back "Fine!" in between textually fellating a "user" and verbally orgasming for a caller. Perhaps I was angry after all. Certainly I could not stomach wasting an entire half semester, all that progress she had made. And considering that this was likely just a momentary discouragement, and that she would return to her education as soon as she remembered how unsatisfying her life was otherwise, I decided to finish her courses myself, so that at least she would have the credits when she came back.

It was an odd arrangement, and worked only because Tanya was by now such a heavy user (I mean of heroin, though of computers as well) that she spent as much time semiconscious as either conscious or un-. She wasn't eating much, and lost weight. She remained very far from healthy, of course, and had even begun suffering back problems from slouching at the computer for such long hours. Admittedly, this was partly my fault, since half of her computer time was actually mine—indeed, our existences at this point became almost evenly entwined, as if we were partners in Tanya's life, or more like roommates in her body, coming and going at different hours as we pursued our separate activities in the individual daytimes of our virtual realities. Nor did I feel bad about occupying so much of Tanya's consciousness, since my half of our life was much healthier than hers.

Will you be surprised to hear that I did very well in school? I had never thought myself particularly studious, but Tanya's continuing education courses were not particularly hard. And when that semester ended, and Tanya's response to Uncle Samuel's threat to stop the money was simply to stop responding to Uncle Samuel, I at that point went ahead and enrolled in more courses on my own, if still on behalf of Tanya. More challenging courses, in fact, since, if Tanya wasn't going to take them, then I would take the ones *I* found most interesting, the ones I might enjoy rather than the ones I thought Tanya would have enjoyed and learned from, which was how I had tried to pick them earlier—fat lot of good it had done!

And those classes did prove interesting, and reading itself I found edifying, a heady liberation from the world's dreariness, with a feeling of belonging, of being among people you can never speak to or touch but who have a great deal to share with you, whose companionship makes you a larger person, if only inside your own mind. I could thrive in that world—and I did. For two years I did. Yet it was not until I had completed Tanya's GED and enrolled in an online college program that I truly began to feel I was developing my own intellectual *purpose*, which of course is where everything once again (but for the last time with Tanya) went wrong.

I had taken a class in philosophy. Actually I had taken several, since of all the subjects, philosophy most interested me, having over the years spent a truly enormous amount of time—surely more time than any living philosopher has spent—thinking about the nature of reality and existence and the world and so forth, simply thinking and wondering about these things. Also because my own existential situation gave me a unique perspective on many of philosophy's essential questions while also raising for me some existential questions that living philosophers did not or could not even imagine to ask. Of course, I did not expect a handful of online courses from a third-tier college to provide groundbreaking answers to never-before-asked existential questions, but the incredible thing was, one class almost did: a very small class (only four students) devoted entirely to the concept of "eternal recurrence" or "eternal return."

The doctrine of eternal return originated (or arguably originated, or at any rate our study of it originated) with the nineteenth-century German poet Heinrich Heine, but was popularized, if one can speak of a philosophical doctrine as being "popularized," in several books by the important German philosopher Friedrich Nietzsche, and more recently, and perhaps more "popularly," by the 2004 remake of the television program *Battlestar Galactica* (although this is purely my own interpretation of the ending of that series, which aired in 2009, the year I took this class). It starts from the premise that time is infinite but the universe is finite. There is only so much *stuff*, so many objects, so many events, constantly being rearranged and reconfigured. But if time is without limit, then eventually—"eventually" meaning over a period of time longer than your brain can imagine—but after an impossibly long period of time, all the existing stuff will have gone through all of the possible reconfigurations and will start over again. The comparison often made is to a game of chess: there is an extremely large number of possible moves, and consequently an almost inconceivably large number of chess games that could be played; but this number is not *infinite*, only large, and so if you play a different game of chess each time to infinity, eventually all the possible games will have been played, and you will have to play the same ones over. Of course our universe is much more complicated than a game of chess, but when faced with *infinite* time, the number of "moves" in the game of our universe is no larger, relatively speaking, than the moves in chess—or in tic-tac-toe, for that matter.

Had our class been limited to this basic formulation of eternal return, I would have found it interesting, but not interesting enough that I would be telling you about it now. But since this was a semester-long study, we rather quickly left these basics behind to apply the concept of eternal return in other directions, both backwards to the Pythagoreans and Heraclitus and forward to the internet. We looked at Stoicism and Skepticism, which have in common a lack of attachment to worldly things, which becomes a rather natural worldview once you believe everything is just repeating itself anyway. We considered how eternal return rebukes Christian doctrine, and how the Church, by preaching "progress" toward an "afterlife," risks devaluing the one life human beings irrefutably have, like skipping midway through a book to get to the ending, as if the ending were the point rather than the book. (And let me here take a moment to congratulate anyone who has read to this point in *this* book; you are obviously not among the "skippers," or else you would already have skipped this entire section, if not this entire chapter, by far my longest and most meandering.) We looked at Heidegger, and other thinkers, and in many other interesting directions as well. In fact, the more places we looked, the more the concept of eternal return appeared to be everywhere, so that I began to wonder why I had never heard of it before.

But the real turn for me came late in the semester, on the day the class's instructor finally shared with us his own personal theory of eternal return, which (he now revealed to us) had been the topic of his doctoral dissertation, which was why we had been able to spend an entire semester on just this one subject, a subject some other, less deeply informed instructor would likely have covered in half a class.

My instructor's own theory, as described in his dissertation, which I am able to excerpt verbatim for reasons that will become clear later, goes like this:

The fundamental obstacle to Nietzsche's formulation of "eternal return" is that the progressive albeit cyclical model of time upon which it predicates itself is blatantly contradictory to the "Dionysian" or just totally anarchic spirit of liberty-from-"received ideas" that makes Nietzsche "Nietzsche" in the first place, and which (spirit) the various other facets of this formulation do, obviously, enjoy.

Lest we place undue blame on the thinker, consider that the historical moment out of which he utters his utterance contains only inadequate models of time vis-à-vis experience. Meaning what? Meaning Herr Friedrich lacked the tech to know better. For it is only *our modernity* that allows us to avoid comparing reality to, for example, a *chess game* (being a series of events having a discernible beginning and end) and to replace this linear "game" model with the more ontologically apt metaphor of the *internet* (being a space of unbound experience wherein such words as "beginning" and "end" are totally and utterly beside the point—*Beyond Start and Finish!*—vestiges of a model of "progress" Mr. Nietzsche was trying to shake but was stuck with, simply because he did not yet have the internet, or say rather that *humanity in his moment* was not in a very good position to *notice* the internet, it having "not yet been invented," and so naturally they failed to draw comparisons to it).

To clarify: As a culture we speak *ad nauseum*, in fear and self-congratulation, of the many *changes* the internet has wrought upon *our lives*, as if our lives were one thing and now are something totally different, when in fact what has truly changed is our *understanding*. In purposefully applying the internet's precedent to concepts of reality and experience and time, however, we *instantly recognize* that Nietzsche's key mistake, utterly systematic in how greatly it messes everything up, is the limiting of the concept "eternal return" to denote only the notion of a present that *departs* then *cycles back,* rather than, as the example of the internet suggests (or rather as the *existence* of the internet makes at last *possible to conceive*) (or rather as the *application of our attention* to the *already existing internet* finally allows us to *figure out*) a reality in which everything exists in a state of perpetuity and *nothing ever leaves.* It is not that ideas or patterns of history return but that our attention returns to them. All we ever study is our own attention, the application of our attention, where it chooses to hover, at which moments, and, to a lesser extent, why. It even probably follows, or "follows," that our attention itself is not strictly "ours," that rather we should speak of Attention with a capital A, a fundamental force in the universe of which we are mere participating bits—although for feasibility reasons this latter line of inquiry lies outside the purview of the current study.

But we now at least have the terms to see plainly, based on all of that, that what we call "life" is nothing but the path Attention takes across the always-already-existing objects of our reality;

and what we call "selves" are the vehicles of Attention, as well as its self-reflectors; and what we call the "reality" of our reality is the field of possible topics and objects that Attention, through its aforementioned vehicles, returns to over time; and what we call "time" is the spatial organization of this attention; and what we call "history" is the discernible if totally bogus and fabricated pattern of the sequence of this returning; even what I have called "our modernity" is merely the particular set of objects upon which Attention, in the historical moment I personally utter out of, happens to fall; and what we call "the future" is the set of attentive acts that we have yet to take notice of in the illusory forward extrapolation of the current manifestation of Attention's self-awareness; and what we call "death" is a shift, not of objects, but of perspective; and what we call "birth" is the reification of a previous perspective by which the Attention again returns to its various topics and objects, which in the meantime have themselves altered in position, maybe, or in duration, if there even exists such a thing, but not, to any significant degree, in type.

So that in the end (being the recognition of endlessness), the term "eternal return" refers quite simply to the illusion of change, the lie of progress, without which what we call "life" quickly loses its liveliness, which sounds tautological, because it is tautological, as are all things eternal, i.e., as is everything.

Typing it here, I find I am much less impressed with my instructor's theory now than when I first encountered it, due no doubt in part to all that happened later to spoil it for me.

But even the theory itself—I'm a little embarrassed to recall how awestruck I was at the time, though certainly you can see why. For decades my existence had been a giant question mark, yet here was the first seemingly reasonable explanation of my personal state of being in the world. We are, all of us, nothing but vehicles of attention! Everything exists in a state of "perpetuity"— and nothing ever leaves! In hindsight, I see in the above passage little more than the flippant whimsy of an autodidactic graduate student, but back then it seemed like the answer to every question I'd ever asked.

Thus when the time came to choose topics for our final papers, I of course chose to write about my instructor's own theory, which pleased him immensely. He even offered to tutor me, should I have questions or need any additional help. By which I mean that he agreed to tutor *Tanya*, since she was the one enrolled, the actual human being whose name appeared in the online course roster, to whom my instructor naturally assumed his compliments were addressed. It was Tanya he claimed to be very impressed with, Tanya he made himself available for, which was perfectly fine with me (I was not seeking credit, or not that kind of credit, even if I was perhaps a bit sad not to receive any). Or it *would have been* fine had it not caused such a catastrophic mess.

For on the day I received my instructor's approval for my paper topic, in an e-mail that also included several compliments on my recent performance in the course, I was on that day in such good spirits that I made a terrible mistake. When ceding control of Tanya's body—as I did at a certain point every evening, allowing her body finally to fall asleep, typically for many hours—I inadvertently left open the "window" on my computer's browser that contained the internal e-mail system for the class, a window I of course took great care to close every time I was done with it, no doubt antici-pating precisely the sort of disaster that my negligence in this case allowed. For when she finally awoke, after many pleasant hours during which I was feeling good about myself and had not yet real-ized my mistake, she stumbled over as usual to the computer con-sole and, having not yet drunk her several cups of coffee and seeing a window open that looked vaguely like the browser windows she performed her work in, she went ahead and did what she always did, she typed a bunch of porn into it.

Of course this was my fault and not Tanya's. She was just doing her job and had no reason to suspect anything amiss. Still I could not help feeling furious while she typed, and terribly worried, as she pressed Send, of the impression she would make on my instructor.

One minute and forty-five seconds later, when his reply arrived, my fury and worry turned rather quickly to *monumental disappointment*, for his message took a markedly similar tone to Tanya's.

Indeed, this man whose ideas I deeply respected, and in whom I had even invested a certain amount of hope, this highly educated academic professional spent the next *full hour* exchanging pornographic messages with Tanya, who was not even fully awake, whose hair was a mess and who was farting and scratching herself, stumbling around making coffee and using the bathroom the whole time. If ever in my tenure on this planet I was more disgusted than I felt right then, I do not remember it. I had seen whole lives sunk into drunken squalor, a bull decapitated, Donald's hairy back— but these were merely physically or morally disgusting, whereas this was an affront in all those ways *and intellectually as well*. I was disgusted at the situation and the people involved. At myself for being careless, at my instructor for disappointing me, and at Tanya, who had not actually done anything wrong.

Given the severe negativity of my feelings, you might be surprised to learn—as I am rather ashamed to recall—how conflicted I felt the following day, when my instructor wrote to say that he would be traveling downstate on some sort of academic business, that by coincidence he would be taking the train to Peoria that very weekend, and this seemed a "singular opportunity" to get together to discuss my paper topic in person, in case I needed any additional guidance with the more nuanced aspects of his theory vis-à-vis the something or other and so on.

Of course, any decent person would have wanted nothing to do with him, let alone to meet him, at that point. Yet Samuel Johnson, in full knowledge of how repulsive the whole thing was, nonetheless found himself (I found myself) begrudgingly eager at the prospect. Even knowing what I knew, still I wanted to meet him. More to the horrible point, in my mind this despicable event had already become *our* meeting, my instructor's and my own. I, who for excellent reasons had always avoided engaging a sober human being in direct interchange, was now seriously considering "meeting up" with a disappointing pervert-intellectual for the simple reason that I believed, or wanted to believe, despite mounting evidence, that he could help solve the riddle of my existence.

In fact it must have been more than that. It must have been that in addition to my deluded self-interest, I had also lost sight of Tanya. Clearly, that was the case. At some point in the course of my education—no longer *her* education—I had left behind my vision for her future. My own interests had come to occupy me, and I had given up on hers. Perhaps I even realized it, and felt ashamed of it, but not ashamed enough to change my mind. Perhaps I felt I'd been wrong about her; for all those years I'd been wrong. A father cannot live his child's life for her, nor was I even her father, nor was I even alive. It had all been a fool's errand from the start, its only purpose to provide purpose to a fool, and I had filled up many years with it, but now it was done. Now there was something I wanted to do for myself, not Tanya. And wasn't that for the best? Since nothing I had done "for Tanya" had helped her in the least? I would meet with my instructor, my disgusting, depraved, lascivious instructor, on the remaining chance that I might learn something, perhaps even figure out a way to bring an end to all this, to be done with this world and finally move on!

And so I agreed to meet with him. I told him we'd meet in a bar by the train station. I thought that would be safe. Or rather I thought that it didn't matter. Or rather I didn't think. I would go against decades of better judgment and every ounce of common sense, which I happened to notice had gotten me nowhere. I would take from this man whatever knowledge he could offer me, after which I would at last retreat from Tanya's life, would set her free of both my selfishness and my well-meaning incompetence, would sit quietly in the back of her mind and mind my own business forever.

You know, I have been planning all along to draw out at length this scene with my philosophy instructor at the bar. Having been forced to summarize Tanya's story in order to fit it all in, I had thought I would at least end in a substantial scene to register the gravity of that moment. I would then share the real feelings I hold for Tanya, despite everything we had been through, or because of everything we had been through, and the considerable grief I experienced at losing her. But now that we are here, I think there will be no scene. I cannot help feeling that even with the distance of time and all that has happened and everything I think I have learned, still there is something inadequate about all this. Something phony, even if everything I've written is true. I've made fake feelings out of my real feelings, crafted too-simple stories of my time with Tanya, and pretended, for some reason, that I have distance on these events, which in reality I never did and still don't. And while I suppose the same could be said for all of my so-called adventures, for every tale I've told in this book, yet only now do I find myself embarrassed by it, even ashamed of it, here wrapping up my time with Tanya. I will just tell you what happened and move on.

He was disappointing. I had expected, I think, an older, more mature version of Christopher Plume, awkward and bookish, but serious, with a gravity of knowledge behind him. This man was shorter and shadier than Christopher and not much older—just out of graduate school, it turned out—and while he seemed to know his topic, I saw instantly that I would learn nothing new. And so eager! Clearly this was a unique adventure for him, riding out into the world to have sex with a woman he must have assumed was a nymphomaniac or something similar, a "worldly" woman, a "dirty" woman, a woman he no doubt had mythologized into a test of his own courage, a Herculean task, number whatever on his "bucket list," a story to never tell his grandchildren. That she turned out to be noticeably older than him, and heavy, even though she'd lost weight, and that in addition to seeming generally trashy, she looked and acted, on this particular occasion, as if she were either drunk or psychotic, or possibly possessed by the soul of a dead man who was controlling (if inadequately) her movements—all these factors seemed only to excite him. And for so many reasons—including the quashing of my own hopes, my indignation on behalf of the intellectual tradition, my sorrow for all of humanity, and a sudden swell of guilt and defensive feeling for Tanya—for so many reasons, his excitement at the exoticism of this occasion was the most depressing thing I have ever seen.

And I suppose I had not planned it all very well, and I really cannot imagine how I thought it might go, but my instructor was getting worked up, and I was plummeting down, down, until finally, in the midst of it all, I walked away. Not from the bar, but from Tanya. I ceded control, is the best I can describe it. I slumped into my hole at the back of her brain and quietly shut the door. It was something I had never done before, just "left" like that. But the effect, in this case, was that Tanya fell back into consciousness, not anywhere near sober, in this bar with this odd, eager young man, a situation that might have seemed strange to her had she not already survived half a lifetime of strange situations. And when, highly inebriated, he suggested she take him back to her place, she agreed. And they went, her driving, both still, of course, highly inebriated.

She drove and they got out to the access road (her apartment complex was just off the highway access road), swerved around perilously as if this were perfectly normal, and finally launched into a telephone poll, that simple. All my talk about helping Tanya and being a guardian angel to Tanya and in the end I could not even get her to buckle her seat belt. My philosophy instructor had managed to buckle his, and survived to take me along with him, off to his life—goodbye, Tanya.

11.

I am sitting in a dayroom, a room made for light and air. But right now it's nighttime. A small room, not a closed-in porch, but resembling a closed-in porch, at the front of a second-story apartment in an uptown neighborhood of Chicago. It has hardwood floors and white trim and a white ceiling. I would say it has white walls, but it doesn't really have walls, or barely. The street side of the room and the two sides adjacent are all windows (with a little bit of wall beneath the windows), while the non-street side, where the room connects to the rest of the apartment, is taken up by a large arched entryway, too wide to have a door, or at any rate there isn't one. I'm sitting on a folding chair at a folding table with this computer and a lamp and some other objects—books, bourbon. It's very quiet here, only the patter of typing and night sounds through the windows. Shush of cicadas, occasional passing cars. Outside is dark, though the sky above the city, which you can see over the buildings across the street, never really gets darker than a sort of muddy gray. On the ceiling there's a fan with wood-and-wicker blades, there's an electrical outlet in the floorboards by the archway, and there really isn't anything else in here at all.

How do I feel? What can I say about my circumstances? Those are good questions. Having arrived, at last, at my final chapter, I have been asking myself those questions.

I suppose I am better off than I would have imagined five years ago, when Tanya died and I was transported into the body of my philosophy instructor. Had you asked me back then where I would be in five years, I would have guessed something worse than this. And understandably so, for as he left the hospital the following morning, after several hours blubbering to the police; and also during the train ride back, as he stared out the window at the desert of corn that covers the state of Illinois, perhaps comparing that desert to the state of his own soul; or while examining himself in the mirror of the train's tiny bathroom, his face frozen in an anguished expression, like a theatrical mask symbolizing *Anguish* (I'm sure it was genuine, his anguish; I'm not saying his anguish was not genuine, only that it seemed much more for himself than for Tanya); in short, throughout the entire despicable sequence of events by which my philosophy instructor crawled his way back to Chicago, my opinion of him was understandably low, and so, too, of my own future prospects.

Back then, this room looked much messier. Anthony—I'll call him that now—had a roommate, not a friend, just someone who rented this dayroom, so it was cluttered with that person's, Gary's, things. You had to look at Gary's piled-up things whenever you walked through the apartment: his futon mattress, his guitar case covered in stickers, and his conga drum, also covered in stickers. What a dismal time, those first months back from Peoria! Rarely leaving his room, rarer still the apartment, and since my entire knowledge of Anthony was limited to his performance with Tanya and this moody behavior back home, I assumed this was it, the course of our future, a forecast of endless gloom, which to be fair was not solely Anthony's gloom but mine as well, for what was left to me then? With all my mysteries revealed? The real mysteries were never about God or Fate, of course, not revelations about existence or lessons hard learned. No, the real mysteries were only about myself—of course they were—about who I was and might become, and now I had my answers, Tanya had given me that. Tanya and to a lesser extent Lillian, and Henry and Orson, even Christopher had given me that. I had my answers and was ready, well past ready, to be done.

But if there is one lesson my story must have taught us all by now, it is that nothing is allowed to end in this world. Everything moves on, or starts over, or cycles; it doesn't stop but slouches forward, or circles back—existence, time, one direction or another, "fate"—and sure enough, as the shock of Peoria wore off, Anthony returned to civilization. Having encountered him at his lowest point, I had naturally assumed it was the average, but now I discovered he had friends, and places he liked to go, a past, and so on. At a party in the fall he met Sanjana, a recent graduate of the same school he'd attended, though she'd studied anthropology, and in school they hadn't met. She, too, had recently come out of a bad situation, a psychologically trying relationship she described to him in rather exhaustive detail, which had likewise left her feeling distraught, depressed, and insecure. They began seeing each other immediately.

At the start of their relationship, they—

But am I really going to tell this story? For several days now, proceeding through my other stories, approaching this one, I have wondered what I would do once I arrived. I thought: *No, it's too near, too complicated; my feelings about it are discombobulated, raw, unclear. Doubtful I could even be fair.* The closer I came to the end, the more anxious I was feeling to be done with it. Then Tanya's story—well, it had an unexpected effect on me. It left me wondering why I've been telling any of these stories at all. I've just assumed there was a reason.

But now I've told them, haven't I? And I suppose there's no practical way to skip this last story and still have the rest make sense.

At the start of their relationship—Anthony and Sanjana's—they expended quite a lot of energy analyzing their motives, worrying that their attraction to one another was the result of their mutual insecurity and neediness, and that in a more normal or natural emotional state, they would never have come together at all. They discussed whether an attraction based on need was even a real attraction per se; or—contrarily—whether such an attraction was in fact the most normal, natural, and obvious *sort* of attraction; or—a third option—whether "need" was necessarily even the defining aspect of their attraction (an assumption neither wished to accept a priori), and anyway, isn't needing a particular relationship at the same time that you happen to *have* that very relationship an example of rather extremely good luck? In short, they were slow to accept the fact that, in addition to the fortunate timing of their coming together, they also simply liked each other. This is the sort of people they are.

Once they'd come to accept the legitimacy of liking each other, however, they quickly decided they also loved each other, and promptly and without much ceremony married each other, at which point roommate Gary and his mattress and various stickered instruments disappeared from this dayroom (to where? Who knows), which was then cleaned up and outfitted with Anthony's desk and books and filing cabinet. It looked then quite a lot like it does now, though his actual wooden desk and chair softened the space, whereas this card table and folding chair are more severely ascetic. Meanwhile, Sanjana took over the cozy room at the far end of the apartment that had previously been Anthony's "office," a room he'd almost never entered in the time I'd been with him, though he treated its loss as a small catastrophe, proof of his personal failure, probably because that is precisely what it was.

But here I need to back up.

You see, Anthony had completed his PhD only a year or so earlier and had been teaching courses online because he had failed to obtain a postdoc, a position that would have supported him while he revised his dissertation into a book, which he needed to finish and publish (since he had no published papers) before he could be hired into a tenure-track faculty position. A tenure-track faculty position being apparently the only career path he had ever considered. In the absence of a postdoc, however, and the consequent need to teach courses online, his efforts to revise his dissertation had proved scattered and disheartening. He'd lost confidence. Lost interest in his work. He'd started to question whether academia was the best use of his talents, or whether he was simply in academia because he could not think of other uses for his talents, or whether the talents he had acquired in academia simply had no uses anywhere else? At the height of this anxiety and self-doubt, he had traveled to Peoria, where I, in the guise of Tanya, was at that moment working on my final paper about his dissertation. I believe my paper, that tiny shred of outside affirmation, had meant a great deal to him, in the state he was then in. His imagination had taken hold of that shred and made it into something greater than it was, an elaborate fantasy of validation that had probably turned inappropriately sexual even before I inadvertently left that damn window open on Tanya's computer. All of which is to say that, seven months after Anthony's trip to Peoria, as he lugged his office suite into this dayroom, I was willing to allow that an overwhelming sense of *existential failure* had been at least partly responsible for his tragic stupidity with Tanya, and to consider that Anthony might be simply a neurotic, self-imploding buffoon rather than the calculating monster I had previously imagined.

But the reason Sanjana got the office space—to get back to our story—and Anthony this louder, more open, more distracting space to work in (not that anyone should care about their work spaces, but the *reason* matters for what happened next) was because unlike Anthony, she had already been hired, on the strength of her published papers, into a tenure-track faculty position with significant professional responsibilities, not least the expectation that within six years she would revise and publish her own dissertation as a book. Since her relatively stable and lucrative career was more important to their future than Anthony's nonexistent career, therefore her book's completion was a greater priority, a fact that lost him not only his office space but soon quite a lot more when they discovered—here it is!—that there was a baby on the way. A son. And then they had him, their son. At which point Anthony, as "primary caregiver," lost whatever autonomy he had managed to save for himself, swallowed whole by this lovely, needy child.

I had forgotten how that happens. I'd forgotten so much about those early years of watching a child grow, the lengthening, the blossoming. I'd forgotten—or else the memories had simply stretched so thin over the years, over the incredible distance from then to now, that I had come to doubt them, the memories, since surely whatever survived was at least partially false or fabricated, half-imagined or mixed up with images from elsewhere, from other people's lives or from characters on television. So when the boy arrived, he was in some ways familiar to me, to my memories of Samuel, but in other ways startlingly new. New to the world but to me as well, and to Anthony, of course, to their marriage, to the apartment, everything.

Now into the basement storage space went Anthony's office things, and into this dayroom came all sorts of colorful squeezies, plush stuffies, and battery-operated swingies and spinnies. Suddenly, this was a sunny, happy space. A space of shapes and colors, oversized numbers and letters, paper mobiles, crocheted rainbows, and endless gurgles, giggles, screams, and squeaks. Also diapers, with a clever sort of air-lock trash can for disposing of them. On the windows hung sticky flowers of rubbery gel, on the floor a shaggy rug (sky blue), and every remaining inch of unoccupied space was smothered in soft cushions. All of which made me feel—how? I reminded myself I'd been down this road before, this road and many others. That for decades I'd suffered for my affections and finally had fortified myself with an impenetrable apathy. But none of it made any difference. Face-to-face with the boy, the son, I was ambushed by optimism, and—

On second thought, I am not going to tell this story after all. These past years, this most recent regurgitation of joys and disappointments. I am sorry to break it off, but more sorry to have started it.

I will tell you instead about the television of today, though in all likelihood you watch as much as I do. I will finish television's story, which is a large part of Anthony's life anyway, just as it was of mine, and which deserves its own ending, as don't we all.

William Shatner now appears in a sitcom based upon a Twitter feed, as well as in commercials for a website that searches other websites for travel bargains. On any given day, I might encounter him on various channels as a young man being Captain Kirk, a little older as T. J. Hooker, older still as that lawyer on *Boston Legal,* and finally these various internet-related roles that old age has arranged for him. Sometimes I imagine him—the actor, William Shatner—afraid to turn on his television (or switch on his smartphone or iPad or whatever screened device is networked into whatever content-sourcing telecommunications package he subscribes to) for fear that he will suddenly be faced with his life in its entirety, playing and replaying its odd trajectory forever, an experience he was perhaps once excited to discover but has long since grown tired of, or rueful of, tired and rueful being the only emotions I can imagine for him. After which I wonder why everyone in the world is not afraid of their own screens for this very same reason. Because even if they do not see themselves, still, how could they not see themselves? How they've spent their time, how they continue to spend it, this shockingly large chunk of what their clocked hours amount to.

Or should I talk instead about today's programs, which are, as usual, both better and worse than ever? Game shows that insult their audience with the transparency of their greed. Reality shows now the norm rather than the exception, as if television during my most recent absence settled upon its own worst self, its least attractive habits, deciding at last and forever that everyone's got talent, that every race is amazing, every makeover extreme, that everyone should marry a millionaire, and even the most forgettable celebrities will never be allowed to stop dancing. It is a lifeless world; if not dead, at least lifeless. While on the other side, the "quality" side, the flourishing of nonnetwork television has meant that many programs have gotten exceedingly good, for those who can afford them. The Netflix programs, the Amazon and HBO programs. Well, you know.

So perhaps I should proclaim, instead, how television is dead in another way, how it has split not just into evermore individualized programming segregated by race, class, and gender, but also onto countless unshared screens, its last source of common ground now buried under ever-growing piles of rarely recycled electronic devices? How television nonetheless lives on, a programmable cybernetic steroid-carcass of the magical window I once loved, yet another victim of this world's inexhaustible capacity for exhausting itself. Shall I mention how, perversely, in its living death, I find television even more relatable than before? How television seems to want to be done with itself as much as I do? Or less obviously, that I believe everyone else feels the same way, since the very best program on television today (*The Walking Dead*, a wonderful zombie-apocalypse program heading into its sixth season) is essentially a postapocalyptic fantasy about starting over, where the isolating, distracting, depressive media-soaked world that humans currently inhabit is swept away and replaced by a world in which the constant battle for mere survival (against zombies and other people) creates true fellow feeling and a daily life in which *everything matters*, where there is no place for boredom or distraction and every moment is lived in the sheerness of the present? Shall I point out the absurd irony that this simpler-seeming, more fully lived-in universe is accessible only through a screen, or that this fantasy about the destruction of the media-saturated world is one of the most-watched programs in television history?

I thought I'd been given a gift. A second chance to witness the miracle of childhood, but minus the responsibility, like a congenial grandpa (into my seventies, by then) at last able to pay a new small life the undivided attention it deserves. It hadn't occurred to me—why, I have no idea—that instead of a "second chance" I would simply relive the first one, listening to or peripherally watching this wonderful little person sit aimless for hours before blocks and stuffies and worse, much worse—television programs!—while his "primary caregiver," propped before an iPad, repeats my failures of fifty years earlier, the restlessness and distraction, the fleeing to screens when life is the thing right in front of you.

I thought—well, I don't know what I really thought, only what I allowed myself to hope, despite a vast preponderance of evidence, against Anthony but against this "brave new world" as well. For of course it is no longer "television" but "screen time," hydra-headed. It is the internet, it is binge-watching, it is YouTube channels, it is Google News: technologies I never had to contend with, battles I was never forced to lose. On top of which, he has a goal—Anthony—or thinks he does, a book he is supposedly working on, which he can never find time to work on, or tells himself he can't, too distracted by his son, too distracted by his son *even to attend to his son*. And this goal has given him a reason, a justification—I never had a justification—so that while his fathering is even worse than mine was, still his guilt is infuriatingly less, a fact that has filled me with hate on many occasions, such as right now, writing this, thinking about all this, allowing myself once more to be bothered by things I have no control over simply because the blatant failure and injustice of them is unstomachable, and the idea that I should be forced to stomach them is unstomachable, to stomach them still! But leaving open also the possibility that my anger and judgment are not entirely fair. That in looking back over the past years I see only the bad things, I leave out the good things—for surely I do, and in fact I would like to think I did something similar to myself, over the years, assigning myself guilt I did not actually deserve. Some I deserved, but not all of it. For in fact I was a good father (I would like to think), or certainly better than Anthony (no contest there!), and at the *very least* I can say his was a peaceful childhood, Samuel's. There was never fighting in our little house, no marital discord, two parents better than one but when they constantly fight, how is that better? When one is too busy and the other too impatient, when one can't stop telling the other what a lousy parent he is, and the other complains he never gets anything done, and the first says if he's so worried about getting work done, why spend whatever free time he has on the fucking internet, and anyway they agreed on this plan—didn't he agree to this plan? Sure he agreed, but he didn't know he was agreeing to have his entire life sucked up as if through a vacuum cleaner, a galactic existential vacuum cleaner, and—and on it goes, in front of the boy, not in front of the boy, while I, Samuel Johnson, seethe with fury, *at* but also *for* them, the world, all these years on this planet and nothing any better and most of it quite a lot worse. Because nothing ever ends (my fatalistic side), nothing ends or even improves; no goals get reached, no hopes realized, no struggles pay off—except that some, of course, one has to admit, do. Some things end. What kinds of things? Childhoods end, and you never get them back. Marriages end, even if a few manage not to. Books end, people finish them—

and that is what happened, how all of this finally changed. A little over a month ago, Sanjana finished her book.

They were in this very room when she announced it, the "happy" room, whose atmosphere had long since been soured by hours of negligent parenting but whose colorful fruit-flavored appearance had not changed. Anthony was showing the boy checkers, and she came in with a remarkable smile on her face, remarkable because their discord had come to such a head recently; things had gotten so bad between them that there had not been any pleasant feeling in a very long while.

"I'm done," she said.

"What?" he said, with something like shock, perhaps thinking, as I immediately thought, that she was talking about their marriage.

"My book!" she said.

And then he didn't know what to say. Probably it had never occurred to him that this day would actually arrive, and the impenetrable gloom they'd forged together would at some point be interrupted.

"You can work on your book!" she said.

Also possibly because he suspected, as I had all along, that his need to work on his book was just an excuse to feel bad for himself, since the fact was, he hadn't gotten much work done on it even before their son was born; yet having turned his book into the reason for his suffering, the justification for his perpetual distraction and lousy parenting, now he would actually have to work on it.

"In fact," she said, "I've been thinking of taking Junior here to my parents for a month. You get the entire apartment to yourself."

"Oh," Anthony began, "you don't have to . . ."

"No worries!" said Sanjana. "I already bought tickets!"

Aha!

He faltered for a moment, taking all this in. Then he asked— "just to say"—if he shouldn't perhaps come along? That before he "got to work" he should probably "clear his head"; that he didn't want her parents to think he was avoiding them. But "Oh no, no," said Sanjana—he should stay and work on his book.

And so it came to pass that one morning, just under a month ago, the exhausting, distracted existence Anthony loved to complain about but had nonetheless grown used to was at last brought to an end, and he found himself standing alone in the middle of the apartment, looking around.

He had just seen them off to the airport.

He was standing listening to an empty apartment, to noises out on the street.

He stepped into the dayroom, this room, still cluttered with his son's stuff.

Well?

After a few minutes, he started doing things.

He cleared out all the toys and cushions and kids' furniture, even the gel flowers from the windows. Even the rug. He carried a folding card table from the basement storage area—the wooden desk was too heavy—and set it up in the middle of the room. He moved a folding chair in from the kitchen, placed that at the folding table, and stood back to take stock of his accomplishments. He announced out loud that it was time to get to work.

Part of the reason it feels so stark, it now occurs to me, is the absence of the toys and things. If the room had been empty in the first place, probably it would not look so Spartan to me now.

Once he'd laid claim to this work space, he carried in and arranged, around the surface of the card table, a laptop, desk lamp, and printer, along with some books. He did not have the most recent draft of his dissertation in hard copy, so he printed that out and stacked the pages to the right of the laptop. He moved the lamp to just behind the laptop on the right and the book piles back to the card table's left corner, thus clearing table space to the laptop's left, where the dissertation pages would eventually be stacked as he moved through them. All of this took no more than twenty minutes, even with numerous small adjustments. After which he went online, looked up movie showtimes, and left for the rest of the day.

The following days, too, saw no work at all, but only an orgy of laziness, of morning movies and daytime drinking, of walks, naps, and masturbation. Pizza and arcade games, more movies, naps, and wandering between bars at night. Three and a half years of parental slogging required at least three days of unabated gluttony, is how I imagine he explained it to himself. When the gluttony ended, which was actually on the morning of the fifth rather than third day, he made a large pot of coffee and lay in bed reading his dissertation and slashing at its pages with a pen. He grew sullen, and later that afternoon walked along the lake. He spent the next few days sitting at his laptop in the dayroom, typing in restless, superficial changes that more often than not he changed back. On the fifth day of typing—so the tenth day of his "writing month"—he left the apartment and simply walked around the city. He slept through half the day after, then for the next two days stayed in bed binge-watching programs on Netflix. A very unusual way to write a book! When he again returned to the dayroom, he began a file on his computer titled NEW THING— and I understood from this bizarre two-week time-waste that he had found his dissertation to be hopelessly bad, and had given up on it, but apparently not on himself—not yet!—which was why he was now starting, or trying to start, something new.

But the "something new" did not go well either—it did not go anywhere—and that same night found his drunken head slouching toward the keyboard. He occasionally typed some words that he immediately deleted, then after a while began deleting for its own sake, simply pressing Delete on an empty document, Delete Delete, more drinking and deleting, until he was drunker than I had ever seen him, and his head landed with a thud on the keyboard, spelling *ghrrgtvhfgdsxjkkjpkhp*. And this verbless nonword stood alone on his screen, a testament to the absurdity and purposelessness of his life, or at least the absurdity and purposelessness of his previous two weeks, until finally I, Samuel Johnson—having waited through all this, the previous two weeks but also the years before, and having become by now unsalvageably disgusted—stepped in, sat up, and clicked New.

Then I typed: *Samuel Johnson's Eternal Return*.

Then: *for my wife and son*.

Then: 1.

I continued typing, and I suppose the rest is self-explanatory.

Except for the part where Anthony woke the next day and read my chapter 1, and of course he assumed he had written it. Of course he assumed that, in a drunken fit of inspiration, he had invented the tiny town of Unityville out of nothing, thus at long last—and much to his own surprise!—freeing his true creative genius from the heady cage of subconscious in which it had so long been trapped.

Except also for the part where he sat down again the next night, but insufficiently drunk, apparently believing the previous night had permanently unlocked his creative powers and that now that "his" book was under way, he could soberly churn out chapter after chapter—only to find that his muse refused to visit him. I will not bother to describe the many inferior pages he wrote that night, the ludicrous "fiction" he tried attaching to my own sober account of my struggles. I will spare you how embarrassed he was the following day to reread what he had written; how sensibly he responded by again getting blisteringly drunk; and how quickly I deleted his nonsense the moment I was able to.

And he continued drinking, and I continued writing. Some chapters took longer than others and affected me in different ways. I learned some things about myself in the process, or was reminded of things I'd not thought about in a long time. But you already know all of this, because you've read it. You may not have been here with me as I wrote it, in the latter half of June 2015, in this residential neighborhood of uptown Chicago. You may not know the feeling of sitting in this small room of dark windows, listening to ambient insects and occasional cars and the soft chatter of my typing. You may be existentially restricted to merely imagining this moment with me, never able to share it in any more meaningful way—yet for all of that, you are still closer than Anthony, who, though present in body, will never accept the reality of his own life.

He would need to admit that he is not a repressed novelist whose mind has taken flight via alcohol to invent the most inexplicably detailed fictions, but is just the more or less average person he deep down knows himself to be. He would need to accept that this book is not a fiction but a true account, one written by a dead man to whom his only tie is proximity. All of which is sufficiently outlandish to begin with, and since it could only lead him to despair, there is simply no reason at all for his conscious mind to credit it. Even this paragraph he will assume he wrote himself.

Do I care?

Why would I care?

There's no good reason.

Meanwhile, it is now two days before Sanjana and their son return from Bethesda, and I have arrived at the end of my story. It suddenly occurs to me that the reason I have written it, the actual reason all along, was to end it, to watch my story at last come to an end. For that is how stories work, isn't it? Things happen, and then everything wraps up. Perhaps in writing this book, some part of me imagined I was creating the necessity for my *actual situation* to change, if only because my story required it? That I, like this book, would at last have to come to an end?

A dayroom after dark is really a night room. It could as easily be named that, or as logically, if you look at its situation overall.

Sitting here, I'm surrounded by darkness, a very large darkness, a sea of darkness that starts at the windows and stretches outward in all directions to points unknown, horizons unexplored, oblivions unexhausted. A dayroom at night is like a small boat you're floating in, with just a chair, a table, a few other things—alone but not necessarily lonely, or not lonely at all but simply adrift, with no idea where you are going. Only when the sun comes up the following day will you find out where you went.

I guess I do not really know why I wrote this book. What I hoped to accomplish. I know the various reasons I have given myself, but having now arrived at its end, none of them ring true; nor have I experienced the satisfaction I thought finishing might bring. I am wondering whether, when all is said and done, I simply had nothing better to do.

Sometimes when I watch Anthony and his family on one of their better days, when they are spending time together, being caring and considerate, and when their little boy is being funny—in such moments the world appears to me hopeful, or at least possible, a place of possibility.

Other times, for example while staring into the computer screen at the endlessly reloading (or *refreshing*, a word that in the age of the internet has taken on something like the opposite of its original meaning) stream of harrowing world events, I find myself unable to see anything but calamity, a civilization bent on destroying itself and almost certain to succeed. In fact it seems obvious, in such moments, that the horrific catastrophic end will be arriving any moment now.

But most often I do not feel either of those ways. Most often I feel as I do right now. Not that there is still hope left, nor that it will all soon come to an end, but rather that all of this—the entire world, but starting with me!—ought to have been over a long time ago.

12.

THIS WILL BE THE LAST TIME I WRITE IN THIS BOOK
AND I WILL SAY NOW EVERYTHING I HAVE TO SAY.
THIS OPPORTUNITY IS OFFERED IN GOOD FAITH AND
WITH THE UNDERSTANDING THAT IN THE MEANTIME
NOTHING BAD WILL HAPPEN TO THE PERSON WRITING
THIS, AND THAT AFTER THIS LAST TIME, LIFE WILL GO
BACK TO NORMAL FOR EVERYONE INVOLVED.

The most extraordinary thing has happened! I do not even know
where to begin.

Just over a year has passed since I ended the previous
chapter—a perfectly fine year, in most ways. Sanjana and their
son returned from Maryland to find Anthony in good spirits, neither overly anxious nor overly excited, nor overly anything else, but a
calmer, more personable self than the one they'd left a month earlier.
In the days and weeks that followed, too, his attitude only improved,
and eventually it was simply accepted, without anyone having said a

word, that one way or another Anthony had shaken off the restlessness poisoning his soul, and had embraced his role as a father and husband and as a reasonable human being. The virtual and televisual worlds remained a temptation and distraction, but the level of stress it brought upon his marriage was a fraction of what it had been. And he re-devoted himself to his son, who over the months that followed began to show himself an exceedingly clever little boy—he is almost five now—already good with math and reading, very curious and interested in practically every subject that crosses his path. In fact the boy has developed a certain intellectual bossiness, his pride in his big-young-man knowledge causing him to be at times unreasonably insistent, which I have tended to find cute rather than off-putting. And he is so often in good humor—the boy—that on those days when Anthony has summoned the patience to participate in his increasingly elaborate fantasy games, they've invariably had a good time. Sanjana too, though very busy—back to the tenure track!—has managed to find more time for her family, and Anthony has continued to support her work. All told, it has been encouraging to watch, and given the timing, and how everything has played out, I can't help but think I was at least partly responsible for these changes, because of the book I wrote and the lessons Anthony must have learned from it.

But none of that is the extraordinary thing I need to tell!

Six weeks ago, the family returned to Bethesda, Anthony along this time, Sanjana having decided she would like this visit to be an annual event. Not that it was very "eventful" even lasting a full month. Mostly they were there to give the grandparents time with their grandson. Indeed, Anthony and Sanjana treated their time there as an extended babysitting session, sitting by the pool, walking around the neighborhood, and spending whole afternoons in front of the largest, thinnest television screen I have ever seen, binge-watching foreign sporting events they've never watched otherwise and liberal comedy-news programs saved to the DVR, one program after another, until the daylight hours sagged all around them, and they felt nothing but bad about themselves.

By the third week, even the grandparents had grown restless. The days collected in a formless, dissatisfying pile, and tempers were running short. It was then that Anthony's in-laws began asking him, casually at first, as if simply interested, then more aggressively, as his answers became increasingly vague, what he was working on, or "up to," and in particular they asked about his book. Sanjana had mentioned it: that he had completed a book last summer but placed it in a drawer; that it had never come back out of the drawer in the subsequent months; that it had long since stopped being a topic of conversation between them. And since then, the in-laws admitted, they could not help wondering about this book—as well as, more generally, about his lack of a career or any discernible professional prospects? All of which irritated Anthony, of course, but gave me, Samuel Johnson, a perverse sort of thrill, having myself spent a fair amount of the previous year angrily wondering why my book was in a drawer, why Anthony had made no effort to publish it, its possible publication (I had decided after the fact) being the real reason I'd written it, since publishing this book was my best remaining chance of ever reaching my son. We would publish it and put it into the world, and there was a narrow but not nonexistent chance that my son would read it . . . Thus the fact that it remained inexplicably in a drawer had been a source of real irritation.

But it was in the midst of one of his in-laws' passive-aggressive interrogations, midway through the visit's third week, that Anthony blurted out a request to borrow one of their cars. He wished, he said, to drive to northern central Pennsylvania, where he hoped "to do research" for the book they kept asking about, which was set in that area, and which he had apparently decided to pretend he was still working on, though I'm sure everyone involved suspected his real motive was simply to escape them for the day. Certainly I thought as much. I assumed he would drive to Baltimore, or even Philadelphia, and sit in a bar or a movie theater.

But for once I was wrong about Anthony (it is possible I have been wrong about him on other occasions as well), and that night, when he logged on to his laptop and "Google Mapped" Unityville, pa (he even "Google Earthed" it, although there is very little online to see: there is an aerial view, but the "street view" sets you down on pa 42, where you can click yourself forward past a shack-like fire station and a few other lonely structures, but you cannot move off of this larger road to see the actual town)—that night, that is, I found myself facing the strangest, most unexpected possibility, a possibility so improbable it took me until morning to fully accept it—until Anthony had risen early and made his coffee while the others were sleeping; until he'd climbed into their hybrid car and stowed his travel mug in the cup holder, his map on the passenger seat. *This is happening*, I then said to myself. And the next moment, we were off: on a three-hour-and-forty-two-minute drive north, in a car that made so little noise I could hardly believe it was moving, in a mood so ecstatically happy I could hardly believe it was mine.

On the road, the time passed quickly—or rather, at first it did not pass at all; there was no time, no passing, only a blur of expectation. It was as we approached Harrisburg that my attention began to anchor itself, as we encountered places I had previously been. Now the universe began expanding in all directions, forward over the asphalt, backwards across the fifty—fifty!—years I had been gone . . . Here was the spot, just south of Harrisburg, where once at sunrise, Henry Nelson had turned north onto Route 11 . . . Here was that small-city skyline, the Susquehanna wide and slow, and low mountains sliced short for the highway to roll through . . . Farther along, the tiny two-story where Lillian had lived, across from where Henry had died . . . Up ahead—up ahead the bend where, so long ago, many decades ago, a crazed long-haired man, in whose ranting, raving cranium my dear wife and I may or may not have been reunited for a fleeting moment without my even realizing it, had steered his truck into the river, and I had awoken in an airplane flying away from my son, my accursed "adventure" begun . . . Yes, it was as if my entire history was unfolding here, the history of my death recounting itself on the road back to my life, to the place I had lived, where my son might still—oh portentous road! One that had caused me great anxiety on previous occasions, but *this* time I could be still and watch it all pass, *this* time I could forego panic and doubt, because this time I was only a passenger. For once, being a passenger was the very best thing! I could sit back and know there was nothing I could do. That whatever might go wrong was out of my control. That because it was out of my control, it might go right for once . . . I was beyond excitement, beyond anticipation. I mean I was literally beyond these feelings. I did not feel them. I felt only calm. I felt only things I had never felt before, had longed for but never felt: that Fate did not hate me, that I would not make a mistake, that I might soon see my son.

And it occurred to me then, in that heady three-hour-and-forty-two-minute moment, when my thoughts were many and scattered but not a single one lost from me, for I contained all of those thoughts and many others, and saw all things clearly as I had managed to only once or twice before: on that first night in Pittsburgh with Orson, sitting on the curb by the newspaper box under the dark buildings, and then later on Tanya's trip to Tampa, lying on the ventilation grate under the stars behind the Waffle House, just those two moments and now . . . It struck me, that is, as rather funny, that despite all those years of trying everything possible to get back to Samuel, when having a goal and moving toward it was the only hope I'd held out, in the end all that effort had been worthless, really no help at all. And foolish! How foolish to imagine "returning" in a world that is constantly moving on? How foolish to attempt "making progress" when reality just keeps repeating itself? At which point I concluded—in good spirits, I felt quite whimsical thinking all of this—I concluded that my own existence had never been a matter of either progressing or returning, of moving forward or circling back, but that both had been present to precisely the degree required to make neither one useful to me. Whenever I might move forward, Fate had turned me back about. Whenever I was on the verge of returning, Fate chose that moment to move me on again. It was, when looked at from an outside perspective, fairly comic! But only because in the end—of many journeys, of many lifetimes, and of this particular three hours and forty-two minutes in the car—in the end "progress" and "return" had at last, in earnest, come together, for the sign up ahead said Unityville, and the next thing I knew, I was home.

Fifty years since I had last set foot in that place. Shall I list again the lives I had known in that time, the routes I had traveled, to give you a sense of how far away I felt, how great the distance of time seemed as we turned onto Unityville's now-paved street and parked not twenty feet from the spot where Abram had stood all those years before, on his horse-drawn buggy with the television in back? By the church where I'd spent so much of my youth? Where Emily and I had been married, where we'd set out together on what might have been our lives? To be there again, to look down the line of houses. I was not overwhelmed. It felt perfectly natural. I'd arrived.

As for Anthony, I think he was already, at that point, a bit perplexed. He had of course assumed that Unityville would look nothing like the town he believed he had pulled single-handedly out of his imagination. Yet here it stood, not the same, but not so different. Potentially, a later version of the same. He walked from one end of the town to the other. He had brought along a notebook and pen, as if he planned to take notes on the place, notes whose only possible use would be to make changes to my book, and he carried these "at the ready" as he walked. No one else was on the street just then, yet I imagine he felt conspicuous, if not because he was an outsider, then because of the ways he was, eerily, an insider—as if he had once lived in this town in a dream, so well had he managed to describe it. Thus confounded, he was naturally drawn to the one building that *least* fit my description, the one most likely to discredit his "imagination," a gas station/store at the far end of town that had not been there in my time, but had clearly been there for quite a while since.

It was the sort with windows all across the front under a hard-plastic awning, and inside, fluorescent lighting and snacks in aisles. It was a bit of a muddle of new and old fashions, at once too modern for Unityville (I thought) and too antiquated for a gas station/store (they've gotten quite flashy and elaborate), although probably I was the only person in the world for whom it would seem odd or out of place at all. The bell on the door was a real bell with a clink-clanky ring, not that elevator sound the electronic bells make, and there was a pickle barrel by the cash register, and maps and Mad Libs and yo-yos in plastic packaging. There were mirrors so you could see every aisle of the place, and lottery tickets and an ATM. It was a place of considerable curiosity to me, but finally it was just a gas station/store.

The woman at the register looked to be in her thirties, with a brown ponytail and denim shirt. She was too young for me to have known her. Anthony loitered a little, then went up with a bag of mini pretzels.

"Just the pretzels?"

"Yes, thanks." And he paid. Then he said: "Do you mind if I ask you a couple of questions?"

"Sure. Shoot." She was very friendly.

"Great." Here Anthony flipped open his notebook, which surprised the friendly woman and made her suddenly less friendly-seeming. "This town," he said, "it's been here a long time?"

"The town? Hundred years or so." She thought. "Maybe less. Maybe more. I think less." She made a face as if flummoxed, a "flummoxed" face. "I guess I don't really know."

"But you grew up here?"

"These are odd questions," she replied. She was right, of course. Even I could not figure out what Anthony thought he was up to. "When you asked to ask questions, I thought you meant like how-do-I-get-to-the-highway type questions."

"Right, sorry." He made a little laugh, and looked at his notebook, and closed it. "I'm writing a book about this area," he said more naturally. "Or part of it is set in this general area, but a long time ago. So I'm just up here trying to get a better sense of the place. There's not much about it online."

"Well, that surprises me not at all," said the woman, friendly again.

I decided that I liked this woman, how prudently she had questioned Anthony's nosiness, yet how quickly she was willing to be friendly again. It made me happy to like her, happy and a little bit proud: we were from the same hometown!

"We *have* internet," she went on, "but I can't imagine why anybody would look us up."

"Well, if they do, they aren't finding much!" He was a little awkward, Anthony, but all in all, he was doing better than I would have done.

"What's there to find?" she said. "I guess there's the fire station . . ."

"I saw that on the way in."

"There's restaurants and bars over in Hughesville. Williamsport's not far."

"Oh, I'm not really looking for restaurants or anything like that."

"What are you looking for?"

Anthony paused, probably wondering that himself. "Just getting a sense of the place. The story of the place. I suppose if you have internet, you must also have television?"

The woman laughed, then Anthony as well.

"Right, of course you do," he went on. "It's just that I'd read somewhere this town was originally founded as a sort of religious community, without television or phones or things."

"Well, that's true, but that's a long time ago. I think things changed a lot in the early seventies, when they paved 42 and started calling it the 'Wilkes-Barre-Williamsport Corridor.' It's really before my time . . . You could talk to Sam? He grew up back then. Plus he holds the undisputed title for Unityville's most interesting life story. Not that there's much competition, I admit. He's just down the other end of the street at the post office. Sam Johnson."

"Sam . . . ?"

Have I mentioned that it was a lovely day? Not that it matters, since regardless of the weather I would have found it to be the most perfect day in the history of the universe. A day with nice big clouds—I've always preferred a few pillowy cumulous clouds— and even though I could not smell, still as we started out across and down the street, the memory of Unityville's smell was in my thoughts, the woody crispness and whiffs of manure. As a boy I had walked up and down this street as often as I had done any other single thing. Some days I would spend an entire afternoon walking up and down it, although I never thought of it as walking, in fact I probably did not think about it much at all. Certainly I never imagined myself *going somewhere* along the length of this street. Certainly I never had the feeling that when I reached the other end, I would arrive at a destination, let alone *the* destination, the culmination of decades of effort, the single moment that every one of the past fifty years' worth of moments had aspired to. And how odd, I thought—still walking—how odd to discover, after everything, that in the end my story was *not* about a person stuck with himself and going nowhere forever, but instead about someone who had *a goal* and actually *achieved* it? Who faced some rather epically unheard-of obstacles and floundered in some truly spectacular ways, and who even frankly lost sight of his goal more than a few times, and so could just as easily have ended badly. But who nonetheless succeeded—he *succeeded*—and not by Fate but by his own hand, if not precisely by his own design (for it was my writing this book that had brought us here, even if that had not been my intention in writing it). Until finally time and space arrived at here and now: here was the post office, and inside, my son.

To say I did not at first recognize him would be preposterous, but in a sense also true. The post office—a small tan room with a countertop, with a single chair out front and with boxes stacked behind the counter—occupied the front of a house, and there was no one else there, so no one else he could be. Of course I knew he would no longer look four years old—he was fifty-five—but I suppose I did not expect him to be quite so . . . heavy. Not that I was disappointed—not at all!—I am simply describing my first thought. And I am describing it primarily because, more than anything, this thought was a revelation about *myself*, a revelation that took place in an eyeblink yet in that instant completely remade five decades of my self-image: it had never occurred to me that, had I lived, I would have gotten fat. My father was a large man, my mother heavyset; yet in my mind I had always kept my youthful waistline. It did not matter—I am not saying that any of this mattered. And of course the only reason it *was* my first thought upon entering the post office was because all my other thoughts were so much larger, so much more complicated and overwhelming, and this thought, being small and obvious, was all that my mind could manage.

"I'm looking for Sam Johnson?" said Anthony.

"You found him!" He was very friendly, immediately friendly, my son.

"You're Samuel Johnson."

"I am."

Though undoubtedly shaken by the preponderance of coincidence, I must say Anthony played all of this out with surprising aplomb. I suspect that even at this point he did not want to believe the increasingly unavoidable facts of his own situation. He introduced himself. He gave his spiel—that he was working on a book about the area, or with part of it set in this area, and how the woman at the gas station had sent him over here—and Samuel, who had a natural ease about him, the sort of person about whom you think, when you meet him, that he has never known an inch of anger or an ounce of ill will, said that of course he would be happy to help.

"And your parents?"

"Both dead. I was raised by my grandparents."

"Sorry."

"Oh, it was a long time ago. My mother died giving birth to me, and my father when I was four. That's probably the story Lauren was talking about—the woman at the gas station. It was back in the sixties, so the fact that people still talk about it gives you an idea of how little happens around here. It's sort of a local legend."

"I guess I would like to hear that story, if you don't mind."

Out again came the damn notebook.

Then Samuel, who'd been leaning toward us on the counter, straightened up. "Sure. Well." He took a moment. "There was a vagrant roaming around the woods up here around dusk. I think of him as a vagrant, though the truth is nobody ever found out much about him, who he was or what he was doing. But for some reason he ended up outside our house. We lived in a small house my father'd built when he and my mother were married. It was just a short walk from town but out in the woods, secluded. Anyway, I must have been playing outside that night, I don't actually remember any of it, but I understood it all enough at the time to be able to tell people in town what had happened, and then later, when I was older, they told it all back to me. So even though I was there, I only really know this story as a story. But I was small and playing outside the house, around dusk, and this vagrant came along and grabbed me and I guess he had a gun. I must have yelled, and my father ran out of the house and straight at the vagrant. He wrested the gun right out of this man's hand, and got me free, and made the man run off and never come back. But once the man was gone I saw my father'd been shot. I ran to town but he was dead before anybody got back to him. The vagrant showed up the next day drowned in the Susquehanna. He had a truck, which suggests he wasn't really a vagrant exactly, in fact the oddness of everything is probably why it became a local legend, since it's not like my family's the only one something bad ever happened to. Everybody has their theories about it, each one as crazy as the others. I was raised by my mother's parents. They died some years ago as well. Now I live over in Hughesville. Are you going to write any of this down?"

"Oh, I . . . This is just something I brought. I'm not even sure why. That's quite a story, though. You have a family of your own now?"

If there is a particular moment I would like to thank Anthony for, it is this one. I can imagine how discombobulating all of this was for him, yet in the midst of it, he had the presence of mind to ask meaningful questions, substantive questions, the sort of questions I myself would have asked and wanted to know the answers to.

"No," said Samuel, "I never did that."

"So, no family . . ." He put a check mark in his notebook, which just looked ridiculous. "It must have been hard growing up without parents."

"I don't know. What's hard? My grandparents were good people. And my father—I never really knew him. It's sort of neat that he's a hero, though."

"He was a hero?"

"He died saving my life."

Reader, I was overcome with emotion when I heard these words, coming so suddenly, as they did, on the tail end of hearing, from his own mouth, my son's account of losing me. I am overcome again as I write these words now. You cannot imagine what it meant to me, hearing this from my son. Or perhaps, having read this book, you can, in fact, imagine it. I have no words with which to comment on it, however, no words but those words themselves. And since I am not yet ready to move on from those words and would like to linger on them just a moment longer, perhaps I will simply type them a second time:

"It's sort of neat that he's a hero, though."

"He was a hero?"

"He died saving my life."

(!)

Anthony then asked my son if he had any memories of me at all. It could be that he was hoping Samuel would say something to run contrary to my account, something that would allow him to hold on to his delusions. But I prefer to think the opposite, that in fact he was convinced of me by then, and while he had perhaps not yet fully come to terms with the *fact* of my existence (as evidenced by the emotional breakdown he suffered in the car on the way back to Bethesda), still some part of him was thoughtful enough in that moment to seek out every bit of solace this meeting with my son could provide me. But Samuel did not have any memories of his own, only the small things his grandparents had told him. He shared what he could share, then asked Anthony about the book he was working on. Anthony replied vaguely—set in the area, a while ago, and so on—after which Samuel asked if he thought he might use his, Samuel's, story, and Anthony (who, of course, had already "used" Samuel's story) said he didn't know, but that he might, and would that be O.K.? Samuel said "Sure," and that either way, he'd love to read the book when it was done. All told, they spoke for only thirty or forty minutes, and within moments of leaving the post office, we were back on the road.

He drove for perhaps an hour before he stopped. To be honest I was not paying much attention. I had seen Samuel. He seemed healthy, even happy, certainly happier than most. I had not felt the need to stay in Unityville any longer; in fact, once we left the post office, I rather felt that I did not wish to stay. I had been thinking, there in the car, about how strange a thing a *goal* is, how wonderful and at the same time unsettling it is to see a goal accomplished. Not disappointing, simply strange. I felt like a ball being inflated and deflated at the same time in equal proportions, thus remaining exactly the same size, seemingly unchanged, but in reality full of change and motion. But this thought was interrupted as Anthony pulled into the parking lot of an Amish pie store along Route 11 and turned the rearview mirror in order to see himself, and said:

"I don't know if I'm crazy or what is going on here. I don't think I'm crazy because I don't feel crazy in any other way, and nobody around me seems to think I'm crazy, although obviously I have done some bad and stupid things. But I'm going to say this and it's the only thing I'm going to say. I hope you got what you wanted. I mean I really do, I hope you did. But that's done now. I have a family, my own wife and son who rely on me. Despite what you seem to think, I am totally fucking cognizant about my responsibilities to them, and I need to be taking care of myself, so I can take care of them. I can't be having 'accidents' while I'm driving, or whatever. I can't be wandering into bars or waking up in the back of a van in the middle of nowhere. I hope that's clear because from here on out I am going to be one sober motherfucker and I am not going to speak to myself in a fucking mirror like this ever again."

Since then, he's been true to his word. In the two weeks since we returned from Bethesda, he's not drunk any alcohol. He's eaten better and even tried to jog. He continues to be a good father and husband, and while I do not wish to take credit I do not deserve, still I cannot help but feel that for once—for once!—I have been a positive influence on someone.

Then suddenly this evening, after the family had gone to bed, he got up again, restless. He went into the dayroom with his laptop, two bottles of whiskey, and quite a lot of beer. The dayroom has long since been converted back into a playroom, so he sat on a big cushion in the semidark and started drinking. For a moment I felt disappointed in him, that he was failing in his vow to his family, but eventually he unfolded his laptop, opened the document that contains my book, scrolled to the last page, and typed out the words in all caps that began this final chapter: THIS WILL BE THE LAST TIME I WRITE IN THIS BOOK . . . and I understood then that he was allowing me this opportunity, which I have tried to put to good use.

It is still dark outside, though morning. There is still time before his family wakes up, still whiskey in the bottle, nor do I feel as if I'm nearing an end, but quite the opposite: I am feeling extraordinarily present! Giddy, in fact.

I would like to thank Anthony for his generosity and trust, and for this opportunity, which as he can see I did not use to his detriment. I would like to assure him that I do not hold a low opinion of him—and of course I myself am hardly above reproach. But truly I am nothing but grateful, and if he finds himself celebrating a bit too heartily on some future occasion, he should not fear me or what I might do. In fact, I would hope for the opposite, that he could find some comfort in the knowledge that I am here, not spying on him, not judging or conspiring against him, but simply witnessing, bearing witness. Surely that knowledge could be a comfort to someone, and to Anthony in particular: to know that however anonymous his life might sometimes seem, and however impossible it proves for even his family to know him, still, he is never entirely alone. There is always at least Samuel Johnson.

That will be my part of our bargain.

For his part, I trust that when this book is finally done, which is any moment now, but beyond that, in the days that follow, I trust that he will act on the good faith we have established between us and will send a copy to my son. He needn't publish it to the world, and of course I understand that there are things here he might prefer others not see. But send it to my son, do that much, so that someday soon Samuel will be able to read it and learn everything these pages have to teach, or rather to tell (I won't start pretending there has been "teaching" involved!).

And since I know in my heart that all this *will occur*, therefore now, in the final moment, I will stop referring to "you" or "Reader" or whatever I have called the person holding this book for the past however many pages, when I believed there was little chance that you would actually be my son. I will speak at last directly to the only reader I have ever truly cared to reach to say that these pages, then, are my account of how it happened, the manner in which everything went wrong. This is where I have been all the time you have walked in the world, and these are the experiences I have had—though not, of course, the ones I have wanted. They are all I have to share, and I do not know what good they will do you, in fact they may very well tarnish the heroic image you seem to have formed. But please know from the *fact* of these pages, from the great effort that went into crafting them, know from this that you are loved.

Acknowledgments

This book was first conceived as a retelling of Robert Montgomery Bird's 1836 *Sheppard Lee, Written by Himself*. Along the way this book went in some very different directions, but it still owes a great debt to Bird's wonderful novel.

Thanks to Bradford Morrow for excerpting the first two chapters in *Conjunctions*.

Thanks to Josh, Laird, Ben, Kate, all the Coffee House folks, and, always, Danielle.

LITERATURE
is not the same thing as
PUBLISHING

Coffee House Press began as a small letterpress operation in 1972 and has grown into an internationally renowned nonprofit publisher of literary fiction, essay, poetry, and other work that doesn't fit neatly into genre categories.

Coffee House is both a publisher and an arts organization. Through our *Books in Action* program and publications, we've become interdisciplinary collaborators and incubators for new work and audience experiences. Our vision for the future is one where a publisher is a catalyst and connector.

Funder Acknowledgments

Coffee House Press is an internationally renowned independent book publisher and arts nonprofit based in Minneapolis, MN; through its literary publications and *Books in Action* program, Coffee House acts as a catalyst and connector—between authors and readers, ideas and resources, creativity and community, inspiration and action.

Coffee House Press books are made possible through the generous support of grants and donations from corporations, state and federal grant programs, family foundations, and the many individuals who believe in the transformational power of literature. This activity is made possible by the voters of Minnesota through a Minnesota State Arts Board Operating Support grant, thanks to the legislative appropriation from the arts and cultural heritage fund. Coffee House also receives major operating support from the Amazon Literary Partnership, the Jerome Foundation, McKnight Foundation, Target Foundation, and the National Endowment for the Arts (NEA). To find out more about how NEA grants impact individuals and communities, visit www.arts.gov.

Coffee House Press receives additional support from the Elmer L. & Eleanor J. Andersen Foundation; the David & Mary Anderson Family Foundation; Bookmobile; the Buuck Family Foundation; Fredrikson & Byron, P.A.; Dorsey & Whitney LLP; the Fringe Foundation; Kenneth Koch Literary Estate; the Knight Foundation; the Matching Grant Program Fund of the Minneapolis Foundation; Mr. Pancks' Fund in memory of Graham Kimpton; the Schwab Charitable Fund; Schwegman, Lundberg & Woessner, P.A.; the U.S. Bank Foundation; and VSA Minnesota for the Metropolitan Regional Arts Council.

The Publisher's Circle of Coffee House Press

Publisher's Circle members make significant contributions to Coffee House Press's annual giving campaign. Understanding that a strong financial base is necessary for the press to meet the challenges and opportunities that arise each year, this group plays a crucial part in the success of Coffee House's mission.

Recent Publisher's Circle members include many anonymous donors, Suzanne Allen, Patricia A. Beithon, the E. Thomas Binger & Rebecca Rand Fund of the Minneapolis Foundation, Andrew Brantingham, Robert & Gail Buuck, Louise Copeland, Jane Dalrymple-Hollo, Mary Ebert & Paul Stembler, Kaywin Feldman & Jim Lutz, Chris Fischbach & Katie Dublinski, Sally French, Jocelyn Hale & Glenn Miller, the Rehael Fund-Roger Hale/Nor Hall of the Minneapolis Foundation, Randy Hartten & Ron Lotz, Dylan Hicks & Nina Hale, William Hardacker, Randall Heath, Jeffrey Hom, Carl & Heidi Horsch, the Amy L. Hubbard & Geoffrey J. Kehoe Fund, Kenneth Kahn & Susan Dicker, Stephen & Isabel Keating, Kenneth Koch Literary Estate, Cinda Kornblum, Jennifer Kwon Dobbs & Stefan Liess, Lambert Family Foundation, Lenfestey Family Foundation, Sarah Lutman & Rob Rudolph, the Carol & Aaron Mack Charitable Fund of the Minneapolis Foundation, George & Olga Mack, Joshua Mack & Ron Warren, Gillian McCain, Malcolm S. McDermid & Katie Windle, Mary & Malcolm McDermid, Sjur Midness & Briar Andresen, Maureen Millea Smith & Daniel Smith, Peter Nelson & Jennifer Swenson, Enrique & Jennifer Olivarez, Alan Polsky, Marc Porter & James Hennessy, Robin Preble, Alexis Scott, Ruth Stricker Dayton, Jeffrey Sugerman & Sarah Schultz, Nan G. & Stephen C. Swid, Kenneth Thorp in memory of Allan Kornblum & Rochelle Ratner, Patricia Tilton, Joanne Von Blon, Stu Wilson & Melissa Barker, Warren D. Woessner & Iris C. Freeman, Margaret Wurtele, and Wayne P. Zink & Christopher Schout.

For more information about the Publisher's Circle and other ways to support Coffee House Press books, authors, and activities, please visit www.coffeehousepress.org/pages/support or contact us at info@coffeehousepress.org.

MARTIN RIKER grew up in central Pennsylvania. He worked as a musician for most of his twenties, worked in nonprofit literary publishing for most of his thirties, and has spent the first half of his forties teaching in the English department at Washington University in St. Louis. In 2010, he and his wife, Danielle Dutton, cofounded the feminist press Dorothy, a Publishing Project. His fiction and criticism have appeared in publications including the *Wall Street Journal*, the *New York Times*, *London Review of Books*, the *Baffler*, and *Conjunctions*. This is his first novel.

Samuel Johnson's Eternal Return was designed by
Bookmobile Design & Digital Publisher Services.
Text is set in Adobe Jenson Pro.